Praise for *Blaze (or Love in the Time of Supervillains)*

"High-schooler Blaze is self-deprecating, hilarious, and geeky in the coolest way possible...One of the most relatable anti-love stories we've come across in a while." *—Seventeen*

"Funny, cringe-worthy and heartbreaking. Don't miss out." *—RT Book Reviews*, 4 ½ stars

"Entertaining reading...the novel forces readers to reconsider the way they treat their peers, especially girls, over their sexual behavior, real or imagined." *—Publishers Weekly*

"Honest and realistic...with a large helping of humor." *—Library Media Connection*, Recommended

"Readers trying to balance life's responsibilities with a desire for independence or those struggling to navigate teen life online will likely find a kindred spirit in Blaze." *—Bulletin of the Center for Children's Books*

"Hilarious and heartfelt!" *—*Jennifer Ziegler, author of *How to NOT be Popular*

"Laurie Boyle Crompton's blend of snark and heart will keep you turning the pages." —Mandy Hubbard, author of *Prada and Prejudice*

"Laurie Crompton has created a character who sparkles…Blaze is spirited and complicated—she absolutely pops off the page. I loved this book!" —Robin Mellom, author of *Ditched: A Love Story*

"Laurie Crompton's super power is bringing the funny. Readers should make this book their trusty side-kick." —Eileen Cook, author of *Getting Revenge on Lauren Wood* and *The Almost Truth*

THE *Real*
PROM QUEENS
OF WESTFIELD HIGH

laurie boyle crompton

sourcebooks
fire

Published by Sourcebooks Fire, an imprint of Sourcebooks, Inc.
P.O. Box 4410, Naperville, Illinois 60567-4410
(630) 961-3900
Fax: (630) 961-2168
teenfire.sourcebooks.com

Library of Congress Cataloging-in-Publication data is on file with the publisher.

Printed and bound in the United States of America.
VP 10 9 8 7 6 5 4 3 2 1

For Trinity, the reigning princess of my reality.

PREVIEW TEASER

Not even the producers of the show could've predicted it would end with the biggest reality-show bitch-fight in history. Just picture six girls wearing prom gowns going at it. I'm talking hair pulling, lipstick smearing, manicured-claws clawing as the television cameras gobble up the bloody chaos.

If you had tried to warn me that a year ago Westfield High's prom would be the scene of such violence, I would've said that despite your obvious insanity, you seem like a very nice person.

And if you'd told me last year that I'd find myself smack-dab in the middle of that battle with a freaking tiara on my head, I would've pointed out that your being crazy won't necessarily stop you from living a long and fulfilling life.

But if you had considered mentioning that I was about to destroy my best friendship, lose my chance at true love, and be utterly and completely humiliated on national television, I have just one thing to say to you: *Where the hell were you a year ago?*

PART ONE

Westfield High Wannabes

CHAPTER ONE

We are closing in on the last day of junior year, and I'm physically in trigonometry but mentally sunning myself on our deck. Mr. Mortimer would be happy to know at least my daydreaming is somewhat mathematical.

Let x equal my SPF number. If the sun is positioned overhead at an 80° angle, and the temperature is 78 degrees Fahrenheit, what is the ideal value of x to achieve maximum tanning without risking melanoma as I bask in my tankini?

My calculations are interrupted when an anonymous underclassman knocks on the door and hands Mr. Mortimer a yellow slip. Without a pause in his monologue on inverse trigonometric functions, Mr. M walks over and hands me the "Report to Guidance Office Immediately" pass.

I quickly pack my books and give my best-slash-only friend, Marnie, a shrug. I realize it's pathetic to feel special over being summoned to the guidance office, but I feel like a kite, cut free after straining against my string all day.

Soaring toward the door, I try to float smoothly past Grace Douglas's desk, but of course she can't just let me pass in peace. She hums a few bars of "We Wish You a Merry Christmas," just loud enough for me to hear. I hang my head in shame, wishing I could disappear. You'd think Grace could at least give the mocking Christmas Carol a rest on days when the temperature rises above seventy. But her cruelty is like the number π. Constant and irrational.

Hugging my books, I watch the hallway tiles as I shuffle my thick black boots past endless classrooms. Students-slash-inmates sit in submissive rows, their bored heads swiveling toward me as I slump by. Classroom by classroom, they all turn back to their droning wardens once they see it's just me. A few kids from Grace's clan actually point and laugh as if I'm their walking punch line. Which, of course, I am.

I'm sure Grace gets a whole different reaction when she walks by. I imagine entire classes standing up and clapping as she stops in each doorway to pose and shake her glossy hair. The only people who ever wave to me are Marnie and "the dweebs," aka James and Rick.

Rick's study hall is coming up on my right, and I slow down for my shining opportunity to act like I'm popular. I peer through his open doorway, a smile heading for my lips.

When I see Rick, my smile drips into my throat and turns bitter. I swallow it.

There he is, sitting right in the absolute center of the

classroom, with—get this—his *socks* hanging on his ears. That's right, I'm talking one puffy white sock on each ear as he casually writes in his notebook. Two girls in the back row are pointing and laughing, but only Rick Shuebert could get away with acting so perpetually bizarre without getting in trouble. Teachers love the guy, and this one is sitting at his desk as if he can't even see the obvious footwear dangling from the sides of Rick's head.

I stand in shock and disgust until Rick must sense my twitching eye daggers and finally looks up. As usual, he seems happy to see me. I clench my teeth and silently hiss, "What the hell are you doing?"

As if his behavior isn't bad enough, Rick is actually the one who helped initiate the incident that turned me into a punch line. No, I'm not getting into that right now, but you can trust me when I say it was awful. In fact, I'd be totally justified in hating Rick's guts forever. But my best friend, Marnie, has been secretly in love with his best friend, James, since grade school, and I just so happen to be an excellent best friend.

I tolerate Rick for Marnie's sake but socks-on-ears is a new low. I shake my head disapprovingly, and he shakes his back at me, his goofy sock ears flopping back and forth. I suppress the urge to laugh and ignore his happy wave as I stomp out of the doorframe and on toward the guidance office.

Rick is constantly coming up with new ways to be antisocial.

Marnie thinks he has an "I'll reject you before you get the chance to reject me" complex, but I think he's just the most clueless smart person I know. He's not even all that awful to look at. I mean, he has nice hair anyway—brown and wavy. His nose is a bit off-center but he could potentially be a semihottie under different circumstances. For instance, if he took his damn *socks* off his *ears*.

The guidance office is in a separate building, so I have to go out the cafeteria doors and down a short walkway to get to it. When the warm outdoor air hits my face, it reminds me what a crime it is to be stuck in school on such a beautiful day. It's much too warm for my black combat boots, but I like the way they make me feel protected. My *I-don't-give-a-shit-kickers*.

I squint up at a fluffy, white cloud trying to get my attention. It seems to be gesturing with its billowy arms. Sailing ahead, it dares me to follow it to the cornfield where the smokers meet. But then, skipping school isn't really my style. Besides, I'm not even close to cool enough to just *show up* in the cornfield without an invitation or a nicotine addiction.

With a sigh, I drag open the door to the guidance office. After my brief fling with glorious sunshine, it takes a moment for my eyes to adjust to the dim waiting room. The guidance secretary gives me her patented consoling smile as I wait for her to finish her phone conversation. Which, from the sound of it, is a personal call.

I look around at the cheap wood-paneled walls covered

in posters of mountain climbers with "ambition" and kittens "hanging in there." *This place is so depressing.* No wonder our guidance staff has such a high turnover rate.

When the secretary hangs up, I slide my yellow slip across her desk.

"Oh yes, Shannon Depola," she says brightly. "You're the last to arrive. Number three."

"So, this is some sort of group thing?"

"Oh, they wouldn't tell me what they're doing with you. But judging by the pair running this thing, it's something *ritzy.* Go ahead, straight down the hall, last office in the back. The ladies went searching for a *real* cup of coffee but should be back in a minute."

As I shuffle past, she leans over and whispers, "And maybe you can give me a hint once you know what's happening." She grins, showing long teeth bursting out of her gums. "They've been *awfully* secretive."

I nod noncommittally. *Incurable gossip—what a darling quality to have in a guidance secretary.*

I move down the dark hallway, passing the rainbow-postered offices of the counselors who haven't given up on us yet.

I never knew the guidance department even had a back room. It smells of fresh paint, and I blink as my pupils readjust to the ultra-white walls and million-watt fluorescent bulbs crowded along the ceiling.

"Told you," says a gruff voice on my right. I look over to see Kelly Marco glaring at me through layers of eyebrow rings and eyeliner.

"I suppose you're right," a soft voice answers from my left. I snap my head toward it and see Amy "The Whale" Waller sitting in an orange plastic chair with the attached desk pressing into her ample stomach. Amy drops her head, and her mousy hair drips forward.

"What the...?" I try to figure out why the three of us are being grouped together. Kelly may be flunking out of something or other, but Amy has passing grades and I'm in advanced classes. Amy may have some sort of depression-thing happening, and Kelly has her pharmaceutical issues, but I'm pretty average in the category of teenage angst. I mean, aside from being a social pariah and all...

And *BAM*—it hits me.

The prank. At least, I'd assumed it was a prank. *It totally had to be a prank.* During homeroom last week, we were handed out a questionnaire. Everyone murmured and laughed and assumed it was some sort of test to see if teachers even read all the crap they pass out to students.

The survey had only two questions. The first one asked us to write down the three girls "most likely to be elected Prom Queen next year." Which, okay, was not the most ridiculous question ever posed to a group of high school students. Premature and idiotic maybe, but not completely ridiculous. We do have our three solid front-runners already in place. It was the second question that had everyone murmuring. It asked us to list the three "*least* likely to be voted Prom Queen, ever."

For me, it was the "ever" that really screamed *prank*. As if unworthiness of becoming Prom Queen is a permanent condition.

It *had* to be a prank.

But now, here we are a week later, the three of us collected in one room. The obvious choices for the bottom three—the recluse, the druggie, and me. Amy is busy studying her desk belt, so I turn to Kelly. "We're not the…?" I can't even say it out loud.

Her face jingles with piercings as she snarls. "Well, we're certainly not the damn Prom Queens."

No, no, no! I say in my head. "No, no, no!" I say out loud as I slide into the desk beside Amy. If anyone hears about the survey results, I'll be humiliated all over again. *I don't think I can take any more.* "This can't be happening!"

"Relax, kiddo," says Kelly. "You're upsetting the whale." I look over and see that Amy is rocking her entire desk back and forth. "Sheesh," Kelly says, "you two thought you were maybe gonna *be* Prom Queen?" She starts laughing. Or more accurately, she starts cackling-slash-coughing thanks to her pack-a-day habit.

Kelly is a burnout druggie who doesn't socialize with the other recreational drug-users at school. They seem like a rather inclusive group, but Kelly keeps to herself. She has a ton of piercings all over her face, which gives the impression her head is perpetually wrapped in barbed wire. It also helps to emphasize her "keep out" attitude.

With a groan, I look over at Amy. As usual, her hair hangs askew as if she's had some tawdry run-in with the hair gel. She's biting on her lower lip, a constant habit that creates pink impressions of her teeth below her mouth. Amy isn't the fattest girl in our class, but she's the one who's the most weighed down by her size so she gets singled out for abuse.

And here I am, the school's resident social exile, sitting between them where I belong. We're the bottom three. I close my eyes and moan. "Maybe the guidance counselors are staging a popularity intervention." Leaning over my desk, I tuck in my stupid black boots and pull my brown hair forward. My breath seems amplified inside the little personal hair-corral I've created. I feel my enormous ears poking out and try to smooth my limp hair over them.

It may surprise you to know that my stringy brown hair and largish ears are not the main reason I'm socially null and void. I was actually doing just fine for myself, before the Elf Ucker Incident.

Unless you go to Westfield High, I'm sure you're wondering, "What the hell is an Elf Ucker Incident?" Well, let me tell you, it is something terrible. And now my mind can't stop replaying it like the *Twenty Most Shocking Reality Show Moments* my sister was watching in the living room last night.

I might as well tell you, since nobody who knows me will ever forget the story anyway. I'm talking, I could become the first female pope who builds a homeless shelter on the moon, and folks around here will still remember me more for the Elf Ucker Incident.

It happened last year during gym class. We were playing co-ed dodgeball, and the wooden floors had just been redone, so the game was extra squeaky. The smell of polyurethane was strong, which was handy since the hormone fairy had been a little heavy-handed in adding the stink to everyone's sweat. I was one of the final four players still in the game.

I'm not all that athletic, but over the years I've developed this dodgeball strategy where I fall back, unnoticed, for the entire game. Once nearly everyone's out, I grab a ball, charge forward, and usually get taken out pretty fast. But every now and then, I get lucky—one of the really good players is distracted with some other really good player, and I manage to nail them at close range. Then everyone cheers for me like I'm some sort of rock star. It gives the impression I'm a much better player than I actually am.

So anyway, there I was, having the best dodgeball game of my life, completely oblivious to my impending doom. I waited patiently then leapt from the shadows and bumped off Luke Hershman, the most gorgeous of our notably attractive foot-ball players and an accomplished ball hog. As everyone was still reacting to my surprise attack on Luke, I dove to the floor like some action-adventure chick, avoiding a firebomb from my left.

The damned thing must've fallen out of my pocket when I stood back up, and of course I was too busy grinning like an idiot at my cheering fans to see it. I didn't even know I'd dropped it until Rick Shuebert (yes, *that* Rick—Mr. Socks-on-ears) pointed to the spot on the floor where I'd just gotten up and practically shouted, "What the heck is that?"

I looked over and my heart dove into my sneakers because I remembered sticking it in my pocket that morning, and *there it was* for everyone to see. A finger cot. Now, you may be asking: 1) Why was I carrying a finger cot in my pocket? and 2) What the hell is a finger cot, anyway? Well, 1) it's something that's used for a very embarrassing hobby that I'm not ready to tell you about, and 2) it's a rubber thing that looks, well, exactly like a tiny condom.

Quick as a wink, Luke snatched it from the floor and rolled it onto his pinky finger exactly the way we'd all learned to put condoms on bananas in health class.

He waggled his "protected" finger in the air for everyone to see. It felt like gym class had suddenly shifted into slow motion with laughing mouths gaping open from the sidelines. And it was just my horrible luck that Grace Douglas happened to be in that gym class. Besides reigning Westfield Royalty, Grace also happens to be Luke's girlfriend.

I suddenly wished I hadn't thrown him out after all. Luke walked over to the sidelines and continued waving his pinky in the air as he slid his arm casually over Grace's shoulder. Giving me a wicked smile, Grace announced the line that has reverberated in my head like a nightmare ever since.

"What the heck is that for, Depola?" she asked. "*Safe sex with elves?*"

The entire gym froze for a beat before erupting with the thundering sound of everyone's laughter. I felt my face go bright red and suddenly I had to pee real bad. I looked around for help, but the gym teacher, Ms. Gumto, seemed hesitant to interrupt—probably since Luke's demonstration *was* promoting STD protection after all.

I knew laughing along would've been my best damage-control reaction, but I just couldn't force myself to do it. I stood motionless as my humiliation rose exponentially by the minute.

The freshly taped lines on the wooden floor started to run and blur, and I grasped the truth that no matter what, crying in the middle of tenth grade gym class was *not* an option.

So I turned and fled—my flailing run emitting a flurry of embarrassing loud squeaks.

But there's really no outrunning an incident like that. Luke walked around school for the rest of the day with the damned dirty finger cot on his finger, and people couldn't resist repeating Grace's clever comment over and over. By the time school let out everyone was in on the joke and I'd been forever christened the Elf Ucker.

The whole thing stayed in everyone's minds, not just because it was wonderfully humiliating, but because it was a shining moment for Grace Douglas, a girl who I assure you does not lack shining moments. She's so epically popular that, in spite of everything she's done to me, even *I* wrote her in as number one on my Prom Queen Survey. Obviously some sick impulse to get a perfect score on my anonymous pop quiz.

I think I maybe could've lived the whole Elf Ucker thing down if I was the type of girl to just get over it and pretend nothing happened. But for days afterward, I was so aware of people laughing at me that I couldn't make eye contact with anyone. And then, just when I started to think things might go back to normal, the first elf showed up on my desk in homeroom.

When I walked through the door, the creepy-looking thing was leering at me with his long green legs bent at odd angles. I actually screamed when I saw it. Some quick wit called out, "What's the matter, Depola? Your elf hookup coming back to haunt you?" So then *that* story was the highlight of everyone's conversations. It must've been a pretty slow week among the popular clan.

After that, it became a solid running joke for everyone to sneak elves into my locker and backpack. The creepier-looking the better, and occasionally with added phallic appendages. *Ick.* The holidays were a freaking nightmare.

Grace and one of her lackeys named Deena approached me by my locker one December morning and politely serenaded me with a Christmas Carol that had been rewritten called "We Wish You a Tiny Pecker." They wiggled their pinkies at me the whole time they sang it and ended with "We wish you a tiny pecker, on an elf who's not queer." Despite the song's obvious lack of creativity and hint of homophobia, it inspired widespread humming of the chorus wherever I went. Grace even managed to get it on the morning announcements.

I still remember the way my big ears perked up when I heard, "This next message is for Shannon Depola." I couldn't believe it when the school's a cappella group started humming a harmony of the tune over the loudspeakers.

After the holiday break, I came back feeling hopeful that the teasing was behind me, only to be greeted by a floppy elf flung at my head as soon as I walked through the school doors.

It was when the mocking surprise gifts started to include garden gnomes with drawn-on permanent marker penises that the brutal fantasies started.

They began with a rather generic image of my hand slapping Grace Douglas across the face. Next it graduated to me pulling her shirt over her head and shoving her down the school's stairwell. Eventually, in my mind, I was pretty much beating the shit out of Grace Douglas every day.

Of course, I continued to submit to her in real life, practically bowing in reverence as she strode down the hallway. Hunky boyfriend, Luke, on her arm and an entourage of worshipers at her back. Grace Douglas was as untouchable as I became. Except her untouchable was in the holy sense and mine was more like what happens when you've got an extremely contagious disease.

My friends started fleeing in acts of social status preservation that I really couldn't blame them for. Marnie was the only one who never distanced herself. I started trying to look as plain as possible, since wearing something as simple as lipstick or a cute pair of shoes would instigate a fresh round of teasing. "Ooo, Depola," I'd hear, "all dressed up for one of your special little friends?" It's really no wonder I was driven to wearing aggressive footwear.

The final straw was when some clown hacked my profile, changed my status to "in a relationship," and photoshopped a creepy-looking elf with his tongue in my ear. It was really more than I could handle, and after I regained control of my account, I deleted the whole thing. I stopped existing online and escaped real life by disappearing into my daydreams as often as possible. It seemed like the more I got teased, the more disconnected and weird I acted. It became a vicious cycle.

Now here I am, officially elected as a hopeless loser who couldn't be voted Prom Queen *ever*. I guess I deserve it. Between my scuffed-up *I-don't-give-a-shit-kickers* and my frequent breaks from reality, it seems like I was sort of campaigning for a bottom three position without even knowing it. In retrospect, I maybe should've joined the Future Homemakers of America alliance with Marns when she begged me to. Or maybe at least the left-hander's club.

I can't imagine why the guidance office is getting involved in my loser status, but I'm starting to think I should've run off through the cornfield chasing that fluffy little cloud after all.

In fact, right now, *any* escape from reality will do.

CHAPTER TWO

The door swings open and two women stride purposefully into the room. One looks city-like with a crisp business suit perfectly tailored to her sharp angles. Her black hair is short and slick, and it seems likely her pale skin would combust if it came in contact with direct sunlight.

The other woman wears a low-cut dress and is pretty in that showy way that clearly requires a lot of maintenance. Nobody's hair falls naturally into the long, loose waves that are happening on her head. She reminds me of an older version of Victoria from season six of *Make Me a Model*. My sister, Josie, made me watch it with her, and I remember Victoria getting slammed by the judges for doing pageants and being too "commercial" even though she was the prettiest contestant that cycle.

The women are both way too thin to be local. Pinned to each of their chests are big sets of lips covered in pink rhinestones. I recognize those lips as the Nŏrealique Cosmetics logo and wonder why some makeup company would be involved in our "popularity intervention," or whatever this is.

"Hello, girls!" announces the one with the slicked-back hair. "I'm Mickey, and this is Victoria."

Victoria flashes a smile, and my eyes widen as I realize she *is* that pageant girl from *MMaM*.

The silence stretches on as the two of them analyze us with narrowed eyes. Amy starts rocking back and forth again, and Kelly crosses her arms on her desk and drops her head on top of them, which is her usual desk-sleeping position. I try to cover my ears with my shoulders. An uncomfortable stretch of time passes as the women whisper to each other. I want to go home and bury myself in bed for a week until the safety of summer vacation arrives.

Finally Mickey smiles. "Well, congratulations to you all!"

What? I grin. *We totally jumped to the wrong conclusion.* I blame Kelly for all the panic and hear Amy grunt beside me.

"Yeah, thanks." Kelly lifts her head to glare at them. "I'm thrilled to be lumped in with these losers as the toxic ooze of our junior class."

Mickey's eyebrows jump, then she concedes, "I assume you've figured out this little meeting is related to the preemptive Prom Queen election that we had here the other day."

Amy whimpers and my heart sinks.

"Duh!" says Kelly.

"And by the looks on your faces," Victoria says, "you probably know you three were voted least likely to become Prom Queen." Her expression conveys talk-show-worthy concern, which strikes me as odd since she was a stone-cold bitch on *MMaM*.

"I understand this comes as a disappointment," Mickey says sternly. "But I assure you, what we are about to tell you will make you realize this is actually the best news of your young lives. You will look back on this day as the beginning of all the good things that are to come."

Victoria gestures to us with open palms. "How would you girls like to become reality television stars?" Her smile is so huge I instinctively look behind me to see who she's grinning at. All that's back there is a poster of a puppy resting his head on an enormous bone with black letters commanding us to DREAM BIG.

"We're proposing the most unique unscripted show ever conceived." Victoria raises her arms as if forming an invisible billboard and announces, "*From Wannabes to Prom Queens!*"

Kelly mocks, "Cause *The Greatest Loser* is already taken, right?"

Ignoring her, Victoria goes on, "You girls will be treated to full makeovers during your six-week stay at Prom Queen Camp, which is being set up at this very moment in a *top secret* location. Then, your new Social Advisement Coaches will help guide you *up, up, up* the social ladder while hidden cameras capture your *rise to success!*"

Mickey seems more businesslike. "The show will be exploring

the factors that control a girl's level of popularity at any given point in her high school career. The complete average-ness of Wakefield High makes it perfect."

"It's Westfield," Victoria corrects under her breath. She pushes her shoulders back and asks perkily, "What factors turn an otherwise normal girl into a social liability?" She looks around as if this isn't a rhetorical question, then answers herself. "Looks. Social skills. Boyfriends. These are things we can give you!" She holds her arms out toward us, and I glance behind me again. The puppy has made no progress on his bone. "This show is an amazing opportunity." Victoria practically explodes with joy. "It's part hidden-camera reality show, part makeover show, part competition! It has *everything!*"

Kelly leans back in her chair, crosses her arms in front of her chest, and rolls her eyes so hard I'm afraid she'll strain her eyeballs. But Amy has stopped rocking and appears to be listening.

"At Prom Queen Camp, the three of you will receive complete and total, head-to-toe, physical and mental *makeovers*," Victoria says. "Your classmates are going to go crazy over how you look when you walk into this school building in September. And our hidden cameras will catch every head as it turns to watch you."

"With our team of professional experts guiding you from behind the scenes," Mickey says, "we are confident any one of you can meet the steep challenge of winning that ultimate badge of popularity and acceptance—being crowned Prom Queen!"

"Count me out," Kelly deadpans. "I'd be mortified to be the Prom Queen."

This whole thing feels too surreal for me to speak, and I cram my shoulders more deeply into my ears. Mickey gives Victoria a nod, and Victoria's eyes start dancing. In a totally obnoxious game-show-host voice, she raises her hands over her head and announces, "The girl who is voted Prom Queen will also win…"

Mickey joins her in shouting, *"One! Million! Dollars!"*

Amy lets out a small laugh and doesn't bother shutting her mouth afterward. Even Kelly uncrosses her arms and leans forward. My head just echoes *one-million-dollars-one-million-dollars-one-million-dollars*. Teenage millionaires do not exactly exist in our town. It could offer me a whole new thing to be known for.

The women look smug. "So, are you girls ready to turn this school's social order upside down?" Mickey challenges.

"Are you wannabes ready to become Prom Queens?" Victoria calls out, in a way that makes me suspect we're already being taped.

The screen in the front of the room flashes to life with, *From Wannabes to Prom Queens*, written in giant pink letters.

Mickey turns all business and begins pecking at a laptop as Victoria lays out the production plan. After the two-hour premiere highlighting our six weeks at Prom Queen Camp, there will be twelve episodes documenting our status rise over the course of the school year that will be recorded via strategically hidden cameras placed throughout the school.

The footage will be edited and ready for the show's debut next spring, which will require signed permission slips from all our classmates who appear on camera. Mickey glances up from her computer to assure us that collecting signatures won't be a problem. "We're professionals at getting consent."

Victoria explains that everything will build up to the big finale, "which will be taped *live!* at the prom where one of you will **fingers crossed** be crowned queen and win the *One! Million! Dollars!*" Her voice goes so high it actually squeaks on "dollars."

So basically they're planning to construct a miracle so they can televise it. And let me tell you, there are easier miracles to pull off than turning the three of us into potential Prom Queens. Kelly keeps laughing, and I have to admit, the whole thing would be hysterical if it weren't so mortifying. I wonder if maybe this is some new version of the show *Gotcha!* where instead of pranking celebrities, they now prank total nobodies. It doesn't sound like a very good show.

The screen in front flashes with beautiful headshots of Grace Douglas, Kristan Bowman, and Deena McKinnley.

"You must know thine enemies," Mickey says ominously, and Kelly gives a hiss in response.

Victoria says, "These are the three girls voted most likely to become Prom Queen next year." My hand balls into a fist as I glare at Grace's image. "If any of you hope to win the crown and the *One! Million! Dollars!* you must displace these girls from their positions at the head of the social hierarchy."

"I'd love to displace their heads," says Kelly.

"Hey, it's up to you how far you get," Mickey says. "Just remember, this is a competition. For *One! Million! Dollars!*"

Yeah. We heard.

• • •

Kelly, Amy, and I each have a catalog-sized questionnaire to fill out. It asks everything from our favorite color to our most embarrassing moment. Mine was definitely the Elf Ucker Incident before today. In the answer space, I write,

Being voted least likely to become Prom Queen, ever.

Mickey gives us thick release contracts to sign, which Amy does happily, right then and there, on account of her being eighteen already. Apparently, her parents decided to hold her back from starting kindergarten for a year to give her an edge over the rest of us. Looking at her, I can't help but think they made a perilous miscalculation. Any developmental benefits were canceled out by the fact that, even in grade school, Amy was a little on the large side. She's been Amy Whale-r for as long as I can remember, and it isn't because she loves *Moby Dick*.

Since we're under eighteen, Kelly and I have to get our parents to sign if we're going to do the show. Mickey and Victoria are coming to our homes to meet with our families and answer any questions, but they stress that it's up to us to sell our folks on the idea first.

"They're your parents, and you girls have been negotiating with them your whole lives," says Mickey. "You're the ones in the best position to convince them to sign."

"This is your big chance," Victoria adds. "Don't let the *'rents* stand in your way!"

I shuffle my boots. I hate it when adults try to use slang like that. And the persuasive techniques Mickey suggests don't exactly thrill me either. She wants us to stress the *One! Million! Dollars!* as much as possible and maybe act as if it has always been our secret dream to be voted Prom Queen. Kelly scoffs at that. "Yeah right, like I've privately been trying on tiaras in my closet."

The image of Kelly sitting in her closet with a sparkly crown on top of her burned-looking hair makes me giggle in spite of being in shock. She glares at me through her heavy black eyeliner, and I cut off mid-giggle.

I'm dying to escape this room and discuss the show with Marnie, but I'm not even allowed to tell her about it. The entire thing has to be kept secret for the whole school year due to the candid premise. If we spill to anyone outside our immediate family before the show airs, we're disqualified and lose our shot at the *One! Million! Dollars!*

Instead of following us around the school with handheld cameras, which would be a definite tip-off to our classmates, they'll be using super high-tech hidden cameras to capture nearly every move we make. I imagine getting caught doing something gross like scratching my butt, and the thought makes my bottom itch. I cross my legs.

"Shannon?" Mickey says sharply, making me realize she's been talking.

"Huh?" I click back to the present.

"Do you think your folks will sign off on this?" Mickey asks, possibly for the third or fourth time, judging by the controlled impatience in her voice.

"My mom," I correct. "Not my 'folks,' just my mom."

"Oh, I'm so sorry." Mickey sifts through papers. "I don't see any indication of a divorce here in your file…"

"It happened a long time ago. Now it's just me, Mom, and my little sister, Josie. She's fourteen." I don't add that Josie is the polar opposite of me. She has friends coming out of her butt. In fact, she's already on a trajectory to *be* the damn Prom Queen her senior year. But the look on Mickey's face makes me afraid to draw us severely off topic. On top of my daydreaming, I have a tendency to pull conversations on tangents. It's a gift. Marnie and I even do a little hand signal, palm to the side as we call out, "Tangent!" when I do it.

"Um, so yeah," I say, "I think my mom'll sign. I mean, free clothes and a shot at a million bucks, right?" I smile weakly. "Who wouldn't sign?"

Except for, here's the thing—no way is my mother signing anything.

Raising two girls by herself has made my mom really tough. She's suspicious too. Tough and suspicious add up to her reading over every fine-print item placed in front of her. It may be one of the reasons she decided to become a contract lawyer when she went back to graduate school. Mom hasn't been a lawyer for very long, but legal speak is pretty much her second language. People *literally* hire her to write ironclad agreements. Getting her to sign this book-length television contract will take a minor miracle. And I'm not even sure it's a miracle I'm interested in attempting.

Mickey and Victoria send us off, bulging paperwork in our arms, with the reminder not to tell a single soul about any of this. "At least school's almost out for the summer," Victoria says brightly. "Just think, if everything goes well, the three of you will be at Prom Queen Camp in less than two weeks!" She sounds so happy, I wonder what sort of twisted summer camp she went to as a teen.

Making my escape behind Kelly and Amy, I can feel the curious secretary trying to catch my eye. I just focus on the coffee-stained carpet the whole way to the door.

Thankfully, eighth period is over by the time we step back out into the sunshine, and it's time for us to go straight to our buses. Except for Kelly, who lives in the sprawling trailer park across the street from the school. From my bus window, I see her, head down, lit cigarette already in hand, as she moves across Westfield High's huge front lawn.

I'm startled by a tapping on the glass window next to my face and see Marnie giving me her patented raised eyebrow. It's not especially humid today, but her hair is a ball of frizz like usual. Looking at her flushed cheeks, it feels like the reality show is a big lie that's stuck in my throat. *How can I not tell her?*

I shake my head and pretend to strangle myself to indicate the guidance office sucks, and she laughs. I think about how much she would freak out over my news. The only reality shows she ever watches are the sewing ones, since she sews most of her own clothes. But here's the thing—Marnie is horrible at sewing. I mean really awful. Like, the clothes she makes are hideous. She knows it too. It's just her way of expressing her anti-corporate branding resistance. She also pulls the brand-name labels out of the things she buys at the thrift store or uses fabric paint to draw strike-out buster signs through logos. She's all about rejecting consumerism.

I look at the hand-sewn dress she's wearing today and think it's a good thing she's cute enough to make loose threads and lumpy seams work.

She and I agree to talk on the phone after school using our highly evolved top secret best-friend sign language. Which basically means she puts her thumb and pinky out and holds them to her ear like a phone and mouths the words "call me" while I nod in agreement. She pats the window before moving toward her bus, and I have to resist the urge to knock on the glass and spill my news.

But it's not as if there's any best-friend secret way to pantomime the fact that I've been invited to star in a reality show based on how much of a loser I am. And now I've essentially begun lying to the one person who never thinks of me as the Elf Ucker.

I must admit, it would be pretty sweet if the show helped me lose that damned nickname for senior year, but I have no idea how I'd keep it from Marnie that long. Besides the fact that she can read my mind, I suck at lying in general. Like, even when I start in with my daydreaming during a conversation, the other person can totally tell, which is probably why I need my own reality show and a whole team of professionals to make me socially acceptable.

Just as I ease into my comfortable gutter of self-loathing, who should come bouncing up the aisle but my darling little sister, Josie, and one of her upbeat friends. Josie is so bubbly and popular, it makes me wonder how we can possibly be from the same gene pool.

She ignores me as she bounces by, but I grab her arm and pull her into the seat beside me. She and I might not have much in common, but she's family, and so she is one of the only two people I'm allowed to tell about the show.

"Ow, hey," she says. "I'm *sit*ting with *Tif*fany."

"I have to tell you something," I hiss.

Josie slaps my arm. "Oh my God. You're pregnant! Mom's going to kill you."

I resist the urge to slap her back hard. "I'm a virgin, stupid." I stop and ask, "Aren't you?"

"Yes, of course, but I don't know what goes on in your world. You could've lost your virginity along the way."

"Like I would somehow misplace my virginity!" I say loudly enough that heads whip in my direction. Tiffany stops whining, "*Jo*sie, when are you coming *back* here?" and the whole bus goes silent. Josie stifles a giggle, and I fling my head back and pretend to be passed out.

Once the bus is moving and interest in the Elf Ucker's sexual status has finally worn off, I open my eyes and whisper to Josie, "You know your obsession with reality shows?"

Josie nods, and we're tossed against the seat as the bus lurches left.

"Well, what do you think of me being on one?"

My sister sits, blinking at me, and asks, "They're making a reality show about you losing your virginity?"

"Shhhh! Can you *please* drop the subject of my virginity?"

She shakes her hair. "So uptight."

"Shut up and listen." Scanning for potential eavesdroppers, I launch into a description of the show in hushed tones. As I share the whole story, Josie's wide eyes grow wider. She begins bouncing more and more excitedly, making the green seat squeak as I lay out Mickey and Victoria's "amazing, life-changing opportunity."

"I don't know," I say, "I mean it would obviously be nice to ditch the *Elf Ucker* thing." I don't actually say the words Elf Ucker, just mouth them silently, but Josie knows what I'm talking about. "Well? What do you think?"

Words burst out of my sister. "This is it! I really thought I'd be on my own show first, but this is the way this sort of thing happens. The premise sounds like an elaborate version of *Switch*. Have you seen that one?"

I shake my head no.

"It's where they take people who have a dream of becoming someone else and make it come true."

"I never asked to be turned into the dang Prom Queen."

"I know, I know," she says. "And it's not as if they're going to succeed. I mean, talk about L-O-L. But how can you turn down this chance to be on television? Oh my goodness, you could actually stop being a tremendous loser. Think of what this can *mean* for me."

"Um, okay, so I'm not exactly focused on the impact the show will have on *your* life…"

"Oh, Shannon." Josie hugs me. "We can finally put the stupid Elf Ucker thing behind us!" She says "Elf Ucker" loud enough to turn a few heads and make me blush.

"Who knows?" Josie draws back. "With the show's help, you might even become friends with Grace Douglas."

"I will never be friends with Grace, trust me." Josie doesn't know that Grace is the one who came up with the Elf Ucker in the first place. That information only adds to my humiliation.

She pouts. "You could at least *try* becoming friends with Grace Douglas."

"There is no way Mom will even go for this." I pull out the thick stack of papers Mickey gave me. "You really think she'll sign this mega-contract plus let them install cameras all over our house?"

Josie absentmindedly fixes her hair and sits back against the pleather bus seat. "Of course, I'll need to pick a personality type...maybe I'll be your studious little sister and people watching will wonder how someone so cute can be so smart and serious. Or maybe..."

I tune my sister out as she excitedly plots her onscreen strategy. *Maybe Josie's right.* The show itself sounds pretty cool, something I wouldn't mind watching.

But do I really want to see it unfold from the inside?

• • •

When I get home, I nearly have to sit on my hands to avoid calling Marnie right away. The two of us do everything together. Even something boring like a trip to JippyLube to get the oil changed in the old Coroda my "Aunt" Kate gave me turns fun if Marnie comes along. I picture the two of us bouncing our butts on the stacks of tires until I knocked one over, sending tires rolling in every direction. We laughed so hard as we chased them down that nobody in the shop could even get mad at us.

Marnie and I will probably be just like my mom and my Aunt Kate. Best friends since the third grade, they may not have grand tales of wild exploits, but they've always had each other. Through Mom's divorce and Aunt Kate's breast cancer, they've stuck together. I try to imagine what it might be like to be popular next year with dozens of friends, and I smile at the image of multiple Marnies.

My phone lights up with a picture of her with her tongue rolled and her eyes crossed. Automatically, my hand reaches to answer it, and I practically have to slap it away with my other hand. Missing my talk with Marnie after school feels very wrong, but I need to talk to Mom about this whole thing before I figure out what to tell my best friend.

Marnie and I keep secrets *together*, not from each other. Her secret crush on James, my secret obsession with the movie *Pretty Woman*—for years we've even shared similar secret hobbies. That is, secret up until Marnie had to go all public with the stupid Future Homemakers of America club. She's tried to convince me

I should be proud of my talent, but how can I be proud when the Elf Ucker finger cot catastrophe all stems from this stupid hobby?

How could I be proud of a hobby as lame as quilting? That's right, I'm a quilter. I'd be a big hit with the Amish.

The mini-condom that started the whole Elf Ucker thing is actually a handy-dandy insider's trick to help with hand quilting, so the needle doesn't slip. Which pretty much makes the whole thing even sadder.

It all started with a sleepover at Marnie's house the same night her mom was hosting a stitch-n-bitch with about a dozen women. Marnie and I were still pretty young, like, maybe sixth grade or so, and in our defense, nothing on television was more interesting than the bitch-fest happening in the living room.

I'd learned from my mom and Aunt Kate that with grown-ups, all you have to do is sit very quiet and still and wait for them to gradually forget you're there. That's when you get to hear the good stuff. So Marnie and I parked ourselves outside the sewing circle and got busy disappearing into the background. It was working too. Mrs. Engelbert was just launching in about Mr. Engelbert's inadequate sexual maneuvers when, wouldn't you know it, Marnie's mom noticed us sitting there listening. Instead of just chasing us out of the room, like my mom would've done, she changed the subject and included us in piecing her quilt together.

It was like a giant puzzle but with colors and patterns that had to blend together. Somehow mixing and matching the fabrics made sense to me in a way that's hard to describe. It was almost like hearing a new song that seems familiar, and then when you open your mouth, you discover that you can already sing it. Like it was inside you all along.

So now, I'll be flipping through a fashion magazine, looking at all the makeup that I have no clue how to use, and I'll turn the page to some knee-length, brightly patterned wrap dress on a model with a severe eating disorder. Instead of thinking, *Gee, I think I'll skip lunch to look like that,* like any normal, painfully insecure and damaged teenage girl, I go, *Wow, the material of that dress would look awesome in a Log Cabin quilt design.*

A lot of the time, when it seems like I'm daydreaming, I'm actually constructing new shapes and patterns in my mind. For instance, the day Grace tripped me in the hallway as a part of her ongoing mission to make my high school experience pure hell, I sat in English class afterward envisioning a quilt called *Crushing Grace Douglas's Face with an English Literature Textbook.* It had a Shakespeare-patterned background and a nice swirly design with lines of text and lots of red.

As stupid as I think quilting is, I'm hopelessly into it. Marns and I spend lots of time sitting in her bedroom as she constructs her *unique* outfits and I quilt. This is probably one of the many reasons I'm not exactly on my way to accessorizing my head with a tiara come prom night. In fact, I can picture Marnie and me falling into a laughing heap at the idea of me becoming the Prom Queen.

...

"No, no, absolutely not," Mom says as soon as I've gotten five minutes of her attention to tell her about the show. I didn't even get to the part where I spend my summer at Prom Queen Camp.

"Those reality shows are destroying lives, honey," she says as she scans the massive stack of contract pages. "I hate the fact that Josie even watches them. They edit people's conversations and rearrange everything to appear more dramatic. Not to mention this insane release they expect me to sign." She points to a paragraph that she apparently finds particularly disgusting. "If anything goes wrong, there'll be no legal recourse!"

"Okay, Mom? Take a breath," I say. "You're a great lawyer and can probably negotiate some stuff in there." I slide the contract out of her hand since its presence is not helping. "I want you to think about what a great opportunity this can be. The prize money can help us out with bills, and you can stop working so hard." I look at her meaningfully as I add, "We'll be able to spend more time together as a family."

I'm aiming for her weak spot, and let me tell you, Mom's guilt over working as much as she does is so soft and gooey, it's like a giant toasted marshmallow with a bull's-eye painted on it.

"They may even give me a new car!" I say, which is over-shooting because, apparently, Mom does not feel at all guilty that I'm stuck driving Aunt Kate's old Coroda.

She shakes her head no.

"She should get this chance, Mom," Josie speaks up from where she's been hovering close by. "They will be *fixing* her socially. Do you have any idea how much help Shannon needs?"

Mom raises her eyebrows. It isn't very often that Josie and I double-team her, which is why it can be so effective when we do. Mom shakes her head in disbelief, which is a good sign she realizes we're determined to wear her down.

"If becoming popular is something you care about, why don't you just work on your people skills?" Mom says. "Josie, you can help her—*without* involving nationwide viewers. Have you even thought about how embarrassing this could end up being?"

I am, of course, familiar with the concept of manufactured drama among the contestants-slash-participants-slash-stars of reality shows. But really, who wants to watch real reality? I may as well sit at our bay window watching the little old couple across the street argue with each other. We call them the Bickersons, and let me tell you, they can get into it over anything. Whether or not the right front tire of their car is low on air—*it's not*. Whether or not it's going to rain—*it did*. Whether or not Mrs. Bickerson needs to "shut the hell up already"—*she does*. Sorry, *tangent*. I did warn you.

As I've been daydreaming, Josie has been trying to work Mom over, and I tune in just as she blurts out, "Did you know Shannon's been getting bullied at school for over a year now?"

Mom swings on me with her nostrils flared. "What?"

"Thanks a bunch, Jos," I say, and she mouths *sorry* and heads to her bedroom. Mom asks me if it's true.

"I've been getting *lightly* bullied off and on. Mostly on. But doing the show would put an end to that."

Mom grabs the bridge of her nose. "Please tell me you're not getting called a slut." She takes a deep breath.

"Not exactly. It's just one mean girl that I can totally handle. Don't worry." Mom presses me for details, and seeing how upset she is makes the pain fresh and raw all over again. "I'm sorry, Mom." I can't stop the tears in my eyes. "I didn't want you to know."

We sit in silence while I get my emotions under control by fantasizing what it would be like to walk down the hallways at school with my head held high.

"So, voted into the bottom three, huh?" Mom finally says.

"I'd like my senior year to be different," I tell her. "This show can help."

• • •

Mom finally agrees to meet with Mickey and Victoria, which is how she, Josie, and I end up huddled together on our Swedish sofa getting assaulted by a full-color multimedia presentation right there in our living room.

No way is Mom being swayed by this *One! Million! Dollar!* game-show pageantry complete with thumping dance music.

She puts her hands over her ears, and Josie stands up to start working damage control. "Hey, Mickey," Josie yells over the music. "This sounds like a fun show that will be really popular and all"— Mickey clicks off the music and Josie glances at Mom before going on—"but I think what we're most concerned about *here* is Shannon."

"Yes." Mom sits up. "Teenagers tend to speak and act before thinking. In a situation like this, Shannon's *life* could be ruined."

Mickey must be pretty slick, because she snaps her laptop shut right then and looks Mom square in the face. "Your concern is perfectly normal," she says. "It's important to us that you feel comfortable with this."

Josie and I trade a private smile as Victoria looks back and forth from us to the spot on the wall where the blazing video presentation has gone dark.

Mickey softens her voice and goes on. "Raising two girls on your own must be very difficult, Ms. Depola. I must say, from what I can see, you're doing a fabulous job."

Eep. Josie and I grimace. Condescending to our mother is not going to get Mickey anywhere except ejected from our house: projector, laptop, slick suit, and all.

Victoria leans back. "Shannon graduates next year," she says. "Do you think she's maybe ready to start making some decisions on her own?"

Mom frowns at this, and I see Mickey toss a warning look in Victoria's direction. She seems able to read Mom, as if she's playing a game of hot and cold, zoning in on the best way to manipulate her.

"I've been producing reality shows for seven years now," Mickey says briskly. "Did you ever see *Spring Break Sweethearts?*" Thankfully, Mom has not, since she probably isn't in a huge rush to sign me up as a wet T-shirt contestant.

"Besides developing *Sweethearts*," Mickey goes on, "I've been in charge of casting over sixteen reality shows. Normally, when we cast these shows, we audition for particular types."

"They look for over-the-top personalities," Victoria says. "Kids that will clash with each other and create lots of drama."

"Those shows encourage the drama normally associated with reality television. But this show is different," says Mickey. "The girls never asked to be on it. It's the next wave of reality television. You don't come to us; we come to you."

"This isn't just a makeover show," Victoria says, licking her bright-red lips. "It's a show about helping the girls discover who they really are."

Good, I think. *Load of crap…but good.*

"Plus of course there *is* the *One! Million! Dollars!* to consider!" Victoria adds and I wince.

Mickey intercepts Victoria's fumble. "There will be a team of professionals, or Social Advisement Coaches as we call them, to help the girls make good decisions over the course of this year. Shannon will be challenged to consider her future."

"Have you been thinking about college, Shannon?" Victoria asks me pointedly.

"Um." I glance at Mom. "No?" And that's how Victoria stumbled on the exact right thing to say to crack through that rock-hard single-mother exoskeleton. Mom wants me to go to college. And even though I could probably earn scholarships thanks to my grades, I'm pretty okay with taking a year off.

Part of the problem is the fact that I'm best at math, but I don't really see myself as a mathematics major. I mean, what does a mathematician even do all day? Sit in a room with a giant calculator and zero windows? No thank you.

Mom asks me, "Are you *sure* this is something you want to do?" and smiles circulate around the room because everyone knows that's the first step to her caving in.

CHAPTER THREE

After Mickey and Victoria leave, Mom starts the process of reading through the stack of releases that need her signature and enters lawyer mode, stabbing at the pages of the contract with her red pen. She negotiates with the studio over the course of the next few days, and it takes near divine intervention for her to agree to cameras all over our house, but she finally gives her reluctant consent.

Meanwhile, I'm having a really hard time keeping my massive secret from Marnie, James, and Rick as school winds down. Thankfully my default setting is "distracted," so I'm not acting *much* odder than usual as I make my way through finals week.

Marnie is heading on a mission trip to the Bahamas with her church's youth group once school ends, so thankfully I won't have to suppress my secret much longer. I was a little bummed when she first told me she was dedicating her summer to Habitat for Humanity, but now I get to go to Prom Queen Camp with a clear conscience.

And I won't have to worry about Rick and James looking to hang out over the break, since we're more or less just friends by default. On top of Marnie's secret love for James, the four of us usually sit together at open study hall where, as long as we use our "indoor voices," we're allowed to work on trigonometry as a group. Rick and I can get insanely competitive over cosines, but this one time I saw him grab a phallic-enhanced gnome off my desk and throw it away before it could upset me. The whole thing is pretty much all his fault, but we're friends enough I suppose. Friends of least resistance.

Marnie wags her head in amazement as the four of us eat in the cafeteria together on the final day of school. "So, besides the party Saturday night, the next time we're together, we'll be seniors?"

I'd forgotten about the party. A kid who used to be in our advanced classes before he got fast-tracked to graduate a year early invited us to a celebration at his house tomorrow night. I've heard buzz that a Neanderthal football player named Pete is having an epic house party tomorrow night as well. But of course, we didn't get invited to the epic one.

"One more year of this torture, and we're outta here," says James. "I'd like to say I'm going to miss it…"

"We know, we know," Marnie says. "The soul-crushing oppression of high school, blah, blah, blah." Marnie always acts like James annoys her, which is the most obvious cover for being madly in love with him.

The urge to shout out, *I'm going to be on TV!* is welling up in my throat, so I blurt, "So, what are everyone's plans after gradu-ation next year?"

Rick flashes me an amused grin. "Shan-non!" he accuses. "You haven't fully tuned-in to a single conversation this month, have you?" *Um, no.* I have a tendency to go into extreme daydreaming mode when the topic switches to something I'm trying to avoid thinking about. Like, for instance, college.

I realize that putting off thinking about college is probably the way folks end up with a career at Royal Burger. I picture my super-successful friends visiting me at work, where I'll be wearing a greasy orange apron and a paper hat on my head.

"…and of course Rick is staying in PA to study science at Pelham," James recites their future plans as I start designing a quilt for the four of us in my head. *The Friends of Least Resistance Quilt.*

James is easiest; with his button-down shirts and all-business buzz cut, he'd get stiff material sewn into neat right angles, but with a cow photo-bombing one corner, since he lives on a dairy farm. Marnie's section would have rows of corporate brand logos with buster signs drawn through each of them. I'd be a day-dreamy cloud pattern, cut into wispy swirls that curl around in a decoupage overlay.

Leaning forward, I consider Rick. He's a bit of an enigma. I take in his goofy expression, his blue eyes, his brown waves resting on his neck. Looking down, I smile with inspiration. His BlackSpot sneakers. He's wearing checkered ones for the last day of school, and they perfectly capture his irreverent sense of humor. He wags his shoe, and I look up to see him watching me with an amused look. I grin back and then remember: *the finger cot*, Elf Ucker Incident, social banishment. I look away as my mind shreds his sweet sneaker quilt square.

I tune back in to James asking, "Do you think there'll be a keg tomorrow night?" He's trying to sound cool but comes off like a little kid, excited about a birthday party that's rumored to have a piñata.

"Well, just in case, we should ride together Saturday," says Rick. "Who wants to be designated driver?"

"I'll do it," I volunteer. If there's going to be alcohol, I like the idea of having an excuse to avoid drinking. I can act flaky enough sober, and besides, there's apparently some bad gene in my family that makes certain members turn into asshats when they drink. It's the reason my dad's not in the picture. I figure I'll hold out as long as I can before feeding that asshat gene some booze, just in case I have it.

· · ·

On Saturday, it's obvious right away when we show up at the party that we didn't need to bother with the designated driver routine. But it is a very good thing the four of us came, since we make up nearly half the party guests.

We sit awkwardly in a row, trying to make a dent in the massive bowls of chips and Cheezy Poofs the graduating kid's mother lined up along the table. The discomfort is so strong I can't help but focus on it.

I try escaping into a daydream of being home, getting a little quilting in before the show starts. We were each given a thick packet of Prom Queen *dos* and *don'ts* to study. It included a spreadsheet of acceptable hobbies, and quilting is very much *not* on that list. I won't have much time for sewing anyway, since I'll apparently be participating in various afterschool activities such as pep club. *Yay.*

I take a sip of apple juice that makes me cough, and everyone turns to look at me. I shake my head and wave them off. "Nothing." I croak, pointing to my throat. "I'm just choking a little." The silence creeps back in, but everyone keeps watching me, sort of smiling and nodding. Finally, I drop my head and curse my plastic cup of apple juice.

Marnie springs up. "I know what we can do!"

"*Leave*?" I whisper hopefully.

"Let's play the adverb game!"

Which, I have to tell you, ends up totally saving everything. At least the poor kid won't have nightmares about his graduation party for the rest of his life because those of us who are there end up having a pretty great time.

If you've never played the adverb game, you should. It's loads of fun. What you do is divide into two teams and write down a bunch of adverbs on slips of paper. Then each team picks an adverb from the other team, like for instance *happily*, which no one would actually use because it's too easy but this is just an example.

Next, you make up a two-person scene that the other team has to act out in a way that illustrates the adverb. So, like, with *happily*, whatever the scene is, even if one guy is robbing the other guy, they both have to act happy so their team can guess the adverb. The ten people at the party make the perfect number of players.

We all go from bored out of our skulls to laughing as we shout out a jumble of obscure adverbs. Our team comes up with a scenario where one kid is trying to bluff his way into a bar with a phony ID and the kid who is graduating plays a bouncer. The adverb is *fanatically*, and so the two of them go into this idiot savant mode that has us laughing so hard we're practically throwing up. Next, Rick plays a driver trying to get out of a speeding ticket with the adverb *deprecatingly* which is really tough to guess, since he's pretty much just acting like regular Rick. It's a good thing Marnie is the cop, because at least there's a contrast to her normal upbeat personality and I manage to guess the word.

I'm glad things are in full swing by the time it's my turn to act, since I'm not really much of an actress. Rick and I are picked to be a couple on a first date who are falling instantly in love. I roll my eyes at that and Rick laughs, but we both groan when we read our little slip of paper. It says "fervently."

The two of us dive in and try our best, but nobody is guessing the word. They all just think we're getting really into the "falling in love" part. The whole party is whooping as we go deeper into our charade. At one point, the two of us are practically rubbing against each other as Rick passes me the imaginary salt shaker and I hear James call out, "Yeah, Rick, go for it."

"Are you guys even guessing?" I snap, realizing our teammates have turned into a gang of voyeurs. I push Rick off of me and say, "New tactic." Fanning myself, I pull at the collar of my T-shirt and act as if the thermostat just jumped about a hundred degrees.

The guessing starts back up, "Hotly!" "Sweatily!" "Feverishly!" At feverishly, I say "Almost!"

"Oh," says Marnie, "fervently!"

"That wasn't as much fun," Rick teases, and I give him a shove. He catches my hand and pulls me close. "Who knew you could act so fervently, Shannon?" The way he looks at me, up close, with his pale blue eyes, sets off a sudden chain of memories in my brain.

I see Rick leaning playfully against my locker as I try to get my books—I see Rick bending to whisper a wry comment in my ear as we move down the hallway in perfect sync—And I see Rick looking at me in amusement as I get caught daydreaming over and over again.

I'd thought he was just method acting for *fervently*, but the two of us are still sitting so close, and I realize: *Rick has a crush on me.* He must read my thoughts, because he gives me the slightest nod.

His eyes trace my face, and the intensity sends a thrill through my whole body. I feel a sudden urge to find out what his brown waves of hair feel like and have to clench my fist to stop my fingers from reaching for it.

We must be sitting like that for a while, because the other team is already organizing themselves into a skit when I finally break our gaze. I look over to Marnie, who's smirking at the two of us. *Leave it to Marnie to know more about my love life than I do.*

As Rick and I awkwardly disengage, I think about how this new development could affect my life. I mean, how cool would it be to get a boyfriend *and* not have to involve any new people? But then, won't it reflect poorly on me to have a boyfriend who puts fluffy white socks on his ears when he's bored? Does dating a dork make one more dorky or in some way less dorky by comparison? Not that my social status could sink any lower, but at least we'd have all summer…

And I remember.

Prom Queen Camp! Not only will I not see Rick all summer, I won't even be able to tell him what I'm up to. I'm hit with fresh doubt about doing the show.

As we continue through the adverb game and then the rest

of the party, there's no denying the fact that things have shifted between me and Rick.

His eyes follow me wherever I go and a private smile plays hide and seek with me on his lips. When his hand brushes my arm on its way to the bowl of Cheezy Poofs, it feels like an electric current just zapped me. Everyone is having so much fun since Marnie's game saved the party that we're all surprised when the kid's mom shows up in her bathrobe to announce it's after eleven o'clock. We have to rush for Marnie to make her midnight curfew.

After some dramatic good-byes to the graduating kid, the four of us pile into my Coroda and head home. Rick sits directly behind me, his face barely illuminated by the dash lights. As I drive, our eyes keep meeting accidentally-on-purpose in the rear-view mirror. I'm having a tough time watching the road, and Marnie grabs the armrest for support more than once.

I feel as if my whole view of Rick is changing even as we zoom along the winding roads. I mean, sure, his hair always looks a little goofy right after he gets a haircut, but his pale blue eyes are—*wow*.

I drive up James's long driveway to drop him in front of his farmhouse, and we all go through the "see you in September" routine that breaks Marnie's heart, I'm sure. Then I'm faced with a very important decision. I need to figure out who I'm dropping off next. On the way to the party, I picked up Marnie first, of course, but now she's the one with the curfew and things are a little more complicated. I glance at Rick watching me in the mirror and smile.

"Shannon!" Marnie shouts. I swerve to miss a squirrel, who has mistaken the Coroda's headlights for a spotlight where he thinks he's auditioning for *Squirrels Got Talent*.

"Sorry."

Marnie asks, "Can you try to focus a little better?" I don't tell her I'm pretty focused already. Just not on the road.

If I drop her off first, Rick will obviously move to the passenger seat, and we'll have to make conversation. Not even radio-fiddling for a distraction, since it doesn't exist.

Aunt Kate was generous enough to give me the car, but her husband insisted they sell the sound system. I like driving in silence, so not having a radio isn't some huge tragedy the way it might be for normal people my age. But I don't have time for this radio tangent right now because the turn-off is approaching, and if I drop Marnie off first, Rick and I can either sing car karaoke or we'll be forced to discuss *that look*.

I immediately launch into a very off-key and audibly painful version of "Lousy Romance" and drive directly to Rick's house.

When I stop the car in his driveway, he opens the door quickly, gets out, and slams it shut. My arm is resting on the edge of my open window, and when I put my head out to say good-bye, he leans down at the same time and startles me.

The two of us are nose-to-nose as his blue eyes stare into mine. I think about reaching out to touch his hair but pull back and drop my gaze to his lips. Imagine drawing him close…"Shannon?" He gives me a loopy grin.

"Sure, yeah…I mean, what?" I stammer, pulling my arm back into the car and refocusing. "Uh…what?"

"Goodnight."

I smile and turn the key in the ignition. Of course, the car is already running, so it makes that angry grinding sound that I hate. "Oops." I wave as I back out of Rick's driveway. He laughs and watches until we're out of sight.

"I thought for sure you were going to drop me off first," Marnie says.

"Oh yeah? Why?" I ask, keeping my focus on the road.

"Shannon, really!" she says. "That *look*? Between you two?"

"What? During the game? We were acting."

"Neither one of you can act."

"Gee thanks."

Marnie stares at me. "You are *not* going to try to tell me there's nothing's going on between you and Rick."

"There's nothing going on." I laugh. "You know. We're friends."

"Okay, you can believe that if you want to," she mocks lightly. "But I'd swear I saw you crushing on him tonight."

"Crushing? Naaah." I glance her way. By the dashboard light, I can see she knows I'm full of shit.

"Well, we'll see what happens." Rolling down her window, she says casually, "Slow down?"

We're passing the BG gas station on Route 8, and BG happens to have caused the most recent disastrous oil spill. Marnie throws her head out the window and screams at the top of her lungs, "Burn in hell, BG!" She calmly rolls her window back up and asks me what I plan to do if Rick calls.

I tell her I don't think him calling would mean anything, but it isn't easy for me, driving and lying at the same time. I'm not great at multitasking. I pull into her driveway, and she jumps out of the car moments before curfew.

"Love you," I say, putting the car in reverse. "Have fun saving the world one beach at a time." I've been teasing her about going to such an amazing spot on a "mission trip," but apparently the island she's going to was ripped up by a recent hurricane and people are now homeless.

"Love you too," she says. "Promise me you won't totally isolate? Quilting while you watch *Pretty Woman* on repeat is no way to spend your summer."

I wave and start backing slowly down her driveway. She calls after me, "Say you'll try something you've never done before!"

"I promise to try something new," I call back. Which is the truest thing I've told her all night.

CHAPTER FOUR

At least at home I don't have to pretend everything is normal. It clearly isn't, as evidenced by the fact that Josie and I are getting along. We're talking late into the night about the show and what it can mean for each of us. I warn her that she might not be on camera all that much. "My school life will be the main focus once the season gets rolling," I say, but Josie's clearly psyched to be getting that cool older sister she's always wanted, and she's determined to help me prepare.

"A girl from *Make Me a Model* said the best advice she got was to take her top off when she was too cranky to deal with the cameras," she tells me. "You're still underage, so they can't film you nude."

"Um, thanks?" There's no way I'm taking my shirt off in front of anybody.

The two of us are sitting on the couch in the living room with the first season of *Biting Reality* playing on instant watch. Josie keeps pausing the show to make comments. She thinks I should focus on riding this opportunity to bigger and better things. "Like the ultimate, writing books!"

As she goes off on a random tip about how to be the center of drama without being labeled a drama queen, I watch her happy expression and feel warmth toward my little sister. She genuinely wants to help me do well, and I realize I've underestimated the sister bond that—

My phone rings from where it rests on the coffee table, and Josie lunges to grab it before I can see who's calling. "Hello, Shannon Depola's phone," she says as I try to snatch it back.

She hits mute. "*It's a BOY!*" she says. "Who's Rick?"

My heart beats in my ears. Slashing my arms back and forth, I mouth an exaggerated *NO*.

"So sorry, Rick," Josie tells him. "She's out and forgot her phone here at home." After a pause, she laughs. "Yes, it *is* just like her." She catches my eye and says, "I'm not sure when she'll be back. Can I give her a message?" Josie happens to be a great liar. I suspect it's a standard popular-girl feature, but she's usually not a bitch about her powers.

After she hangs up, she threatens to call Rick right back and tell him I've got herpes if I don't give her the scoop. Like I said, she's *usually* not a bitch.

"I do appreciate your sudden interest in my life," I say, "but there is no scoop here. That was just Rick."

"That much I know. He says to call him when you get in. I want to know why his call made you freak."

"I think he may be kind of into me," I say. "That's all."

She repeats *"That's all?"* as if a guy being into me is a holy miracle. "How do you feel about him?"

I think about the way our eyes kept locking in the rearview mirror. I shrug, but Josie must read my expression because she says, "Okay, so you like him. What's the problem? Is he a real uggo?"

"No." I'm suddenly defensive. "He's not an *uggo*. I'm just not sure if I like him and anyway I'm leaving in a few days for Prom Queen Camp."

There's a pause where Josie could be telling me to skip the show and go for it with Rick. But she isn't.

"It'll work out," I say. "I think he'll wait."

Josie raises one perfect eyebrow. "Or maybe, after your make-over, you'll snag someone better." She starts rattling off a list of my attributes that need improvement, and I shove her off the couch.

My mind swings to what may have happened if I'd dropped Marnie off first on Saturday night. I imagine the look Rick gave me growing more intense and…

"Shannon!" Josie cuts in. "You are so annoying! Did you hear me?"

"Um, you asked what I want to do with my final free days before camp?"

"No." She sighs. "But never mind. What do you want to do?"

"Finish the binding on my Blue Jean Quilt." I grin widely.

"Gah! I cannot wait for them to turn you into a normal person."

• • •

So now I just need to ignore Rick's phone calls until he catches on and gives up, which, to be honest, takes longer than it should for someone with a 150 IQ. He continues calling at different times for the next few days as I work on finishing my quilt.

Marnie calls to say good-bye before heading halfway across the world, and all she wants to talk about is why I haven't spoken to Rick. "We keep just missing each other," I say. "But you have a great trip." Like she's going to the beach to sunbathe instead of constructing homes for people who are devastatingly poor.

Finally, Marnie and I hang up and she flies away and I'm free from having to lie to her. That is, until she sends me an email from the Bahamas asking if I've spoken to Rick yet. I email her back saying my mom just grounded me from the computer all summer for having a messy room. Except that Marnie knows my room is always super-messy and all Mom asks is that I "keep the door shut on that godforsaken pigsty." At least I know Marns will forgive my awful lies once my real excuse is revealed.

I just hope Rick will too.

The day before camp starts, technicians come to the house and install minicameras and microphones everywhere. Taping won't start until it's time for our "good-byes," but just knowing the cameras are there freaks me out. Josie must feel it too, because she retires her shabby yellow nightshirt with

"Super Chick" printed on the front and is wearing an adorable cotton short set as pajamas. She also has on a pair of faux
black-framed glasses and is curled on the couch reading. *So
much for reality television.*

Victoria comes by and coaches us to wait for filming to begin
before getting emotional about my going away. Oh yeah, and if
I can manage to look significantly unattractive for my good-bye
scene and trip to camp, that would be great.

"The limo will swing by to get you at eight tomorrow
morning," Victoria tells me as she heads out the door. "Feel free
to stay up late tonight eating salty snacks so you're nice and puffy
for the cameras."

The moment she sashays out the door, our home phone rings.
Josie checks the caller ID, looks at me, and silently mouths *Rick*.

My last chance to talk to him before I leave. I glance up at the
camera in the ceiling with its unseeing glassy eye and marvel that
I'm about to be watched relentlessly.

I surprise Josie by taking the phone out of her hand. Glancing
at her and Mom, I hit *talk* and head down the hallway toward
my bedroom.

"Hey," I say once I'm behind my closed door.

"Hey, yourself," says Rick. "You are not an easy girl to get
ahold of."

"Um, yeah, sorry, I lost my cell phone." Actually, Victoria just
confiscated it until after camp.

"This was my final attempt, so I'm glad you picked up," he says, and I realize what a huge mistake I've just made. I didn't even think through what I was going to tell him.

"I was wondering if you maybe wanted to go out?" he says.

"Out? You mean, like, on a date?"

Rick laughs. "Well, if the term 'date' makes you uncomfortable, we can call it a very small gathering, just the two of us. How about the movies? This Saturday?"

This Saturday I'll be up to my neck in makeover paraphernalia. I blurt out, "Sorry, I'm getting my hair done."

"Oh, okay," Rick says. "All day?"

"Pretty much. It's a *very* intense process."

"O-kay." He draws out the word as if he's looking for more of an explanation, but I don't have one.

Finally, Rick breaks the weird silence. "So, maybe we can talk sometime next week?"

I think about the show. "I'm actually leaving for a big competition, Rick." Even the truth sounds like a dirty lie in my mouth. "I'll be gone all summer."

There's another long silence before he asks, "What kind of competition?"

I look at the nearly completed quilt at the foot of my bed and answer, "Quilting!"

"Quilting?"

"Um, yeah," I say. "They're having a big competition in New

Castle this summer. I'll be staying there and working on a quilt. My quilt. That I'm…quilting."

"Oh," Rick says, and the silence is back.

"Listen," I say, "this summer is going to be crazy, but I just want you to know…" *What?* I sigh. "I wonder if I can accept your offer for a very small gathering, just the two of us, but pushed back a bit."

"Pushed back how far?" Rick's voice is tight.

"Until after the summer?"

"Sure. Because, hey, you have your marathon haircut and big quilting competition," he says. "I'm curious, Shannon, just how do they judge quilting anyway?"

This is a question I can actually answer, but I'm not about to get into "Exemplary Piecework" since he is clearly mocking me. I spot a finger cot lying on my dresser and feel inspired.

"Do you remember tenth-grade dodgeball, Rick?"

"What does that—"

"Remember? The gym floor was redone and Mrs. Gumto would have a hissy fit if anyone walked on it wearing anything but sneakers." At his silence, I add, "I used to imagine her lying on it and caressing its glossy smoothness after everyone went home at night." His snickers give me hope. "So, anyway, we were playing dodgeball and I was one of the last players standing…"

"Yeah, you were always really good at dodgeball."

I take a breath. "A finger cot fell out of my pocket."

"A what?"

"The elf condom. The stupid thing that Grace turned into—"

"I remember." The silence is even heavier than before.

"Well, finger cots are used to help with quilting," I say. "I've been quilting for a long time. I'm actually really good." My insides relax at my confession.

"Shannon? I never told you this, but I always felt really bad for pointing out the, er…that thing on the floor."

"Everything pretty much changed for me that day."

"Grace and Luke are a couple of shit slices," Rick says. "I've wanted to apologize for so long…"

"So why didn't you?"

"I guess I hoped you'd forget I was involved. I'm so sorry."

I shake my head to loosen the memory.

"Yeah, well, you should be sorry."

"I am. And I want to make it up to you." His voice deepens. "I've been thinking about you a lot since the party. I can't pretend to go back to the way things were."

I envision Rick crawling through my window and repeating what he just said in person. But I can't acknowledge the flip-flopping way his words make me feel.

"Um, thanks?" I say.

"Thanks. Yeah." His voice is tight again.

"Well, I'd better go spend time with my family," I tell him, trying to deflect the accusing tone of his voice. "I'm not going to see them, so this is our good-bye night."

He mocks, "Well then, happy good-bye night."

"Okay," I say. "Hope you have a good summer—"

He cuts me off, "Yeah, good luck becoming a well-coiffed Queen Quilter."

I laugh. "Who uses the word 'coiffed'?" But he's already hung up.

Stupid reality show. I just hope that this is worth it when the summer ends and my new makeover knocks the socks off his ears.

PART TWO

Prom Queen Boot Camp

CHAPTER FIVE

"I wonder what our makeovers will be like," I grunt as I drag my brown suitcase up the stone stairs leading to a huge columned porch. I have matching bags under my eyes, courtesy of staying up all night to finish my quilt. I categorically qualify as "significantly unattractive" for my big TV debut. *Victoria will be thrilled.*

Kelly raises her nose ring into a snarl as she pushes past me, dragging her scuffed black duffel bag behind her. We follow Amy through the enormous double doors and cross the threshold of what will be our luxurious home for the next six weeks.

The three of us didn't talk much during our shared limo ride here. Amy was completely mute, clutching the small case that coordinates with her plaid luggage and biting her bottom lip the whole time. I picture hours of footage filled with awkward silence and wonder how long before our show gets canceled.

As we stand in the yawning marble foyer, I take in the crystal chandelier, the ornate gold wallpaper, and the Nõrealique Cosmetics posters mounted on the walls. Marnie would hate all the blatant commercialism, but the contrast inspires me to make a mental quilt featuring gold paisley embossed with the trendy red-lipped logo of Nŏrealique Cosmetics.

I'm naming my design *Lip Service to Our Sponsor* when Amy leans in to whisper, "I just hope I don't completely embarrass myself." *She speaks.* I nod and smile, suddenly hyper-aware of the fact that we're being filmed. Besides the two men dressed in black circling us with handhelds, there are hidden cameras all over the house.

I'm so busy envisioning how my every eye blink is coming across that Victoria's big introduction is just background gibberish about how we're not to look directly at the cameras. I notice she's wearing unnaturally bright-red lipstick that goes perfectly with her artificial demeanor.

Amy listens intently while Kelly examines one of her short, black fingernails with disdain. I'd put big money down on Kelly getting into a brawl at some point during our show's run. I picture her crumpling Victoria's perfect highlights in her fist as she smears that bright-red lipstick with her knuckles.

The non-smeared version of Victoria in front of me nods and smiles as she gestures upstairs. I lean over to ask Amy what's happening as the three of us start making our way up the grand marble staircase.

"We're going to see our bedrooms," she says. "Then meeting in the Beauty Room in two hours to get our makeovers."

"Sweet," I say as I heave my suitcase up step by step. "I can't wait to see how they reveal our transformations."

"How simple are you?" Kelly's heavy breathing tarnishes her cool façade.

Amy looks over her shoulder at me. "Victoria just went over the whole layout of the show. Hidden spy cameras will follow us through our senior year. Nobody will know about it until the show airs the first episode in the spring." Amy puts down her plaid suitcases. "They'll start with a two-hour premiere episode of us here at camp. Then the rest of the season will cover senior year, leading up to the *live!* finale at the prom when we find out if any of us wins the money."

I look at Amy. "I think that's the most I've ever heard you speak." She blushes as we continue up the stairs. "And thanks, *live!* finale at the prom—got it."

"Girls, girls, *GIRLS*!" An angry voice cuts in. "Stop! We need another take!"

The three of us turn to see Mickey wearing a headset and walking up the stairs behind us. "What we're looking for today is more excitement, more enthusiasm, and especially more *paying attention* to the fact that you're about to see your Exciting New Bedrooms." She smiles coldly. "I need you three to drop your suitcases in the foyer and have a race up the stairs. Feel free to shove."

Amy and I rest our bags on the steps in front of us. "What the—?" Kelly breathes heavily as she sits down beside her duffel. I imagine she'll need an oxygen tank if she's going to make it down and up the stairs again for the cameras. Amy obediently starts working her way back downstairs, easily hauling three times the weight of Kelly's bag.

"Do *you* want to lug this thing back up here?" Kelly snaps.

Mickey smooths her slicked-back hair. "If the three of you can properly convey how *thrilled* you are with your new bedrooms, we'll get somebody to not only carry all your bags, but unpack them as well."

I thunder back down the stairs where Amy is already standing dutifully beside her pet suitcases. Kelly drags herself to the foyer and flings her bag onto Amy's stack. There's a clear sound of breaking glass, and Amy's face goes crimson. Either Kelly just busted her bong, or Amy packed something fragile. A waft of powdery-smelling fragrance fills the foyer and Amy says apologetically, "Baby's Pink Perfume."

Kelly growls and bats at the air as if she's being gassed.

"That fragrance needs to be confiscated anyway," Mickey says. "The *only* products featured on this show will be Nŏrealique products." She raises her headset's microphone to her mouth and says, "So if Kelly has *finally* caught her breath, we are ready for *ACTION!*"

We all head back up the stairs trying to look like we're putting a little energy into it.

"Much better!" Mickey calls. "Whoever gets there first gets

the big bedroom!" Which is what she should've said in the first place. Kelly is left in the dust as I clamor to be first but Amy proves to be more agile than she looks. We get to the top together and when we open the door to the first room, I'm amazed by how big and fancy it is. It has to be the best one, so I shove past Amy, dive onto the bed, and lick the pillow to claim it.

Amy is undaunted and squeals with delight as she runs from room to room, giving the exact sort of footage Mickey's looking for. Kelly stands in each doorway, trying to look cool, but her quick half-smile makes me think of a cat who totally loses it watching a rolling toy then goes back to acting all bored. I can't blame her covert excitement because honestly, the rooms are chock-full of amazing. In fact, my room turns out to be one of the smaller two. But it's plenty big with pearl-white walls and so many pretty silver touches, it has me thinking this reality show thing was a good decision after all.

• • •

We have two hours before our pilgrimage to the Beauty Room for our makeovers, so I decide to practice being sociable by visiting the other girls in their bedrooms.

Kelly's full duffel bag sits in the middle of her purple carpet waiting for the guy who's coming around to unpack us. She's lying silently on her bed, arms folded over her chest like a corpse, her clunky black clogs crossed and twitching. I stand in the doorway, trying to draw her into a conversation.

Me: "So, what do you think they'll do for our makeovers?"

Her: *silence*

Me: "I really hope they don't cut my hair super short."

Her: *silence*

Me, holding my hair back to reveal my goofy ears: "'Cause my ears are pretty goofy."

Kelly continues staring at the ceiling. She ended up in the room that's decorated in deep purple and reminds me of a witch's lair. *How fitting.* Finally, she rises to glare at me and says, "Shannon? You mind shutting the fuck up?"

I smile. "That'll get bleeped, you know." She doesn't smile back, and I give a sarcastic, "Alrighty then," as I move toward the powdery scent of Amy's room.

Amy is hovering over a guy dressed in all black who's unpacking her stuff. "No, that shouldn't really go th—here, let me do it." She snatches a stack of folded clothes from his hands. "Thank you, I've got it." With a hasty nod, she starts rearranging her drawers. The guy shrugs and leaves, presumably to go unpack either my room or Kelly's.

"Be careful," I warn him in case it's the latter, and he shoots me a weary glare. "Oh, don't worry about my stuff. It can go anywhere." I flap my hand and laugh. "I meant be careful if you're unpacking Kelly. She's in a bit of a...mood."

"Kelly seems to live in a mood," says Amy. *Look at Amy, dishing it.* I move into her room, thinking she may make a decent Prom Queen after all.

"Great bedroom," I say, a little envious I settled for my smaller one.

"Yeah, like *wow.*" She pauses to take in the pink walls, full-length mirrors, and four-poster bed. As I watch her unpack, I decide it's a good thing she got the biggest room, since she brought a crapload of stuff.

"Didn't they say not to pack too much?" I start poking around, opening drawers and sniffing bottles. "We're getting new wardrobes and makeup and everything."

"Yeah, I suppose so." Amy moves to take the diary I'm leafing through. "I just like to be prepared. They might not have stuff that fits me, you know?" She bows her head and smooths a hand over her belly.

"I guess we're all walking into this blind," I say. "But today's makeover should be fun."

"I can't wait to see what they'll do to each of us." She bites her lower lip.

"The makeovers are always the best part of these shows," I say. "And I am seriously in need of a drastic one."

Amy grins at me. "This is going to be great!"

• • •

"This is going to suck!" Kelly growls as the three of us walk down the stairs toward our future selves. "I like my hair like this. I like my clothes like this. I have no interest whatsoever in being the damn Prom Queen."

Ignoring Kelly, I think, *This is it.* Fairy godmothers come in all shapes and sizes, and mine just so happens to be showing up in the form of a squadron of beauty experts.

We enter the large marble "ballroom" where an enormous floor-to-ceiling thick gold curtain covers one wall. There's a huge Nőrealique Cosmetics logo in the center of it, complete with huge kissy lips. It strikes me as funny since the only thing big enough to leave kissy lip marks that giant would be a *Tyrannosaurus rex.* By the time Victoria finishes her pre-camera primping and we're ready to start rolling, the image in my mind has developed into a group of kissy-lipped dinosaurs dancing in a music video. I push away the picture of their big dino butts swaying in sync as their itty-bitty arms pump the air and focus on what Victoria is saying.

"Kelly, for you, we'll be going shorter and layered, with some highlights in the front and soft wisps framing your face." Victoria widens her eyes and pretends to pull invisible wisps of hair around her face. "Then we'll bring your piercings down to no more than three above the neck. And that *includes* earrings."

She seems pretty excited. Victoria, I mean, not Kelly. Kelly looks grossed out. "You'll be ditching the black kohl and getting a softer makeup look, using the Nǒrealique Naturals line of cosmetics. It puts a strong focus on pink tones."

"Oh goodie. Pink," Kelly says icily.

"Cut!" Mickey shoots out from behind the kissy-lip curtain.

She strides toward us, and Amy actually flinches. "Okay, girls. *Kelly* in particular." Mickey glares at her. "I'm only saying this one more time. I realize the three of you are not the typical contestants whose one lifelong dream is to be on television." She puts her hands on her hips. "But the show won't work if we can't get you to display some enthusiasm. You're about to be treated to professional instruction from top makeup artists, hairstylists, nutritionists, and lifestyle coaches. You will have all the help you need for one of you to slap a tiara on your head and put *One! Million! Dollars!* in your bank account."

Kelly crosses her arms, and Amy looks like she's trying to shoot enthusiasm out her pores. I'm still stuck on how strange it is to keep hearing "Cut!" in the middle of our "reality" show.

"You know what you'd do with that money, don't you, Kelly?" Mickey says. "Maybe help out your family?" Kelly drops her gaze to the floor. "Good," says Mickey. "Now, we're looking for *lots* of energy. I need strong reactions, girls. Get excited!" She turns away, pauses, and turns back.

"And it's okay if your strong reaction involves crying by the way." *Because girls crying hysterically over their hair makes good television.* But I don't care if they decide to shave my head; I'll never be *that* girl. Of course, no one could think that giving my ears full exposure is a good idea.

Mickey disappears behind the Rex-Lips curtain, and Victoria starts describing Kelly's makeover from the top. Kelly must've gotten Mickey's point, because she reacts by saying, "Oh really?" in an exaggerated tone. "Shorter hair? Fewer piercings? I sure didn't see that coming." Her sarcasm is barely veiled, but Victoria seems unfazed as she describes the rest of our makeovers.

The swarming team of hairstylists must have gotten a peek at my goofy ears because my hair is staying long. Victoria tells me I'll be going blonde, blonder, *blondest* and I don't need to fake my excitement. I've always sort of wanted to be a blonde in the same abstract way I've always sort of wanted to be Prom Queen.

"You'll be treated to the Nŏrealique Elite Diamond line of premium cosmetics," Victoria tells me. "Think rich heiress celeb-utante meets girl next door." She pauses a moment and glares at my *I-don't-give-a-shit-kickers* before adding, "And those boots are getting burned."

Amy will become a shoulder-length redhead. And not just any redhead. She'll be a dramatic, fire-breathing redhead, "forced to stop playing wallflower." Amy grins maniacally but there's terror in her eyes.

"You'll be wearing Nŏrealique Glamour products," Victoria explains. "Think diva, with an extra splash of Va-Va-Voom."

Victoria also casually offers Amy gastric-bypass surgery, which

I find obscenely rude. I mean, sure, Amy's overweight and all, but as she points out, she isn't a whole hundred *pounds* overweight.

"You might not officially qualify for the surgery yet," Victoria tells her cheerfully, "but you can probably put on a little quick weight to make yourself eligible."

"That sounds healthy," Kelly says.

"I've done research on the procedure." Amy dips her head. "I think I'm still too young to consider something so drastic."

Victoria looks disappointed a moment then brightens. "How about a little lipo?"

"Um, well…" Amy stammers and blushes so hard her face turns purple.

"Butt, abs, chin, thighs—whatever you'd like." Victoria acts as if Amy should feel grateful rather than insulted. "That goes for the rest of you, as well. We'll be putting you all on a strict diet and exercise regimen, but a little liposuction can be a girl's best friend."

I look to Kelly in amazement. I'm pretty average-sized, but she's downright skinny. "Nobody told us we signed up for Fat Camp," she grouses.

Amy still seems taken aback by the news that she might need major surgery to fit into a tiara.

"We are not officially *recommending* you undergo any procedures," Victoria says. "We're merely making options available. Anything you'd like, rhinoplasty"—I grab my nose— "breast implants"—I grab my chest—"tooth veneers"—I hold my hand across my mouth. "We can even get those ears of yours pinned back, Shannon." I slam my hands over them but can still hear her. "There's no shame in giving Mother Nature a little help, ladies."

My heart beats hard and fast. Making fun of my own goofy ears is one thing. Having some beauty queen suggest I have them surgically altered is something else entirely. I imagine myself as one of those makeover show freaks lying on the operating table with my eyes taped shut and my blood everywhere.

"And don't forget, even at your age, Botox can be a girl's best friend." Victoria gives a creaseless smile.

"I thought you said liposuction was a girl's best friend," Kelly says.

"Let's just start with hair and makeup, shall we?" says Victoria brightly. "You three think about what other beautification procedures you may wish to have while you're here."

"In case we want to look as plastic as you?" Kelly asks with mock innocence.

Victoria's face reddens behind her thick foundation. Insulting her looks is a low blow and, to be honest, I don't think she even looks all *that* plastic. She calls out, "Cut, cut, CUT! I don't need this abuse!"

"It's fine." Mickey has reappeared. "That will all be edited out." I hope that includes the part about my ears. "Let's take five and then we'll move forward with makeovers. This scene will be all about a fun day in the salon." She takes two strides away before twirling back and commanding in a deadly tone, "Have fun with it!"

She flings the curtain back with such force I catch a glimpse of a whole separate room behind it. It's filled with electronic equipment, rows of television screens, and at least a half a dozen people dressed all in black. I shouldn't be surprised there's a behind-the-scenes staff, but for some reason it chills me. I think a lipsticked dinosaur wearing gold lamé hot pants would've been slightly less disturbing.

I check to see if the other girls have spotted our hidden company, but Kelly is already gone. Probably outside for a cigarette since smoking is not allowed inside the mansion. Amy has inched over to Victoria. "I think I'd like to see the consultant about some possible liposuction," she says softly, which visibly rejuvenates Victoria. Putting a toned arm around Amy's waist, she says, "Thank goodness at least *one* of you knows what's good for her."

• • •

I realize outpatient surgery isn't the worst thing Amy could experience here at Prom Queen Camp when I see the blazing orange extensions they are weaving tightly into her hair. Her bleeding scalp might not be so bad if the extensions looked great, but they're horrific.

On the other hand, the makeover squadron does Kelly a huge favor by making her processed hair magically healthy-looking and replacing her thick black liner with more subtle makeup. I had no idea she was actually pretty underneath all those piercings.

When the team moves in on me, I look back and forth between the beautiful nymph Kelly has become and the wreck that is Amy and want to scream and start slapping them away. *Mickey would love that.*

I lean back, and my head is quickly engulfed in eye-watering bleach. I blink against the sting as I submit to my makeover.

After my fairy godmother squadron finishes pulling and tweezing and forming me like a claymation figure, I'm ready for my Moment of Truth. Slowly, I face my reflection, camera lens in my face, ready to capture my reaction.

"*Eeeeeeee!*" I squeal, and I can tell you, I'm *not* a squealer. Looking in the mirror is an out-of-body experience. My lips are hot pink and lush-looking, and my eyes shine, but the thing that absolutely mesmerizes me is the glimmering honey-blonde shade of my hair. I'm instantly obsessed.

Even after everyone else has gone to bed, I stay glued to my bathroom mirror. I hope the show has us walk through giant paper "before" photos of ourselves at some point, because my transformation is so "Holy shit!"

Not even Marnie is going to recognize me. The new blonde me. The blonde me who is being watched by all of America.

Remembering the hidden cameras helps me suppress my newfound inner narcissist. I drag myself away from the mirror, turn out the light, and flop onto my bed.

My scalp is itchy from the bleach, but I resist the urge to scratch. Best to not seem lice-infested on camera. I fan my new blonde out prettily on the pillow and tell myself to sleep very still so I'm not all mussed in the morning. Josie drilled it into me that one of my top priorities is to avoid looking ugly on camera. I may have to resort to sleeping in a sitting position.

I've just closed my eyes when I hear what sounds like an animal whining in the next room. I sit up, thinking maybe Amy has smuggled in one of her cats. That girl has "crazy cat lady" written all over her future with a big black permanent marker.

As I listen, I realize it isn't a cat sound after all. It's muffled sobs. I lay back down, staring at the dark ceiling as the crying noises rise and fall. *Maybe Amy's weave is making her upset.* She certainly wouldn't be the first girl on television driven to tears over a hair weave.

The sobbing gets so loud, I finally climb out of bed, and with a flip of blonde, I head toward the hallway. When I get there, I realize the sobs aren't coming from Amy's room at all. Kelly's door is slightly open, and the sound is clearly coming from inside her witch's cave.

I tiptoe closer to Kelly's door and am startled when somebody places a cold hand on my back. "Eep!" I jump and the sobs cut off. I spin around to see Amy waving at me sheepishly. She's wearing pink flannel pajamas, and there's a tan bandage across her nose.

"You got a nose job already?"

"No." She covers her nose with her fingertips. "There's nothing wrong with my nose. It's a BreatheRight strip. I snore."

"So you think wearing *this* on national television is less embarrassing than snoring?" She bows her head, and I feel bad for insulting her ugly tan snore strip.

Kelly's voice shoots through the dark, "What the hell do you two want?"

I move toward the open doorway, and Amy moves in behind me. I lean forward, and she matches my movements exactly. I pause and Amy pauses. It's like I have a chubby shadow with a frizzy orange weave glued to my back. I turn and give Amy a few sissy slaps. "Would—you—please—stop—that?"

She finally moves out of my personal space, and I peer into the moonlit room. I can barely distinguish Kelly's silhouette sitting up in bed.

"You okay?" I ask.

There's complete silence. I shrug and turn back, only to step on Amy who's directly behind me again.

"Ow, ow, ow!" she hops up and down, holding her foot inside its fluffy white slipper.

Kelly shoots, "Will you both please quit the knuckleheadedsidekicks routine?" After a pause, she sighs and adds, "You can come in if you want."

Amy and I bustle across the room and sit on the edge of her bed. "What's the matter?" I ask. "Is it your hair? Because it looks great."

"Yeah, you should try dealing with itchy orange clown hair." Amy slaps at her scalp.

"It's not my hair," says Kelly. "As if I'd cry over something so stupid."

Amy stops slapping her head, and the silence grows and spreads.

"It's this whole thing." Kelly sounds like she's about to cry again. "I mean, Shannon, I know you need to ditch the Elf Ucker thing." I draw my breath in sharply at the name, but Kelly goes on, "And, Amy, it's obvious you're hot for that stupid tiara, but me? I'm only doing this for the money. I'm the biggest hypocrite, letting them turn me into something I despise. I hate all this shit."

"But, Kelly," Amy soothes, "you look fantastic."

"Stop it!" she snaps. "I know I look great—you honestly think I didn't know how to apply makeup? I'm an artist, for shit's sake!"

Amy says, "So why haven't you…?"

"Because! Okay? Just because!" Kelly sits, breathing heavily in the dark. When she speaks again, her voice is calmer. "Have either of you ever seen my mother?"

I say, "I don't think so."

"I've seen your older sister picking you up at school a few times in the rain," says Amy.

"No, no, no! My sister's only twelve. *That's* my mother."

"Wow, your mom's hot," Amy says.

Kelly sighs. "Aaaand that's my problem."

"Your problem is that your mother is hot?" I ask.

"Yes! I mean, no. I mean…" Kelly takes a deep breath. "The problem is, my mother is obsessed with her looks. All she cares about is finding the next boyfriend of the week."

"So, your problem is…your mother acts slutty?" Amy asks, and I shove her.

"What?" she defends. "She said it."

"I'm saying my mother has a screwed-up value system, where beauty matters more than anything. I've always rejected that, and now here I am, letting these freaks turn me into a damn fashion doll."

"But you look so great!" Amy says.

"You're not getting it." Kelly sighs. "I'm acting just like her, using my looks. I'm a complete sellout."

"Well, looking pretty is the weirdest way of selling out I've ever heard," I say. "People have done much worse."

Kelly chuckles and leans in. "Ever hear the joke about the guy who propositions the pretty blonde in a bar?"

"Oooo, I love jokes," Amy says. "I have a good one about a mushroom."

"This better not be one of those dumb-blonde jokes." I fluff my hair. "I'll be utterly offended now."

Kelly goes on, "So, *anyway*, this guy sits on a barstool next to the blonde and asks if she'll have sex with him for one million dollars."

Amy says, "There's a barstool in my joke too." We just stare at her in the dim light until her grin fades. "Sorry."

"Anyway," Kelly goes on, "at first, the blonde is shocked and offended, but then she thinks about the way that kind of money could really change her life. So after some thought, she tells the guy she'll sleep with him for one million dollars. The guy smiles at her and asks, 'So, will you sleep with me for forty bucks?' She slaps him in the face and says, 'What kind of a girl do you think I am?'"

Kelly pauses. "So the guy responds, 'Oh, we've already *established* what kind of girl you are. Now we're just negotiating a price.'"

Amy gasps, and I give a short nose-laugh then don't know what to say. The three of us sit silently in the moonlight.

"I'm a *whore*!" Kelly shouts, making Amy and I jump in surprise. "I'm a whore. Willing to do anything for one million dollars. I'm establishing what kind of girl I am. I'm a freakin' *WHORE*."

And with that, she flops back down and slams the covers over her chest.

"At least you look pretty," Amy says helpfully.

"Get the hell out of my room!"

Amy and I shuffle back to the hallway, and I try to figure out what Marnie would do in this situation. She'd find some way to help Kelly talk through her obvious mother issues. Maybe convince her that her mom is doing the best she can. Marnie would stay until she and Kelly were friends, except that Kelly clearly doesn't *do* "friends."

In the hallway, I whisper to Amy, "I've never seen anyone get so upset over looking pretty." Amy takes a deep breath through her nose strip and heads back into Kelly's room.

She stands in the middle of the dimly lit carpet a moment then launches in. "So, a mushroom walks into a bar and climbs up on the barstool." Amy mimics settling her bum on a stool. "The bartender looks at the mushroom and says, 'I can't serve you!' And so the mushroom says to the bartender, 'What's the matter?'" She holds her hands out. "'I'm a Fungi!'"

I laugh, and Kelly groans and throws a pillow in our direction. But we can hear the grin in her voice as she tells us goodnight.

Once I'm back in bed with my hair fanned out prettily, I have a hard time quieting my mind to go to sleep. I can't believe how much Kelly's and Amy's makeovers have made them open up. Who knew Kelly Marco even had tear ducts? Maybe they've been glued shut with black eyeliner all this time. It makes me wonder what ways my makeover might change me.

I try to construct a quilt in my head called *Star of My Own*

Reality Show so Go Uck Yourself Grace Douglas, but the designs and colors are too jumbled to take form. I suppose I can't know what anything will look like until our show is all edited together.

CHAPTER SIX

The next morning, I wake up to Victoria's voice booming through a bullhorn from downstairs. "You're burning daylight, girls!"

I pull the covers over my head. *Daylight comes too damn early.*

The next thing I'm conscious of is Victoria's voice booming through a bullhorn—from my doorway. "Shannon! Time to seize the day!" I groan and fling the covers off my head. I'm greeted by the fat lens of a camera being aimed at my face by a man dressed in black.

"That's just wrong," I accuse.

"Up and at 'em!" Victoria sings happily.

I sit up in defeat, and she gives me a triumphant smile before spinning around and exiting with her bullhorn held high. I scowl at the cameraman.

Victoria's amplified voice blasts from the next room. "*Kelly, wake u-up.*"

"Bite me, bitch!" Kelly doesn't need a bullhorn. I stifle a giggle.

"Now, now, no need for profanity." Victoria doesn't sound at all discouraged. "After fifty-six pageants, I know how to deal with attitude. Miss Detroit once sabotaged my deodorant with superglue. I just smiled through the swimsuit competition with one armpit glued shut. It will take more than some sad, lonely high school girl to get the best of me."

I hold my breath and wait for the sound of Victoria's skinny body hitting the wall, but Kelly just mumbles, "Lonely, I wish."

I hear Victoria in the hallway next, commending Amy for being up, showered, and dressed already.

"Okay, girls." Bullhorn Victoria is back. "We need to *seize* the day! Meeting in the foyer in ten minutes." Except she says "foyer" like it's spelled "foy-yea" or something. At least ten minutes means I can sleep for another nine-and-a-half. I stick my tongue out at the cameraman and pull the covers back over my head.

When the three of us finally drag ourselves downstairs, we're each followed by our own personal paparazzi ninja, and Amy's the only one who looks ready to seize the day. Her weave is pulled back, and she's already put on her Va-Va-Voom Red lipstick, which I have to admit looks pretty good on her. Plus, it seems to remind her not to suck on her lower lip.

Thankfully, Victoria goes over our schedule sans bullhorn. The day is going to be a patchwork of Personality Adjustment Class and Physical Boot Camp Conditioning with consultations with a licensed dietician thrown in for Mealtime Management Support. Our first day of Prom Queen training will culminate with Poise Perfection Class, which sounds like it might be painful.

Victoria leads us to the kitchen where the needle-thin dietician is already waiting for us. It's obvious right away that Perky Patty is going to be a lot to take this early in the morning. Gleefully she tells us about the magic trick of eating grapefruit for breakfast. Too bad it will also make me *magically* super-cranky, since I'm used to eating actual food in the morning.

Kelly claims she never eats breakfast as she gnaws on her newly pink nails. Amy obediently chews her grapefruit down to the rind as if it's a plate of scrambled eggs, bacon, and hash browns. I just sort of poke at mine, picturing myself squirting grapefruit juice into Perky Patty's eye.

After we finish "eating," Patty waves happily. "See you at lunch! Come hungry. We're having steamed sardines and cottage cheese salad." *Ugh!*

The first class we have is the personality adjustment thing, which is pretty much a waste of time. Our teacher is some low-budget motivational speaker named Larry who mentions the title of his book every third sentence or so. He's teaching us to read body language using *Thirty-five Steps to Winning Friends through Nonverbal Communication* by Larry Phillips. We'll also be learning how to manipulate our own body language to make everybody love us.

I'm counting the number of times Larry repeats, "As I say in my book…" and get up to thirteen before a response of some sort is required of me. Looking around, I see everyone looking in my direction, including the cameras. Grasping for a clue to what he's just asked me, I shrug and say, "Yes?" Larry's look of annoyance tells me his was not a yes or no question.

"Uh…three?" I guess, which makes Kelly snicker. That gets me going. "Yellow? Timbuktu? Kite? Boll weevil?"

Larry's face turns red and he mutters to himself, "Stay positive…focus on the prize."

I'm not sure if it's my hunger, the power of Blonde or maybe just being on camera for twenty-four hours straight, but Larry seems to be bringing out my snide inner bitch. *Camp's working.*

I add, "How about $a^2 + b^2 = c^2$?"

"Okay. Sense of humor, very nice." He gives me a creepy grin. "But how about paying attention?" Wider creepy grin. "Okay, sweetie?"

I realize our motivational speaker might *need* all his positive self-talk just so he doesn't fulfill his true calling as a serial killer.

"I asked you," he says calmly, "how would you describe your outlook on life?"

"Oh, that's easy," I say. "The answer really is yellow." That gets Kelly laughing hysterically. Amy looks nervous, and I can't believe how bold I'm feeling.

"Very funny…Shannon-is-it?" Larry grits his teeth into the widest creepy grin imaginable, and my bold feeling flees. "Would you care to elaborate?"

"I, um…" *I what?* "I like to think of moods as colors, and well, I'm always trying for a nice sunny yellow." *Take that, Mr. Motivation Man.* His raised eyebrows bring some of my boldness back. "Would you like to know how the boll weevil applies?"

"No, that's fine." He sounds tired. "Let's move on. Kelly? Can you please describe your life's outlook for me?"

"Definitely *black!*" says Kelly, which makes even Amy give a snicker.

Personality Adjustment Class ends early. I think Larry has to go reread a few chapters of his book to talk himself out of murdering the three of us.

Next, we discover that Physical Boot Camp Conditioning is a very mean thing to do to a girl. Devices of torture include treadmills, stationary cycles, and a stair-climbing-to-hell machine that nearly kills Amy. Her face gets as bright as her hair, and she is forced to lie flat on the floor catching her breath as a cameraman circles her like a vulture. Then there's mind-centering yoga that nearly kills Kelly. After each pose, she grumbles, "I need a cigarette." Which runs somewhat contrary to the "free and clear" yoga breathing we're supposed to be striving for.

Next up for Boot Camp Conditioning is something called Diva Dance Class. I think they may be trying to combine every reality show ever made into one mega cracked-out, jacked-up production.

"Reality television may have just jumped the shark," I say half to myself as I stand in the ballroom with Kelly and Amy. We're waiting for some technician guy to finish testing the light levels.

"What's 'jump the shark' mean?" Amy asks.

Kelly says, "It's the point when a television show takes things one step too far."

I tell Amy, "There used to be this show called *Happy Days* that everyone loved a long time ago. Then they had this one episode where the main character named Fonzie jumped over a shark tank on his motorcycle, and everyone watching was like, '*What?*'"

"So now," Kelly says, "it refers to the beginning of the end of a show, and I think Shannon's right. We may be jumping the shark for all reality television right now."

With that, Victoria comes clacking in on her high heels with a giant openmouthed smile. "Everybody ready?"

She flings her arms out and announces, "Girls, meet your dance instructor. Direct from *Dancing With Semicelebrities*, it's—*Raul!*" Except she drags his name out so it sounds more like *Raaaaa-uuuuul.*

A young and very sexy Hispanic man steps from behind the gold lip-logo curtain. He strides his gorgeous self to the middle of the room and strikes a few random manly poses. He's wearing tight black pants and a white button-down shirt, and his jawline stubble has me thinking, *Rick who?*

Even Victoria is giggling and flirting, which makes her seem ridiculous since Raul can't be much older than twenty and I'd place her at a well-preserved thirty-five. Amy is biting her lower lip for the first time since her makeover, and Kelly's the only one who seems unfazed by Raul's hot, steamy presence.

I'm so busy daydreaming about Raul I'm surprised when he walks over and sweeps me off my feet. Literally. He actually grasps me firmly—*oh, so firmly*—around the waist and smiles his chiseled features at me as he whisks me around the dance floor like a broom. Apparently, he's trying to gauge what sort of dance moves I have.

I could've told him they're the nonexistent sort.

I have a hard time not looking into the cameras as I'm swung around and am glad when it's finally Amy's turn to get swept off her feet. She's blushing so hard I'm afraid she'll have no blood left for the rest of her body. Raul is obviously a great dancer, but Amy and I don't exactly emphasize his talent.

When it's Kelly's turn, she strides toward him with a bored expression. Raul's amused look turns to one of surprise when she does an aggressive tango sort of maneuver. He quickly recovers and channels her moves into a close partner dance. The chemistry between them is obvious as they dance faster and faster. By the time the music stops, leaving them in a panting embrace in the middle of the dance floor, I think we can all use a cold shower.

Kelly immediately untangles herself and walks back to Amy and me, but Raul keeps watching her. *I'd love to have a guy look at me that way*. I picture Rick in the rearview mirror and remember

I had that and left it behind for all this nonsense. I want Kelly to smile back at Raul, but she's resumed her bored expression, and he eventually regains his cool.

He tells us we'll be practicing our dancing skills for an hour a day for the rest of the summer. Then we'll continue our lessons twice a week once school starts. "As a special surprise," he announces, "the three of you will be performing a musical number at the *live!* finale at the Prom!" He raises his tanned, muscled arms, and I imagine half of our viewers fainting with lust.

But wait. Did gorgeous-man just say—? "Musical number?" I cry out. Kelly and Amy clearly share my horror.

"You'll get to perform *live!* onstage for all of America." Raul smiles winningly. "This is like a dream come true for you!" *I'm never trusting Smoky Latin Hotness again.*

"Do we have to sing too?" Kelly accuses.

"We'll be evaluating your voices, and the show will be tailored to fit your natural talents," he says. "Obviously we have a gifted dancer." He winks at Kelly as if we're not sure who he meant. Clapping his hands briskly, he asks, "So, can any of you sing?"

After a long pause that I imagine the sound editor will fill with crickets chirping, Amy shyly raises her hand. Victoria's thin eyebrows lift, and we all look at Amy while she stares at the floor.

"Well, let's hear it." Raul smiles. "Anything you'd like, Amy. And one and two and…"

She pauses for a few counts, and I wait for her to run away

flailing. Instead, she opens her mouth wide, just as natural as can be, and belts out, "Some*WHERE* over the *RAIN*bow," so beauti-fully I can *taste* the freakin' double rainbow.

After blowing our minds for a few minutes, Amy trails off in embarrassment and resumes her study of the floor. Raul starts a slow clap and the rest of us join in applauding. Amy blushes and tells the floor, "I sing in church sometimes."

"Well, *now* you're going to be singing at the *prom!*" says Raul. "How about you two? Got chops?"

Kelly scowls and gives a few fake karate chops, which makes Raul laugh but doesn't stop him from forcing us to try singing. And *try* is the word you really want to pay attention to here because neither one of us can sing. At all. I'm talking, painful sounds emanate from each of us, like the delusional folks they trot out during *Top Pop Star* tryout week just for the humiliation factor.

Since Kelly can dance and Amy can sing, I get run through a series of random talent auditions. I fail spectacularly as an actor, magician, ventriloquist, acrobat, and juggler, but hold my ground and refuse to attempt fire swallowing. Once I've effec-tively crushed everyone's dreams by proving I have no discernible performance talent, we break for lunch.

I'm so hungry I could eat a tube of lipstick, but lose my appe-tite when I see our green and pink lunch. There's nothing on the menu anyone would want "supersized."

Perky Patty meets with each of us privately to discuss our diets. If Mickey wants me to look anything like Patty, she'll need to use post-production special effects. I wonder if they actually make an anorexia camera filter as Perky drones on about food points. She's developed a program for rapid weight loss that requires a degree in accounting to figure out. I don't mind flexing my math muscles a bit, but our meeting is enough to convince me she is a hateful woman whose skinny body houses a damaged soul.

Looking at the cameraman hunched in the corner, I wonder if we're actually here so they can document us starving to death.

CHAPTER SEVEN

I'm trying to figure out if I can conceivably have a pizza delivered to the mansion while Victoria makes a series of strangled noises deep in her throat. We're all gathered back in the ballroom, and she's getting her voice warmed up to be our trainer for Poise Perfection Class.

Three men dressed in black walk in wheeling racks of clothes like a crew of underground moving men. They line them up across one wall and are quickly swallowed by the big-lipped curtain.

At Mickey's command of, "Action," Victoria flips to full power.

"Okay, girls. Welcome to your first challenge here at Prom Queen Camp. When I say *go*, the three of you will head over to the Nŏrealique Fashion Center." Victoria enunciates each word as she gestures toward the racks of clothes, which are apparently a Fashion Center now.

"You will each select an outfit that captures your own personal style and personality, or should I say"—she gestures for effect—"your *Per-style-ality*." She pauses in case we feel like applauding.

We don't. "*Per-style-ality* is a term that Nŏrealique has registered with the U.S. Trademark Office."

When we still don't react, Victoria switches gesturing arms to indicate where three oval mirrors hang on a wall over a waist-high counter. The counter is covered in a crapload of makeup, and according to Victoria, the area has been transformed into the Nŏrealique Wall of Beauty.

"Then, from there"—she gestures to a lip-shaped rug in the middle of the room—"you'll stand on the Nŏrealique Red Carpet and strike a pose." She smiles, looking proud of her own stellar performance.

"Now, girls." Her voice gets serious. "We understand you haven't had any modeling training, *yet*." She smiles wide. "Just do the best you can and have fun with it."

"Wheee," says Kelly under her breath.

I hear a *pssst* behind us and turn in time to see a bald man in headphones point to his watch. Victoria raises her perfect eyebrows and adds, "Oh yes, and…"—she gestures toward the three of us since she's used up all her other gesturing targets—"the three of you will only have five minutes to complete this task."

"Well, at least it'll be over with quickly," says Kelly.

"Okay. And three, two, one…" Victoria barks sharply, "Go!"

Timed tests always freak me out. No room for losing focus, getting sidetracked, taking tangents. *Wait, where do we go first?*

Amy scrambles over to the racks of clothes and starts clawing at the hangers. *Right, find clothing that defines me.* Kelly leisurely plucks something black off the closest rack. How nice to be able to define one's Per-style-ality™ so easily.

"None of this is going to fit me," wails Amy as she sifts through the racks. Finally, she grabs a flowy, floral one-size-fits-all dress and pulls it over her head. *Whoops, better make that one-size-fits-most.* Amy looks down at the snug fabric and sighs before moving on to the makeup counter where Kelly is already scribbling thick black liner around her eyes.

How did that happen? I snap out of my observing and look at what I'm holding. It's a shirt, bright lime-green and fitted. It seems a little too stylish for me, but I imagine I might enjoy being the type of person who'd choose a fitted lime-green shirt to define her Per-style-ality™. That could be me. Fashionable, bright. Lime-green fitted.

I glance over to Amy and Kelly working on their makeup. *Must focus.* I pull the shirt on over my clothes and belly up to the makeup bar. The pots of color are already pretty torn apart, and Amy roots through them like a dog digging up something dead. She's actually doing a decent job on her face.

Whoops again, I think as she puts a swipe of pool-blue over each eyelid. She *was* doing a decent job. Ah, well, who would notice anyway with that muumuu she's wearing. I turn my attention to Kelly, who has apparently misunderstood the instructions and is transforming herself into a zombie bride. She mock hisses at her reflection with approval.

At least Amy has the good sense to see the blue was a mistake and starts scrubbing at it with a makeup sponge. Unfortunately, pool-blue has serious staying power, and she's quickly giving her eyes the Per-style-ality™ of a strung-out stripper.

I elbow Kelly so she won't miss how funny Amy looks, but my elbow hits empty space and I realize she's gone. Amy throws down the dirty sponge and races to the red lips carpet.

I look at my reflection and sigh. It has taken me five minutes to select one green shirt and throw it on over my clothes. Worse than that, the shirt is clearly the only item of clothing on my body that has nothing to do with my personality *or* style. Plus, it's clear that green is not my color.

Smearing on a bit of tinted lip gloss, I slink to the center of the Nŏrealique Red Carpet and pose with the others, sucking in my cheeks and lacing my fingers behind my head. Probably not very model-like, but, as Victoria says, we haven't had any training. *Yet.*

This doesn't stop her from being shocked over how bad we look. Her grimace rises into a plastic smile as she releases an "Okaaaaaaaaaay," attached to a whoosh of air.

Bald headphone guy is grinning from behind the camera, which makes sense. The more cast members embarrass themselves, the better the reality show. I picture Victoria pulling out three giant, hissing cockroaches for us to eat next—and how sad is it that my stomach actually rumbles at that image?

Victoria repositions Amy so her waist twists one way and her torso twists another. She describes the visually slimming power of that stance, and I glance at Kelly. She's bent over with a hand on her hip and a hand on her head and her lips are pressed out so far she looks like she's trying to kiss someone in the next room. I try not to laugh as my arms start burning.

Victoria moves in front of me with eyebrows that would be furrowed if they weren't botulized in place. "You aren't being arrested, Shannon." I drop my hands from behind my head in relief and put them on my hips. She twists me the same way she showed Amy, who's already coming unwound. Frizzy wisps of her orange hair now frame her face, and with the traces of blue eye shadow and fitted muumuu, Amy should really drape a few stray cats over her shoulders to accessorize properly.

"Much better, Shannon," says Victoria. "Now just give it a little more twist…" I pretend my body is two separate sections and twist until I can't breathe. "Perfect!" she says as a spasm of pain runs up my spine.

"Kelly, you don't honestly think that looks good, do you?" Victoria chastises.

"What?" Kelly asks innocently through her pursed lips. "This isn't attractive?"

I admire her commitment to defying authority. I wait for

Victoria to pull out her bullhorn and start yelling in Kelly's face, but she just guides her to stand up straighter and twist herself in half like the rest of us.

"There." Victoria seems pleased to have us tempting paralysis on national television. "Now, you'll be putting on a little fashion show." I look at my fellow freaks and envision the saddest fashion show ever. "Fortunately," Victoria says, "before you attempt to rock the runway, you'll each get rocked by your own personal stylist. They'll help you select and channel your perfect Per-style-ality™."

Three neatly attractive women sashay into the room and start poking at us. Mine shakes her head and clicks her tongue until I feel shame. I just hope her giant tackle box of makeup carries concealer thick enough to hide my quilt-sewing, day-dreaming, elf-ucker punch-line-earning true self.

The three of us are spackled and painted into model shape over the next hour. The stylists make it a point to hold up each Nŏrealique product they use and recite a short love poem to it. The way my girl goes on about a mascara wand for the camera, you'd think it granted actual wishes.

But I can tell you she does know her stuff and transforms me from totally forgettable to actually-sort-of-hot-in-a-nonthreatening-way. A glance tells me Kelly's and Amy's stylists have mad skills as well.

Amy wears a softly tailored skirt and jacket that make her

once-lumpy figure look downright curvy. Her clown weave is pinned back, revealing how striking her face is. When she gazes into the mirror, her eyes fill with tears and her shaking hands cup her face. It's an emotional scene that will definitely get used on air.

Kelly is wearing flowy, sheer layers that capture her creative, artsy side without all the depressing blackness of her usual wardrobe. She seems surprised by how little she hates her new outfit.

My stylist puts me in a hot pink designer dress that shows off my halfway decent figure. I don't know how much it captures my new Per-style-ality™, but I sure do look expensive. *I wish Grace Douglas could see me now.*

Next, a runway is quickly pieced together by more covert moving men from behind the giant-lips curtain. We're each given a pair of spike-heeled pumps and get walking tips from a tall, skinny man in heels who has a sharp tongue and better legs than mine.

As Amy does her back-and-forth tromping, I notice she walks taller and seems more confident already. Maybe Victoria's speech about attractiveness being 80 percent attitude isn't complete bullshit. It still has to be *mostly* bullshit. I mean, how can anyone possibly measure that statistic?

When our runway coach sees Kelly's fierce walk he says, "Wow, I'm impressed." As if it's a surprise that Kelly can channel *fierce*. That girl brushes her teeth *fierce*. The way Victoria and the walking coach rave, you'd think Kelly was curing cancer as she strode by.

When it's my turn, everyone watches me in horror, like I'm committing a crime against nature with my walk. I clomp loudly down the platform trying to remember too many walking tips at once. *Head high. Pelvis forward. Swing hips. Don't swing shoulders.* It's amazing I'm able to move at all.

When I reach the end I pause, pose, and turn. And promptly trip over my twenty-six-inch heels and tumble directly off the runway.

Sprawled out in my least graceful position to date, I look over to confirm, *Yes, of course the camera caught that.* I envision my awkward fall getting played over and over in the previews for the show and resist the urge to run away flailing. My big ears burn as everyone laughs.

As I fantasize about escaping, Victoria starts talking, and I tune in on the word "shopping." Amy looks so excited she's about to pop a rib. "What did Victoria just say?"

Amy asks me, "Did you hit your head?"

Victoria seems pleased to have our full attention for a change. She smiles and announces for apparently the second time, "We'll be adding to these starter wardrobe items during your all-expense-paid shopping trip to the New Nŏrealique Boutique!" She says it as if the store is located on an exotic island far away. "Nŏrealique Cosmetics is expanding its brand into a line of quality clothing and upscale accessories. They've hired three up-and-coming new designers to create a whole new look for each of you."

"So now you're adding *Fashion Project* to this shark jump?" Kelly asks.

Victoria ignores her and lets her voice go all game-showy as she announces, "And you will each be getting...your own... brand-new...Freus Hybrid!"

"*Eeeeee*! New car!" I punch my fist in the air. "I knew it!" I forget all about my humiliation as Amy and I jump up and down, hugging and screaming. Even Kelly grins from ear to ear. Victoria dramatically leads us out front, where our new cars are already waiting for us.

They look like advertising billboards on wheels. Each one has a giant Nőrealique Lip Logo painted across the hood and sides. My Freus is silver and says Nőrealique Elite, Amy's is red with Nőrealique Glamour written in fat script, and Kelly's is green with Nőrealique Natural's lips and leaves logo.

Kelly grouses, "What can be less *natural* than a car with giant lips all over it?" Low blood sugar must be making Kelly stupid, since honestly, *we just got brand new cars!* We can't drive them until the show is announced since they'd blow our cover, but come next spring, the three of us will be the pimp daddies of fuel-efficient chick cars. Of course, my best friend may literally throw up when she sees the blatant product placement. But hopefully the environment-loving low emissions, plus having an actual sound system to listen to, will help her get over it.

Victoria says, "Okay, ladies, you've clearly had a long day." She announces it's time for dinner, and I imagine being led to the backyard to prepare our meal from grass and twigs. I can almost see the three of us wearing native hunting outfits and heels as we stalk small game with our eyelash curlers.

Perky doesn't actually make us catch and cook our own chipmunk dinner, but a major ingredient does appear to be "lawn."

I try to ignore the cameras watching us eat our foliage. Pulling a dandelion out of my "meal," I tuck it under my napkin and take a stab at small talk.

"So, what do you guys think? Ready for six weeks of this?"

"Today was sort of fun." Amy dutifully gnaws a plant root.

"Classic," says Kelly. "We're in beauty pageant purgatory, and the two of you are rating the experience."

I look for some common ground. "Well, yeah, the food sucks."

"I don't know," says Amy. "I kind of like eating healthier."

"That's because you have enough fat stores to survive all summer," Kelly shoots.

"Hey, I'm cranky too," I say, "but you don't have to take things out on Amy."

"Oh, you're cranky?" Kelly spits, "Try spacey! It's a good thing they finally matched your hair color to your dingbat personality." *Ouch.*

There's silence before Kelly gives a quiet, "Sorry."

"I can't believe we're doing it already." The two of them look at me. "I mean it. Girls on reality shows always end up fighting and I know this is supposedly a *competition*, but hating on each other already? What breed of bitches are we?"

The three of us fall into an awkward silence.

"I'm really sorry, guys," Kelly sighs. "I just want a damn cigarette. I know you're not dumb, Shannon. And that was a really cute mushroom joke you told last night, Amy."

"And your voice is amazing!" I add, which makes Amy blush. "You should totally try out for *Top Pop Idol*. I mean, after this show's done."

"Your makeovers look really great," Amy says shyly. "I especially like your Per-style-ality™, Shannon."

I grin. "The school is going to *freak* when everyone gets a load of us."

"Come on," Kelly says. "Do you honestly believe new threads and a little lipstick will change the way the rest of the school sees us?"

"Will any of this even make a difference?" Amy asks.

My imagination must be on the fritz because as hard as I try, I can't picture how people are going to react to the changes in us.

PART THREE

The Reveal

CHAPTER EIGHT

When Amy, Kelly, and I walk down the hallway of Westfield High on the first day of our senior year, it's like we're the end result of one of those shows on the baking channel. You know, where some cook mixes a bunch of goopy ingredients in a bowl but then sets that mess aside and pulls this gorgeous finished cake from the oven.

Here we are. Hot out of the intense oven of Prom Queen Camp. And we're gorgeous.

The three of us are doing our best runway walks down the newly renovated hallways, and I have no doubt when this scene is aired, we'll be in slow motion with dramatic music playing in the background.

Our classmates cup their hands and whisper to each other as we strut by. Nobody even seems to recognize us as the gooey cake-mix losers from last year. Amy and I glance at each other in amazement. *Go us.* Kelly keeps pace between us, quietly chanting, "I'm-a-whore, I'm-a-whore," with each stride.

The heady feeling of having everyone's attention actually makes me giggle. Then I remember Larry's body language training, or "brainwashing" as Kelly calls it. I shake my blonde hair, tilt my chin slightly upward, and smile in the inviting way I've practiced all summer. As we move smoothly down the hall, eyes widen and feet point toward us. In body-language speak, that means everyone is interested in knowing more.

It's no big surprise either. We look amazing. I'm wearing perfectly tailored clothes with pink pumps that show off how excellent I am at walking now. My slumping shuffle is gone, along with the *I-don't-give-a-shit-kickers*. Victoria wasn't kidding about burning them. We had a big, dramatic campfire scene where we each burned items that were holding us back. It started out okay, with Kelly's pack of cigarettes and Amy's Amish-looking dress, but we had to evacuate the area quickly when a huge toxic cloud emanated from my melting rubber soles.

Most of Kelly's piercings have closed up, and she looks beautiful, but with enough edge to save her from being plastic. The boys are falling over themselves to watch us walk by, but I suspect their focus is mainly on her. I've gotten to know Kelly well enough to know she's barely resisting the urge to shout, "What the hell are you lookin' at?" as we pass clumps of gawkers. But Amy and I are loving all the positive attention.

Amy is by far the most changed of the three of us. She has embraced the exercise and diet regime dictated by Perky and even went through with a "touch" of lipo, which, yes, I know is wrong and dangerous and antifeminist and *everything*, but let me tell you, it does look good on her. She didn't go too extreme, and her sexy curves compliment the fiery red hair that's actually been tamed into a striking accessory.

But it's Amy's personality that's completely unrecognizable from last year. Instead of being so painfully shy it makes everyone around her uncomfortable, she's now the epitome of open confidence. Rather than biting her bottom lip, she holds her mouth in a relaxed smile. And she even learned a trick to stop herself from blushing all the time. When she feels her cheeks heating up, she actually tries to make herself blush harder. The first time Larry had her try it, I was a little nervous she would melt her own face off, but amazingly it seems to work.

Even Westfield High has gotten a full makeover. The sparkly new hallways are about five hundred watts brighter, and the light fixtures have a thick black border with Nŏrealique written in white block letters. I recognize the font from the Nŏrealique Metrosexual men's line, which is kind of hilarious to see in such a rural school. I picture James wearing a light coat of ivory foundation on his face as he rides around on his family's tractor. *And perhaps a bit of arm bronzer to accentuate that farmer tan?*

I notice the new locker numbers are on little silver plates shaped subtly like Nŏrealique Lips. Of course they're also fitted with hidden cameras in strategic locations.

The show can't actually air any of the footage they're shooting until releases are signed. Come April, if our classmates refuse to sign consent forms, the show will feature the three of us surrounded by a bunch of blurred-out faces. But as Mickey has pointed out, it's not our job to worry about any of that. Our job is to become as popular as humanly possible between now and then.

Kelly, Amy, and I arrive at the bank of lockers that's been strategically reserved for us. Located at the axis of student flow, we are offered maximum exposure plus given the opportunity to make deliberate eye contact with our public as often as possible.

Across the crowded intersection, I spot Grace, Deena, and Kristan. *The competition.* They're busy smiling and hugging each other as if they didn't just spend the whole summer posing at the pool together. Victoria devoted two full days of Prom Queen Camp to studying their weaknesses and suggesting ways we can overtake them. It's part of our Popularity Plan of Attack, and as Victoria says, it's nothing personal. Those bitches just need to be taken down a notch or three to make room for us at the top.

I'd be lying if I said I wasn't looking forward to burying Grace Douglas. "Just look at them," I whisper to Amy, as she hangs a mirror inside the door of her locker. "So full of themselves."

"And to think"—Amy purses her lips at her reflection—"we can be just like them by the end of the year."

"Yup." Kelly's busy drawing twisted trees and fairies on her locker door with a thick black marker. "You chop the head off the beast that is popularity in this hellhole, and a new one grows in its place. Or in this case three." Her teeny diamond nose ring glints prettily.

"Don't forget what Victoria said," I warn.

"I'll act *pleasant*." She spits the word. "But this is just us." She glances up to the ceiling tiles where cameras are hidden and adds, "Oh, right…aaand the rest of America."

Just then I see Deena glance in our direction and raise her finely arched eyebrows. The universal symbol of unguarded surprise. She whispers something to Grace, and Grace's eyes shift about before latching onto the three of us.

"Don't look now, but we've been spotted by enemy forces," I say.

"Bring it on," Amy growls in a way that makes me wonder if it's really okay to starve a girl for over two months. She looks ready to attack, and I point out that her body language is bordering on aggressive. She relaxes her shoulders and turns her left foot outward to appear more open and friendly. "Thanks, Shannon," she whispers.

I can read by the Queens' stances they're agitated by our presence. Victoria predicts there's no way they'll ever embrace our new status but claims there's a chance they may invite just one of us into their clique in order to enforce their dominance. If that happens, our Social Advisement Coaches will direct us how to proceed, but for now, our best strategy is to stick together as a hot new clique of our own. I secretly hope to get invited to join the inner sanctum of the Alpha Queens. It seems like a lot less work than inventing our own faction from scratch.

As I watch, the Queens decide to flex their supremacy by ignoring us for now. Those who've been watching in hopes of witnessing a confrontation go back to milling around the hallway and openly staring at us. We'll all just have to wait to find out the official royal response.

The three of us stand tall together, smiling and holding our cores open for approach. I've been considering using my middle name, Elizabeth, and constructing a whole new identity. One that nobody would ever in a million years associate with the Elf Ucker. Glancing in Amy's mirror, I tell my reflection, "Nobody will even guess I'm…"

"Shannon!"

The cry comes from behind. *Someone recognized my back?* That makes no sense. Besides my blonde, over the summer I dropped about ten pounds against my will.

I turn and see it's Marnie, of course. "Holy crap. Look at you!" She gives me a huge hug. "You look amazing! Did your Mom win the lotto or something?"

All of my Prom Queen Training dissolves. I feel like my old self, happy to see my best friend after a long summer apart. Kelly clears her throat, reminding me that my curved shoulders and enormous goofy grin go against Prom Queen Code. I've been the one enforcing "camp rules" all morning and here I am breaking them big time.

"But it's *Marnie*," I whine, and Kelly clucks her tongue.

"Shannon? What's going on?" Marnie squints at Kelly. "Do I know you?"

"Oh yes, how rude of me. Marns?" I gently hook my arm in hers. "You remember Kelly. Marco?" I gesture in mock ceremony. "And *this* is Amy. Waller." Marnie's eyes widen in surprise.

"Wow. I overheard someone say something about three hot new girls in school," Marnie says. "Talk about reinventing yourselves."

"Yeah, we've got everyone all a-tizzy," Kelly says darkly.

Ignoring her, I tell Marnie, "We hung out this summer and sort of started this self-improvement thing." Thankfully, camp has helped me get *way* better at lying.

"Well, you guys look amazing," Marnie says. I read her open stance and the way her smile goes all the way up to her eyes— she's genuinely happy for me.

I want to tell her all about Prom Queen Camp and learning to read body language and Amy's amazing singing voice. Not to mention *I'm going to be on television!* In fact, we're *all* going to be on television and are being taped at this very moment. I have to get Marnie talking about herself, quick, before I spill my guts. "How was your summer helping the homeless?"

"Amazing. Sad. Hot. So much work." She frowns. "Is that a

lips logo on your shirt? And why did my emails bounce back saying you were unavailable all summer?" Leave it to Marnie to be the only person on the planet who doesn't want to talk about her own good deeds.

"Who did you get for science?" I try again, but Marnie just laughs and calls *"Tangent,"* as she aims her palm to the right.

"But speaking of science, Rick was so bummed he couldn't hang out with you over the break."

"You talked to him?" I'd love to say I've stopped thinking about the way he looked at me through my rearview mirror by now, but just the mention of his name gets me going. I look around, hoping to glimpse his poor posture. He'll probably be wearing his traditional first day of school uniform—old jeans with his dirty white BlackSpot sneakers.

"He and James were meeting Mr. Hoovler early this morning," Marnie says. "They're determined to rock the State Science Fair for senior year, and today's the first day they can officially present their project idea to their advisor."

"Science geeks unite," Kelly proclaims. I'm surprised she's still interested in my conversation with Marnie, and for a flash, I worry she's looking for a way to sabotage me in the competition. Then again, the summer *has* changed her. She and Raul have gone from smoldering glances to flirty banter to bonding over how ridiculous reality television is. Kelly confessed to Amy and me that it's the closest she's allowed herself to get to any guy. Amy thinks Kelly is starting to get over her mother issues, but anyone can see Raul is just healing her with his Latin hotness.

"Excuse me." A girl who I think I recognize as a junior is standing way outside my personal space in a classic show of respect. "We're trying to figure out...weren't you Josie Depola's big sister?"

"Why, yes." I turn my smile on full power. "I'm Shannon. And you may also recognize Kelly Marco here, and *this* is Amy Waller." If I can't have a new identity, nobody gets a new identity.

Junior girl's body language indicates she's fighting off physical shock. Marnie puts an arm around her waist, ready in case she needs assistance. Nodding dumbly, the girl scrambles off to her waiting cluster of friends. They dip their heads together as she talks animatedly, then collectively they turn to stare at us with gaping expressions. I imagine their dramatic reactions being played over and over when the show airs.

I close my locker smoothly, give Marnie an air kiss with a loud *mwaaa*, and head to my first class, confident news of us will spread school-wide by third period.

Or sooner.

• • •

"Well, if it isn't Shannon Depola." The slick voice slides over me as I put my first-period books in my locker. "What'd you do this summer? Rob a bank?"

I turn to see Grace Douglas scanning my expensive outfit up and down. I face her and give my best practiced smile, showing my teeth evenly and allowing my eyes to crinkle just enough to seem genuine. *Maybe I'll be chosen to join the Alpha Queens.*

Grace wrinkles her nose. "Too bad you couldn't accessorize with a new personality." *Or not.*

I spread my stance and put my hands on my hips, fingers forward, showcasing my crotch. I know it sounds silly, but it's a clear way to display power and aggression. "Too bad you're not fooling anyone with those knock-off Limano pumps." Prom Queen Camp taught us a thing or two about spotting designer knock-offs, and it turns out Grace has been fooling folks for years with her imposter-wear.

She stands with her jaw slack enough to part her lips. Evidence of astonishment. I'm pretty shocked myself. We practiced bitchy put-downs over the summer, but I had no idea I was capable of zinging Grace Douglas so effectively. I suppress the urge to giggle as a few gawkers stop to watch.

Grace's victim body language shifts to aggressor so fast it's terrifying. I continue to mime confidence as my eyes dart around for the best escape route.

"You may have just pulled your head out of a vat of bleach,"

Grace says icily, "but you'd best remember who you're speaking to, because last year just called and it wants its biggest nobody back."

Technically, I was only the third biggest nobody.

I step backward as Grace leans in for the kill. "Did you honestly expect anyone to be impressed by some lame makeover that won't last into next week?"

"Hi, Shannon. Love your hair." Kristan Bowman has precision timing. I give Grace a smug look, hoping the hidden cameras are catching every second.

"Don't waste your breath, Kristan," Grace says. "This bitch will be off the radar by sixth period tomorrow." She hooks her arm in Kristan's and guides her away, calling to me over her shoulder, "I just realized you must be all dressed up for a special date…" She turns and walks backward a few paces as she gives the game-over blow, "Elf Ucker!"

"I don't have a…date with…elf…," I say lamely as Grace cackles in victory. She launches into an off-key rendition of "We Wish You a Tiny Pecker" as she drags Kristan down the hallway.

Mickey and Victoria have gravely underestimated the innate evilness of our school's reigning Alpha Queen. My hatred for Grace burns with reignited passion. I glance around, hoping the cameras didn't capture that after all, and spot Marnie staring at me.

"Shannon! What happened to you?"

"What?" I hold up my palms innocently.

"You changed this summer." She pulls me aside. "Maybe you lost too much weight or something and it's making you act out."

"Marnie, please, I'm not acting out." I smile at a random group of girls walking by.

"You just picked a fight with Grace Douglas," she says. "That's not something you do. That's not something anyone does."

"Well, maybe it's something I do now. You know I have a valid reason to hate her."

Marnie shakes her head. "Your hatred shouldn't be what directs you, Shannon."

I fold my arms. "She started in on me and I had to fight back."

"Defending yourself is great," she says. "But put-downs are not a competitive sport." I don't correct her even though I have literally hours of training that contradict that statement. Finally, Marnie backs away. "I've got to go. I'll see you later in class."

"Sure." I smile. "We'll catch up then."

Except that, here's the thing—I'm not going to be in any of Marnie's classes. Mickey and I decided that all the new extra-curricular "popular girl" activities I'll be enrolled in will make my advanced class-load too much to handle. We also decided that dropping all my advanced classes for my senior year is a minor detail my mother doesn't need to know about.

Fortunately, Mom's been pretty distracted since I got back from camp. Josie and I suspect she's seeing someone, but our mother has never been very open about her dating life. Which is probably for the best because, *Yuck.*

Amy shows up, opens her locker, and immediately starts preening. I give her a subtle elbow prod. We're supposed to portray the perfect balance of looking good without seeming to care. Prom Queens do *not* primp too much in public.

I spot Rick's hunched figure striding in our direction.

My heart spasms as I grab Amy's locker door and hijack her mirror, pawing at my Blonde. With a *hmpf,* she shuts the door in my face and strides away, leaving me no choice but to face Rick half primped. His eyebrows jump at my seductive, open-lipped smile, and he flashes his loopy grin.

"Hey there." I shift my body to inviting without even thinking about it. My feet turn toward him as I tilt my head to the left and make dreamy eye contact. I'm playing with a strand of my hair when I realize what I'm doing and clear my throat. *No need to use my flirt training with Rick.*

"Quilting all summer can really change a person, huh?" he says. I nod with a fake smile as I run through a catalogue of reasons why he might think I've been quilting all summer. *Got it.* I told him that.

Rick has moved into my personal space and his pupils are dilated, a sure sign that he likes what he's seeing. Except he isn't looking at my outfit or even my blonde hair. He's looking directly into my eyes. Looking at me. He gives me a crooked smile, and I notice the sun has lightened the ends of his hair over the summer.

"So," he says, "about that very small gathering…"

"Just the two of us?" I ask, leaning toward him. Scanning my face with his blue eyes, he slowly leans in. *Is he seriously going to kiss me? Right here in front of everyone?* And I remember the cameras. And I hesitate.

And then the bell rings.

I look around and see we're alone in the hallway. And late for class.

"Oops, late for science." He grins, seeming content to stand staring at me for the rest of the period—and FYI, science is his very most favorite subject.

"Oh yeah," I say. "Marnie told me you and James have a cool project already started for the fair."

"Technically we just started this morning." He winks and my insides dip. "It's against state rules to start early."

"What's your project on?"

"Very top secret stuff." He holds a finger to his lips, and I stare at them distractedly until they ask, "What class do you have now?"

"Oh, um…" I fumble my schedule out of my pink leather Nŏrealique clutch. "I'm in room 125 for Spanish."

"I'll walk you." He puts his arm out in mock formality, and I take it playfully.

"Won't you be late for science?" I ask. "Oh, but wait, you

already met with Mr. Hoovler. This morning? Um, about your project?" Why am I acting like a spaz? *A whole summer of Prom Queen training shot to hell.*

"My, aren't you up on all the juicy gossip." He bumps me teasingly with his shoulder. "Oh, but you have *got* to check out the new science wing! So much better than the antique collection of broken Bunsen burners we used to have. There are digital microscopes, Shannon. Digital! Some makeup company donated everything, Nosealette or something."

"Nŏrealique," I correct.

"Yeah, that's it. Their logo's on everything." He laughs. "It's silly, all these kissy lips everywhere."

"Maybe they're trying to encourage more girls to pursue science?" I give him the line I've been fed.

"Well, either way, I'm *loving* the new equipment! It'll help me and James kick ass with our project."

"So, do I even get a hint about this big secret project you'll be *kicking ass* on?" We arrive at the door to the Spanish room, and Rick unhooks our arms and cradles my hand in his. A flash of warmth runs through me as he leans in slowly. *He's about to kiss me for real.*

I tip my head upward and close my eyes as my lips tingle with raw anticipation. I feel my hair being brushed away from my ear and Rick's warm breath on my cheek as he whispers, "Pheromones."

I breathe out a soft, "Oh," as I open my eyes to him smiling and backing away. He flashes me another wink and turns toward the new, sponsor-infused Science Wing. I sigh, admiring his butt a moment before turning the handle and walking into Spanish class.

Mrs. Laconi turns from the chalkboard and says, "*Gracias por llegar mi Reina*," which basically means, "Thank you for joining us, your highness."

Maybe I'm giving off queenly vibes already.

Mrs. Laconi's smile turns acidic. "*¡Siéntate en el asiento y no llegues tarde a mi classe nunca más!*" Which, loosely translated, means something along the lines of, "Now get your ass in a chair and don't be late to my class again!"

So much for my royal vibes.

As the class laughs at Mrs. Laconi's cleverness, I sink into the closest empty desk. Verbal sparring with Grace is one thing, but getting bested by my middle-aged Spanish teacher will not help me get elected Prom Queen. I sit back, determined not to cause any more disruptions, as my mind begins to replay my most recent look from Rick.

• • •

The onscreen version of that look plays on the television in our living room. Experiencing it as I stand shoulder to shoulder with Victoria and Mom is somewhat less exhilarating.

Victoria showed up an hour after I got home, handed me my sizable weekly wardrobe allowance, and explained she'd be acting as my Social Advisement Coach now that school has started. When Mom asked what her qualifications were, Victoria assured her that in addition to her vast reality show experience, she'll be consulting with a panel of experts regularly and passing their advice on to me at our weekly meetings.

"We're more like a Social Advisement Coach *Committee*." *Just what I need.* My very own SAC Committee.

Victoria's gaze is stern as she asks me, "What do you plan to do about this Rick character?"

"He seems nice enough," Mom says. "I just don't know if now's a good time for you to have a serious boyfriend." I resist the urge to call her out for being a hypocrite since I heard her singing an off-key love song in the shower the other day.

Victoria says sharply. "Our experts have reviewed his file, and we do not believe there's *any* benefit to your entering a relationship with this boy."

"Rick and I are just friends." I think of the way he looks at me and feel obligated to add, "Mostly."

Mom moves to the couch. "You're only in high school. You don't want to narrow your options for the future…"

"Mom, stop," I cut her off. "One conversation in the hallway at school does not mean I'll end up a pregnant teen like y—" I stop at the look of horror on her face. All three of us glance at the ceiling where a camera is watching. Victoria seems pleased by my near tangent, but when our mother/daughter moment doesn't escalate into a scream-fest, she asks if she can talk to me alone.

"Fine," Mom says. "I need to talk to Kate before I head out anyway."

"Who are you going out with, Mom? Anyone I know?"

Her face turns red, and I want to tell her about Larry's trick to stop blushing. Finally, she says, "I'm meeting a *friend*. His name is Thomas."

I smile. "Why didn't you just say so?"

Mom heads to her study and shuts the door. Probably so she can talk privately with Aunt Kate about me acting like a giant hormone. I feel bad and remind myself to keep my aggression aimed at Grace and the Alpha Queens from now on.

Once Victoria has me to herself, she turns all business. "Now then, we are quite pleased with your peer's response to your new Per-style-ality™ and use of body language. Grace Douglas is obviously a problem but you handled yourself fairly well. Good start." She nods and goes on. "*But*, if you want an honest shot at winning the *One! Million! Dollars!* you are going to need a *lot* of help." She looks grave. "Your embarking on a committed relationship is not the problem. In fact, studies show that 92 percent of all Prom Queens have boyfriends at the time of their coronation."

"So Rick and I…"

She holds up a hand. "The *problem* is with this *particular* boy." She points to the screen, still paused on Rick's face. His mouth is frozen in an awkward midsentence twist and his eyes are half-closed. I snort a small laugh. It's just like him to look so super-dorky.

Victoria continues with her relationship statistics. "Of those 92 percent, the varsity quarterback is the most common romantic companion, with 58 percent of Prom Queens dating the captain of the football team." I wonder who on earth is compiling all this data.

She points the remote toward the television and replaces Rick's pre-sneeze-like features with a shot of me walking down the hallway toward my locker. It was taken right as I left Spanish class, and I have to admit my makeover looks great on camera.

The shot suddenly veers to the right and closes in on Luke Hershman's face as I walk past.

"He's totally checking me out," I blurt. "Luke Hershman looked at me!" Which, if you knew Luke Hershman, you'd understand this is about the most amazing thing that could ever happen in my life.

I mean, even more amazing than being on some reality show about trying to become Prom Queen. You see, Grace Douglas is insanely protective of her boyfriend, and girls have fallen from social grace just for accidentally flipping their hair at him. Luke is like a trained pack mule who always keeps his eyes front and center to avoid stumbling into Grace's wrath. But he stole a look at me this morning.

"Luke and Grace broke up over the summer," Victoria says casually. Which is like casually mentioning a meteor just slammed into the cafeteria. This has been my impossible dream ever since the two of them tag-teamed me into social exile. No wonder Grace was so cranky this morning.

"There was something or other about him intercepting a text message she got from another boy." I wonder how Victoria's so clued in. I mean, aside from that thing where she has access to hidden cameras throughout the school.

How did I miss this intergalactic news? Despite interacting with our classmates by waving and smiling and "opening our core," I realize Kelly, Amy, and I barely spoke to anyone besides Marnie all day. And Marnie isn't exactly the type to consider popular-couple breakups big news. Heck, she doesn't even care when movie stars split up.

"As you know," Victoria says, "it's Grace's status as half of Westfield's most popular couple that put her in the top running for that crown. This whole game just cracked wide open."

Victoria's right, of course. Luke is a shoo-in for Prom King, and that means Grace just lost her enormous advantage. I can't believe she was stupid enough to cheat on him. I look at the television screen where Victoria has paused the tape again, this time frozen on Luke's face. Of course, he looks like a male model posing in his freeze-frame. A slight smile plays at his lips, and his jaw points toward me in a way that makes my mind reel with possibilities. With him for a boyfriend, I might actually shock everyone by winning this thing. *Wow.*

When I picture that goofy shot of Rick, my heart lurches. I try to envision him with a thick gold crown sitting on top of his head. And then I see his fluffy, white sock ears peeking out playfully.

Victoria moves on to a shot of Marnie and begins to list off the ways my best friend is a "popularity liability."

I let her chatter on, but there's no way I'm dumping Marnie just for a chance to play real-life Cinderella.

Still, spending a little time with Luke Hershman won't exactly constitute a personal travesty. I could certainly use the status bump of being seen talking to him after getting bested by both Grace and Mrs. Laconi today.

I'm not ready for high school to revert back to the rotting pumpkin patch of last year just yet.

CHAPTER NINE

The next morning at school, I'm greeted with a perfectly executed soul-withering up-and-down look from Grace. She turns to share a laugh with Deena that's clearly designed to crush my confidence. I decide it can't hurt to at least say hello to Luke.

My SAC Committee profiled him as a guy who "likes confident girls who aren't afraid to make the first move." In fact, Victoria slipped me a whole Luke Hershman file with an in-depth summary of his preferences and psychological inclinations. I honestly don't want to know where she got it.

According to my debriefing, he's looking for something casual after spending the past two years in Grace's straitjacket embrace. Which is perfect, since I'm certainly not looking to get into a relationship with him either.

"Hi, Luke," I say, walking up to where he's standing with his friends. I keep my nerves in check and my body language relaxed—hand on hip with my thumbs exposed. You'd be surprised how much power and confidence can be conveyed through an exposed thumb or two.

Luke grins at the sight of me. "Hey, Depola, how was your summer?"

I channel all my training into a flirtatious response. "Hot," I purr slowly.

His grin widens. "Sure looks it."

The seductive up-and-down look he gives me erases the nasty one I just got from Grace. I allow my eyes to roam the length of him. At camp, we learned that girls have better peripheral vision than guys do so we can check a guy out without being obvious. This is why we don't get caught ogling the way boys always do. But guys do respond to being checked out, so it's useful for a girl to openly ogle.

Luke's friends walk away, and he and I fall easily into pleasant banter. No wonder he's so popular. I'm careful to keep the conversation focused on him as per my training. We talk about his summer job and football and working out. At his request, I place my hand on his astonishingly hard bicep. He grins at my impressed reaction—which I'm not faking.

"Now let's feel those abs, Depola," he teases and starts tickling me. For the first time, I'm glad for Perky's tyranny. I giggle at his kneading fingers.

"What're you looking at, Shuebert?" Luke sounds amused as he aims his attention across the hallway.

My giggles stop.

Rick is standing frozen as effectively as if Victoria were pointing her remote control at him. My taut stomach muscles drop into the school basement. Rick's eyes lock onto mine, and I read pain and bewilderment. I want to shove the school quarterback out of my way and run into Rick's skinny arms.

But Rick quickly removes that option, turning on the heel of his BlackSpot sneakers. He's wearing one black one and one white one today—a sign he was feeling cheerful this morning. He strides away, *white-black-white-black*, his backpack clinking with the sound of loose beakers. I glance around the hallway, trying to gauge what I can do to fix this.

"So, hey," Luke says, "you want to hang out sometime?"

No, I need to go talk to Rick.

Instead, I look into the deep brown of Luke's eyes and ask, "What about Grace?" According to page six of his file, he only responds to direct confrontation.

He falters a moment then scoffs, "She and I are *so* over, and boy, am I ready to move on." He smiles at me, dialing his dimples up to full adorable.

I imagine Grace getting the news that her Luke is asking Shannon Depola to hang out and picture her head exploding. *Maybe I should see how this plays out.* I smile back and tell Grace's ex, "I'd *love* to hang sometime."

His brown eyes assure me going on a date with him will not be the worst sacrifice I've ever made.

• • •

As it turns out, I assumed too much when I interpreted Luke's invitation to "hang out sometime" to mean he was taking me on an actual *date*. Apparently, he meant he'd toss his impressive bicep possessively over my shoulder and walk me between all my classes.

Kelly reacts by accusing, "Gee, Shannon, you're going all out. Stealing Grace's man?"

"Outwit, Outplay, Outwear." I smooth my fitted skirt. I know Kelly well enough to see she's actually thrown off by my snagging the football captain.

"I thought you liked that Rick guy," she says, and I regret getting so honest with her at camp.

"This could be a total game changer." I ignore her comment. "I don't seem like such a dumb blonde to you now, do I?"

"Have you completely lost your mind?" I turn to see Marnie standing behind me. "I thought you liked Rick."

I realize I'm pressing my lips together in response, which is a sign a person is holding back what they'd really like to say. I'm not even sure what I'm hiding from Marnie but tell her, "I never actually decided whether or not I'm into him."

"I witnessed the adverb game, Shannon. I'm pretty sure you're into him."

"What's the adverb game?" Kelly asks. "Sounds kinky."

Marnie and I just stare her down until she slams her locker and struts away.

Marnie turns to me. "Have you forgotten *Luke* is the one who picked up your finger cot and gave you that awful nickname?"

"Please, don't bring that up." I wince. "*Rick* is the one responsible for pointing out the...thing, and besides, *Grace* is the one who came up with that name. Now that the two of them are broken up, Luke's a completely different person this year."

"He's not the only one," Marnie grumbles.

"Hey, listen, I'm sorry that Rick and I didn't work out. I know that would've really greased the gears for you and James."

"Is that what you honestly think? That I would steer you toward Rick for my own benefit?" Marnie's brow furrows in anger. "Luke is so clearly wrong for you I can't believe you'd even consider going out with him."

"Oh, so now you don't think I'm good enough to date Luke Hershman?" I'm careful not to raise my voice and cause a scene, but my heart is beating so fast I'm afraid the cameras can see it.

"No. I think you're too good for Luke Hershman. But then, you've always had a tough time seeing yourself clearly."

"What is that supposed to mean?"

"It means you've always sold yourself short, Shannon. Like the whole Elf Ucker thing. You just accepted it all as if you deserved it or something."

"Don't you think my being with the captain of the football team proves my self-esteem is much healthier now?"

"No, I think turning *down* the captain of the football team and dating the guy you actually *like* would prove you have healthy self-esteem."

"The guy I *like* is Luke," I insist.

"Well, if you *like* him then by all means *date* him," Marnie says. "But don't expect me to stand by and watch you make a huge mistake."

She turns and walks away, and I call out, "The Bahamas really changed you!"

She doesn't turn back, and I realize this is the first fight we've had since middle school. And that was about which cookies we should bake during a sleepover. I decide I have no choice but to tell Marnie about the show. It's the only way I can make her understand why I'm spending time with Luke.

It seems his default setting must be "serious monogamous relationship," because before I know it, I'm seamlessly inserted into Grace's place as Luke's girlfriend. Which is exactly the position I've been training for.

Kelly continues to act astonished by my achievement while Amy avoids eye contact with Luke. No amount of Prom Queen training could ever cure her shyness around hot guys. Oh, have I mentioned Luke's hot? Really. I'm talking, he makes Raul seem like a girly-boy who dreams of becoming a man.

Over the next few days, he and I are dubbed "Shan-uke" (pronounced "Shanoŏok") by our student body fanbase. It feels like the hallways should be covered in red carpet as everyone stares at us walking past. Including the faculty. I'm getting watched from every angle, and that isn't even counting the hidden cameras.

This competition? Just. Got. Interesting.

Between the pressing demands of shopping, socializing, and meeting with my SACC, a week passes by before I get a chance to call Marnie. When she picks up, I duck into our bathroom with my cellphone for privacy and whisper, "Hello."

"Shannon, are you okay?"

I laugh and keep my voice low. "Listen, I have something I need to share with you, but you can't tell *anybody*."

"What's going on?"

"You know how I was missing all summer?"

"Yes," Marnie says slowly.

I take a deep breath. "Well, you're not going to believe this, but I was actually at Prom Q—"

"Excuse me, Shannon," a vaguely familiar voice cuts in on the line. "I do believe you are under contract to keep certain details of your summer activities private."

"Marnie?"

"Your friend has been disconnected from this call, and we are now placing a block on her number." It's Mickey.

"How are you even doing this? Have you been listening to all of my calls?"

"We have a lot of money invested in you, Shannon. We need to protect our investment and ensure the show is not compromised by loose lips."

"I wasn't going to…" But I can't lie. I was about to tell Marnie everything. "I'm sorry. But you don't understand how cool Marnie would be. She wouldn't tell a soul about the show. I just want her to understand why I'm hanging out with Luke."

"Nobody should need an excuse to date that boy," Mickey says, which is true. "We have high hopes for you, Shannon. You could be the dark horse that wins this whole epic shebang."

"You mean blonde horse," I say, and Mickey gives a cold laugh before hanging up.

I just stare at the cellphone in my hand for a moment. They must've put some sort of chip in it when they confiscated it for the summer. I understand the need to preserve the show's secrecy, but I wonder if Amy and Kelly know our phone conversations are all being monitored. And now how can I explain everything to Marnie?

• • •

"What were you talking about last night?" Marnie is waiting for me in front of my locker. "I tried calling you back when our connection broke, but I couldn't get through."

I glance at the ceiling where a hidden camera—and Mickey—are probably watching me.

"Sorry, I dropped my cell phone in the toilet," I say, sliding it deeper into my purse before she sees it.

"You said something about summer. Where were you?"

"It was nothing. I was just daydreaming about sunny days. You know how I can be."

"No, I clearly heard you start to say something about prom. Is that why you're dating Luke? You want some hunky arm candy to wear to the prom?"

"That's ridiculous. Prom is like eight months away. Why would I be thinking of it now?" I feel my eyes blinking and hope Marnie doesn't know this is my tell when I'm lying. I've been trying to work on it since camp.

Marnie gives me a look that says of course she's aware of my tell. "I don't know what the hell is up with you, Shannon. But call me when you're ready to act like a normal person."

I smile. "You mean normal for *me*, right?"

"Yes, Shannon." She sighs. "Normal for you."

Marnie walks away, and I'm glad that our friendship is strong enough to withstand my odd behavior. At least now she knows something's up. She'll just have to trust that I have a reason for acting much stranger than usual.

• • •

"Maybe your mom can come and catch one of our practices," Luke tells me as I toss a book into my locker. "I'd love for her to see me in action."

"Okaay," I say, "She's usually kind of busy?" The woman never made it to even one of my volleyball games when I tried on a jock persona back in seventh grade. I close my locker and spin the lock.

Luke laughs and puts his arm over my shoulder. "Yeah, sure, I guess your mom gets enough of that at work." Which makes me wonder what, exactly, he thinks she does for a living. But then, I don't want to jinx my tactical romantic connection by demanding an explanation for every peculiar comment he makes. The whole school is in love with us being together.

"The two of you have *got* to be kidding me!"

It takes a moment to find the source of the outraged voice since I'm tucked into Luke's armpit, and we turn around as one singular unit to see who's talking.

Grace. *Of course.* And her body language is not subtle. Arms crossed and foot tapping—she's pissed.

Luke's arm goes slack, and I catch his expression of gloom before his hold on me tightens. His bulging bicep presses into my neck so hard I bow my head before it gets snapped off like a dandelion.

"Well, if it isn't the cheating cheater," Luke shoots at Grace, and I try to figure out a way to disappear. *Perhaps a stop-drop-and-roll maneuver.*

"I told you, that text message had to be a mistake!" Grace says. "I don't even know a Ben."

"Come on, Grace," Luke accuses. "Ben is a *really* common name." He curls his forearm as he speaks, effectively trapping me in a headlock.

"So this is it? You've moved on already?" Her voice catches. "After all we shared?"

"Problem is, I can't know who else you've been *sharing* with." Luke says. "'I had a great time last night' is a really odd text message to get. Especially the day after you *said* you were sleeping over at your nana's house."

I wheeze at Luke, "Who still has sleepovers at their grandmother's?"

"Exactly," he agrees as he slides his arm down my back and rests his hand on my hip. My lungs enjoy a full breath of air.

"Luuuuke," Grace says. "You called the number yourself. It's disconnected. There is no Ben!"

Luke says, "I'm sure *Ben* would disagree that there is no Ben." *Note to self: Do not expect future disputes with new boyfriend to be particularly rational.*

"Fine, don't believe me," Grace says. "Go ahead and paw this skank all you want, but you'll be back. And, Elf Ucker?" I cringe at the name. "Once Luke and I are together again, don't think I'll forget how you threw yourself at my man during our little break."

I'm pretty sure I've just been socially damned for all eternity. This runs contrary to my primary goal of becoming more popular, but Luke just scoffs and maneuvers me past Grace.

As we move down the hallway, I say, "I take it things ended badly between you two?"

"I don't know." Luke shrugs. "She's just working things through."

Glancing up, I see he isn't joking. *Addendum to Note to self: Don't expect a high level of emotional sensitivity either.* He shoots me a quick grin, and I decide I'll survive. Just as long as he doesn't put me into a chokehold every time we run into his ex.

• • •

Luke invites me to a party that's happening Friday night, which is super-exciting for several reasons. Firstly, I'm going to a gathering entirely made up of my target audience, i.e., popular people. On top of that, I'm pretty sure my hot date and I will *not* make up a significant portion of the guest list. It feels like things are really going to start happening to me now.

On my way out of school Friday afternoon, I nearly run directly into Marnie. The two of us stand awkwardly looking at each other's shoes. Finally, I say, "I'm sorry."

"Me too." But there's no emotion in either of our voices.

"Any plans this weekend?" I ask.

"No, you?"

When I tell her about the party, her eyes go wide. "Holy cow, you've totally gone to the dark side."

I grin. "Want to join me? I can give you a makeover."

Marnie wrinkles her nose. "And what? Bury myself in name brands like you? What the hell is with all the Nŏrealique shit all over the school anyway?" Her eyes narrow. "Are you working for them?"

"What? No." *Not exactly.*

"I've heard of this!" Marnie grabs me by the arms. "Big corporations pay students to wear their brands and promote their image. Is that what you've been doing?"

"I'm not…" I start to protest, but then realize this is probably the closest I can come to telling Marnie the truth without tipping her off about the show and getting in trouble with Mickey. I look my best friend in the eyes and say, "You absolutely cannot tell anyone."

Marnie's mouth opens and closes a few times. "You can't do this. You cannot help this mega-corporation hijack our freedom."

"Nŏrealique isn't taking anybody's freedom."

"What about my freedom to go to school in an ad-free environment?" Marnie is practically shaking with rage.

"I don't think that's—"

"That's your problem, Shannon, you just don't think!"

I'm speechless, and Marnie growls. "You have turned yourself into the thing that I hate." She flicks the rhinestone pair of lips on the front of my shirt. "Pimping your brand. You're a walking advertisement, Shannon."

I want to explain to her that I'm contractually obligated to wear this pin, prominently displayed, at least once a week. Instead I ask, "Are you coming with me to this awesome party tonight or what?"

Marnie shakes her head. "You have a good time, Shannon. I'll let Rick know you've definitely moved on."

As she turns and walks away, I'm hit with a pang of regret. "Hey, Marns," I call. But she doesn't turn around.

I think back to the day we became friends in fifth grade. Marnie was still the new girl despite being here for over a year. We were sitting in social studies class while Mr. Bovard challenged the record for the longest droning monologue ever. A record that had incidentally been set by him a week prior. I was fighting to pay attention when a girl's voice floated down from just above my head.

"Is that a wart?"

I remember shooting my hand protectively over the lump on my index finger and looking up to see the new girl's curious face. She'd been waiting in line to use the pencil sharpener and must've noticed my horrible, deforming wart. I shoved my hands into my lap.

"Hey," she whispered covertly and waited for me to look back up.

She yanked up her sleeve, folded back her arm, and aimed her elbow toward my nose. "I've got one too!" Sure enough, there on the outside of her right elbow was a nice, disgusting wart. It was easier to hide than the one on my hand, but it was way grosser, with teeny brown flesh-spikes growing along one side.

Marnie gave me a huge grin.

I grinned right back and we were instant best friends. I know what you're thinking, pretty gross beginnings—but hey, eventually Marnie had her wart removed and mine fell off and at least it won me an amazing friend.

After the Elf Ucker Incident, Marnie became my only friend too. Looking down the hallway at the spot where she disappeared, I wish I could just explain to her how much Nórealique has already done for me. I straighten my lips logo pin and walk the opposite way.

• • •

New outfits are strewn across my bed as I try to decode what the hell I should wear. *What is my Per-style-ality™ again?* I'm so anxious, I toy with the idea of cutting my purple shirt into triangles and quilting a quick pinwheel square, just to calm my nerves. Thankfully, Josie rescues me before I start butchering my wardrobe. With a dramatic flourish, she picks the perfect combination of blue-jean casual and black low-cut sexiness. *No wonder she's so naturally popular. She knows how to dress for it.*

"I'm so freaking excited you're going to this party!" she squeals. "Everyone's talking about it. And I cannot *believe* you're going with Luke Hershman."

I grin at her and feel a surge of warmth toward my little sister.

"Aren't you glad now that you blew that Rick guy off?"

My smile turns sour, but I nod while I admire my outfit in the mirror. "Thanks so much, Josie. You're a miracle worker."

"Um, you've managed a miracle or two yourself here, sis." She gives me a peck on the cheek and looks me in the eye. "I'm so proud of you."

The two of us have always existed on completely separate planes, but now it seems our planes have intersected in a line. And every point along this common line is familiar to her but strange to me. We embrace, and then Josie scurries off to get ready for her big "greeting Luke at the door" scene.

I stare at my reflection after she goes, wondering if Cinderella felt like this much of an imposter. This night is my debutante ball disguised as a Friday night senior kegger. Luckily, I've already nabbed the handsome prince.

When Luke comes to the door to pick me up, he lets out a low whistle of appreciation for how I look. Then he scans the room and asks, "Your mom around?"

Is he hoping for privacy to make out with me? He's kissed me good-bye on the cheek a few times at school, but nothing with any heat.

"No, she's out with her boyfriend" I say and quickly add, "but my sister's here." On cue, Josie pops in from her eavesdropping position in the hallway.

"Hi, Luke," she says flirtatiously. "I'm Josie." I fight the urge to stand between them and block him from falling in love with her.

"Hey," he greets and turns back to me. "You ready to go then?"

"Sure." I pull on my sexy pumps, hopping awkwardly as I try to balance and cursing the rule that dictates I should never be completely when a date arrives. Luke reaches to steady me, and I grin as I take his strong arm. *Okay, so maybe the rule isn't complete bullshit.* He leads me out, ignoring Josie calling, "It was nice meeting you."

It feels good not to be outshone by my little sister for a change. Despite her age, it's far too easy to picture Josie and Luke as a couple. They seem like each other's type—both upbeat and naturally popular.

As I slide awkwardly into Luke's convertible vintage cruiser, I wonder if popularity will ever feel natural to me.

• • •

The party is being hosted by Luke's teammate Neanderthal Pete, whose parents are out of town for the weekend. I follow Luke into the foyer, pausing a moment to savor my big arrival. As the music throbs, I brace myself for a wild, popular-kid party scene, imagining people dancing on the couches and making out on the stairs. We round the corner to the living room and... *Where the hell is everybody?*

The only witnesses to my grand entrance are a bunch of empty chairs set up around the room. It's the graduation party all over again. I fleetingly hope we don't need a clever word game to save us this time. I'm not entirely certain the football players at our school are familiar with the part of speech commonly referred to as the "adverb."

"We're early." Luke leads me into the kitchen where Pete is lining up Jell-O shots. A thin girl wearing jeans sits on the granite countertop with her head bowed. A black, military style cap obscures her face, and her heels kick at the lower cupboard door. Her body language tells me this chick is mind-numbingly bored.

When she looks up, I'm surprised that it's Kelly. She actually brightens when she sees me walking toward her, which I take as a huge compliment. *We really did bond at camp.* She leans in close, feigning a hug hello, and whispers in my ear, "Thank God you're here! Victoria popped in on me at home and made me wear this stupid hat." She bows her head, showing me the embroidered Nŏrealique Lips logo.

"It's not so bad," I tell her.

"There's a *camera* built in, under the fabric of the logo." She grins. "But *now* the footage won't just be about me."

I make a face at her. I'd been looking forward to a little break from the cameras and even considered having a drink or two tonight. I mean, who knows? Maybe I'm a party prodigy of some sort who is magically funny and charismatic after a few wine coolers. Then again, maybe I'm the type of girl who ends up dancing half-naked on a table before she knows what's happening. Guess I'll wait on yanking the lid off of that Schrödinger experiment.

I ask Kelly, "So, do you think Amy'll show up? Possibly wearing a dorky cap too?" I jab her with my shoulder.

"Like I care what I'm wearing," she says. "And you know Amy's busy working out at the gym every spare second."

I nod. "Her conversion from whale to gym rat is complete."

"Oops, I wasn't looking in your direction." Kelly says. "Mind repeating that for the camera?"

I give her a cheesy smile and twist my body into a slimming pose. That stupid hat is going to make this night seem very long.

But at least it isn't boring.

The Queens show up in all their highlighted glory just before ten, and it's as if they grant the party permission to start happening. The music cranks up a few decibels, and the keg starts pumping. I look around and get a sense of déjà vu for every party in every teen movie I've ever watched. It grows increasingly wild with people making out dancing and chanting for each other to "Drink! Drink! DRINK!"

Grace paces back and forth, eyeing Luke like guy-prey as he

plays a game involving plastic cups of beer and a rather unsanitary ping pong ball. She fires a glare my way each time she grabs another Jell-O shot.

I stick close to Kelly, firstly because she's the only person I know at this party and also so I can keep tabs on that damn camera in her hat. But I also harbor the small hope that the two of us bonded enough at Prom Queen Camp that she'll feel compelled to defend me if Luke's ex tries to jump my ass.

"Have you been to this type of party before?" I ask Kelly. We've looped the crowd twice and are settled back on the kitchen counter where we started.

She snorts, "You kidding? This was my home life growing up. Why would I want to revisit this sort of scene?"

"So you're only here…"

"To try and win a million bucks, yes." She pauses and adds, "I mean, of course I'd like to get to know these people for who they truly are." She gestures to her hat and I stifle the urge to giggle. Making snarky comments about our peers on camera could easily lead to an angry teen mob down the line.

Finally, Grace must reach a truth-serum level of intoxication. She shakes free from Deena and Kristan and launches herself toward me with fury in her eyes. Terrified, I try to duck behind Kelly, bracing myself for impact.

Why the hell didn't they teach us kickboxing instead of advanced flirting at camp?

Grace veers toward the table where Luke and his buddies are playing their rowdy drinking game, and I nearly hyperventilate with relief.

She announces to Luke, "We need to talk."

He looks at his buddies as if there's no way he's obeying her, but when Grace yells, "Now!" he scrapes his chair back and follows her outside with his head down.

Kelly turns to me as if it's her job to get a reaction shot or something. I just look at her and shrug. I don't need to get all up in some drunken ex-girlfriend drama on camera. Especially since I'm stone-cold sober.

I sigh and notice a girl wearing a bright swingy miniskirt that I'd love to cut into quilting strips. *And whoops*, I think as she bends over, flipping the back of it up and exposing her thonged behind for her boyfriend to pat playfully. It looks like Kelly is getting all of that on film and I tell her to turn away. "I don't think she wants her ass exposed on national television," I whisper.

"Well then, she shouldn't be exposing it at a party, should she?" Kelly says. "They'd just blur her crack anyway."

Like that's any better.

"Why are you so worried about some drunk slut anyway?"

I stare at Kelly. "She's a person."

"Whatever," Kelly says, but she flips her hat around backward so it's facing the wall of cabinets behind us.

Luke is rubbing the side of his neck when he strides back inside. Tossing a quick shrug in my direction, he rejoins his buddies and swigs a gulp of beer.

"Well, looks like Shan-uke is still alive and kicking," Kelly says. "But I think you'd better plan on driving home."

Grace's tear-stained face appears in the window, and I grab Kelly's arm in terror. But Grace just gestures for Deena and Kristan to come outside. The two of them scurry to scrape their friend's feelings off the front lawn. I almost feel bad.

Then I imagine that gym class with the smell of polyurethane wafting in the air. Grace's mouth twists in slow motion. Saying the thing that can never be unsaid. I picture the first long-legged elf on my desk with a stubby pencil posing as his dick. Mocking me.

I tell Kelly, "I wish I had my car so I could just head home now." I glance up at the backward lips-camera-hat that's blind-but-not-deaf and amend, "I mean, *Wow*, what a great party! I can't believe we're actually here."

"Yes, and to think, it's all thanks to the power of Nŏrealique cosmetics," Kelly says in a commercial-voiceover tone. The two of us dissolve into laughter.

"You whore." I slump against her.

"I know, I know," she laughs. "Too bad Pete thinks I'm a different type of whore." She waggles her fingers at him.

He gives her a solicitous nod.

"Ugh, come on, Shannon. I'll give you a ride home."

It's my favorite moment of the whole party.

• • •

When I say goodnight to Luke, he gives me a kiss that makes my lips tingle with the alcohol from his. He says he's probably sleeping over at Pete's anyway, but insists on taking me out for breakfast in the morning.

Judging by the way only one of his eyes is focused on my face, I'm assuming his "in the morning" is referring to sometime after twelve.

Unfortunately, that doesn't mean I get to sleep in the next day. Victoria pops by at an ungodly early hour to debrief me about the party. My SAC Committee must have spent the whole night going through the video feed from Kelly's stupid hat, and they have a few suggestions. Victoria actually sits me down to go through the footage, which mostly shows us watching the party from Kelly's point of view. Victoria gives me rapid-fire tips for boosting my image the next time I find myself in this type of social situation. I take a sip of coffee from a mug that's as big as my head and try to pay attention.

Apparently I was supposed to make myself the center of attention without acting too obnoxious. It would seem that playfully sitting on Luke's lap would've been a good start.

"You know," I warn Victoria, "Luke is on his way over this morning. You don't want to blow my cover."

"No need to worry." She's unfazed. "We can tell him I'm your cousin visiting from the city."

I look her up and down. "Aunt, maybe?"

Right away, I say, "Just kidding," but she excuses herself to go to the bathroom. When she comes back, I see she's wearing even more makeup. I wonder what made me offer up insecurity as if it were a breath mint, but I pay dearly for my insult. The next two hours are spent painfully going over my behavior at the party frame by frame.

Good Shannon: Laughing with Kelly can be an effective way to seem like pleasant company.

Bad Shannon: Openly laughing and pointing at people as they walk by gives the impression I'm a bitch.

Good Shannon: Not hanging on all the guys at the party like some sort of floozy.

Bad Shannon: Not flirting with any of the guys at the party at all.

Bad Shannon: Not even interacting with my hot date.

Bad Shannon: Not conversing with anyone aside from Kelly.

Bad Shannon: Ditching the party just before midnight was my worst offense, in spite of how well things worked out for Cinderella. *Maybe I should've left one of my designer pumps sitting on the beer pong table.*

"I certainly hope you haven't been stood up." Victoria looks at her watch as she gathers her things to go. "That would be pretty humiliating."

I know she's just paying me back for the "aunt" put-down, but I have to wonder if Luke maybe hooked back up with Grace last night after I left. "He'll be here," I say more confidently than I feel.

Victoria gives a sly nod and heads toward the door. "Don't forget dance rehearsal tomorrow."

I groan. Working on our stupid routine for the *live!* prom finale seems ridiculous. "Prom is so far away," I whine. "And it already feels like we've been practicing forever."

"And yet, you still look like a dancing emu." Victoria smiles evilly. "We can't do everything for you, Shannon. That tiara must be earned."

• • •

Luke finally pulls up to my house at one-thirty. I'm wearing shorts and a tank top when I greet him at the door, and he's wearing the yeasty scent of beer. *Probably still intoxicated.*

I playfully snatch at his keys and ask if I can drive his convertible. The sun's out, the top's down, and I'm escaping the cameras for a while, so I'm pretty keen to get behind that wheel. Averting a potentially maiming car accident would be pretty sweet as well.

I convince him to hand over the keys, climb behind the wheel, and discover Luke's car is a stick shift. I don't drive stick. I blame it on being left-handed, but really, I think it just involves remembering too many things at once.

I try to focus, *clutch, shift, ease onto the gas*, and the car does little bunny hops down the road. Luke thinks this is adorable and assures me he's a great driving instructor.

He tells me everything I already know about driving with a standard transmission. The car still bunny hops. I laugh nervously and finally manage to get us moving. I keep it in first gear despite the engine's moaning to shift into second, and I pray I don't end up stopped on my way up a hill.

As I head along Route 8 toward the Country Kitchen, my blonde hair lifts and swirls around my head so aggressively I find myself driving blindly. I swipe frantically at my hair while smiling prettily in Luke's direction from time to time.

Thankfully, after a while, he leans back against the seat with his sunglasses on. In spite of the wind roaring in my ears, I can hear him snoring by the time I pull into the Country Kitchen parking lot. At least stopping a stick shift is simple enough, but I hit the brake too hard. Luke flops forward, dangling against his seatbelt as he continues snoring.

Yet another victim of my dazzling presence. I rub his arm to wake him so we can go inside and eat.

• • •

After he's scarfed down a huge plate of eggs with extra bacon, I decide Luke has sobered up enough to drive us back to my house. He suggests we play catch with his football on the front lawn as we wait for my mom to get home from her Saturday errands. Which, translated loosely, means her time with Thomas. She actually told Josie and me we might get to meet him soon. Which, translated loosely, means Mom is really gaga for the guy. As nice as it is to have Mom off my back, she's never been this absorbed in a guy, and it's starting to make me nervous.

Her dark green SUV pulls up about an hour after I get sick of playing football—which happened approximately four minutes after we started. Luke looks pretty dashing, clowning around with the ball, and I'm doing my part to act adorable and pretend I'm having fun, but Victoria woke me way too early, and I'm almost ready to pass out.

When Mom's SUV stops in the driveway, I freeze. There's a man with longish gray hair and a goatee sitting in the passenger seat. *The infamous Thomas.* I frown and Luke turns in time to see Mom step out of the car.

With absolutely no provocation, Luke spikes the ball in my direction. The bullet hits me in the direct center of my forehead. The last thing I see is my mother running toward me.

As she pushes past Luke, it honestly looks as if he's reaching out to try to shake her hand.

• • •

When I come to, I'm stretched across our living room couch with a lovely view of Mom, Luke, and the gray-haired, goatee guy sharing a laugh at our dining room table. I wonder what planet I've landed on where my mother is laughing with the boy who just assaulted me with a football.

"You okay?" comes a voice from behind my head. I twist around to peer at Josie. She's reading a book, her favorite accessory since the cameras moved in.

"Nice one," she whispers. "Getting hit in the head with a football makes for classic television. If he'd hit you in the nose, you'd be a shoo-in for the next *Top Twenty Reality Show Moments of All Time*." She glances toward Luke and leans in to hiss, "He's *so* hot!"

I stare up at her double image as I rub my throbbing head. "Why is everyone acting like my near-decapitation is no big deal?"

"It's okay. Thomas is a sports therapist and he looked you over, said you'll be fine." She grins, and I vaguely remember being asked inane questions as I tried to sleep. "He works for the college where Mom's been doing athletic contracts."

"Mom let Thomas examine me?" My voice is weak.

"She's awake!" Josie calls in to the Stranger, my Attacker, and my so-called Nurturer. Mom comes running in. *Finally, a little sympathy.* She kneels in front of me and starts laughing right in my face. *Perhaps not.*

"Oh, Shannon," Mom giggles. "You're not going to believe what's been happening while you were resting."

"*Resting*," I repeat, but she rushes on.

"Did you even know I've been on retainer with St. James State? Thomas got me a position negotiating contracts for all their athletic programs." She gestures to the goateed stranger, and he gives me an amused nod.

"Anyway," Mom goes on in a rush, "I've been reviewing scholarship contracts for them for the past few weeks. Very exciting. It really is the best work situation I could ever imagine." I stare at the pair of Moms in front of me, trying to figure out which one is real, so I can ask it for a hug. "Obviously when I saw what a great arm Luke has, I thought I'd maybe impress my new boss by introducing them."

"Because his pass impressed you when it *knocked your eldest daughter out cold*." My voice drips with so much sarcasm she should be drowning in it.

"Oh, dear, I know. Are you feeling better? I'm so glad Thomas was here to look you over." I lean my head back, which she must take to mean I'm okay, because she resumes babbling. "So anyway, Thomas thought it was a great idea. I made the call, and it just so happened Luke had a junk drive computer thingy with a video of him playing. So we Internetted that right over to them at St. James, and now they'll be watching how he develops throughout the year. Isn't that great?" She finally takes a breath. "If they sign him, I'll actually get a scouting bonus on top of my retainer."

"If I get a starting position, it'll be double." Luke grins at me over Mom's shoulder. I just stare at the two of them, wondering if my urge to knock their heads together is a sign I've suffered brain damage.

Mom finally gets around to looking concerned. "How's your head feeling?"

I close my eyes and cover them with my forearm.

"Thomas is the team's nurse," Mom says.

"Assistant doctor," he corrects, and she giggles in a way that makes her sound like she's not my mother. When I move my arm to glare at him, he shines a small flashlight back and forth in my eyes. "You took quite a hit there, but you'll be fine. Wish some of my players were so tough."

Securing a big client like St. James State is probably the best thing to happen to Mom's career. But honestly, I don't trust any of this. A guy who randomly signs off on my blunt-force trauma via football? And what are the odds of her accidentally scouting my brand new boyfriend?

My eyes widen. I'm not seeing double anymore. I'm seeing red. "Wait a second." I try to sit up, but a harsh pain in my head makes me slide back down and confront Luke from a horizontal position. I make up for my lack of verticalness by sharpening my glare.

"You just *happened* to have footage of yourself playing?" I think of Luke's insisting we play catch, despite my resistance after aforementioned minute four. I couldn't figure out if his obsession with meeting my mom was cute or creepy, but now it seems he must have had a clue about her new position before I did.

Luke swings down to sit at the edge of the couch and grabs my hand in one smooth motion. He still smells like stale beer, but his brown eyes are warm as they meet mine and his voice is deep. "Of course, silly, I'm a senior. Everyone carries tapes at this stage in the recruitment game." He gently brushes my hair back off my face. "I'm so sorry you got hit by that throw." He chuckles. "It was a pretty sweet one too." At the utterly unamused look on my face, he adds, "Are you feeling okay?"

Finally, a little sympathy for the victim.

As he strokes my hair, I can't help but notice Luke is seriously dreamy. It's no wonder Grace feels burned over losing him. And obviously my mother approves. She's excused herself, dragging Josie and Thomas with her, so Luke and I are alone in the living room. Well, that is, alone with all the hidden cameras and stuff.

Luke smiles and leans in. As his gorgeous eyes close, I think, *Well, I knew I'd have to make some sacrifices going into this competition.* I feel his breath on my lips, which, unlike my fore-head, feel just fine. I close my eyes.

I like his kiss *much* better than his throw.

CHAPTER TEN

I'm putting my books in my locker after first period when Rick grabs my arm and guides me into the math room. I try to resist, but he seems determined to get me alone.

He swings on me the moment the classroom door closes behind us. "What the hell, Shannon?"

I want to hide behind one of the desks. I've been so focused on getting even with Grace and winning Luke over to gain a foothold in the competition, I somehow managed to ignore Rick's feelings for me. And the fact that they might be reciprocal.

Rick looks so angry I can't think, and despite all my Prom Queen training, I find myself stammering, "I-I-I…j-just…"

"Yeah, that's what I thought." He takes a step toward me, and I back up to one of the desks. Looking around wildly, I try to figure out whether or not this classroom is wired. If anyone walks in right now, I'm boned.

"What's the matter? Afraid you'll get caught talking to me?" Rick's anger flashes and I want to explain everything. Instead, I keep my palms flat against the desk underneath me and shake my head no.

The emptiness of the classroom fades as Rick fills the space in front of me. Drawing closer until I'm leaning back against the desk, we stare at each other eye to eye. He glances down at my mouth, and my heart gives a dip. I lick my lips and realize my body language is practically begging him to kiss me right now.

Rick wraps an arm around my waist, and I instinctively press forward. He touches my cheek. I close my eyes. I don't care about being a bottom three loser, or getting even with Grace Douglas, or anything except for how much I want his lips on mine. Wait for them.

"Shannon?"

I open my eyes and see hardness has seeped back into his gaze. "What is going on between you and Luke Hershman?"

"I-I-I…" I start stammering again, and the spell is broken.

"Yeah, that's what I thought."

Rick releases me, pushes off the desk, and turns away.

"Wait," I call, but he just keeps walking. At the door, he turns to give me a look of sadness, but I can't think of a single thing I'm allowed to say that will make him stay.

· · ·

It turns out Marnie must have been right about Rick's "I'll reject you before you can reject me" complex, because when I try to tell him later, "It's not what you think," he won't even look at me. Instead, he gets suddenly absorbed with something buried deep in his backpack.

At the end of the day, when I walk by his locker, he starts studying his BlackSpot sneakers as if they've sprouted wings.

"All right already," I say to him, holding my palms up in surrender. "I get it."

Some of us don't need a 150 IQ to know when we're being blown off.

The cameras must have caught Rick dragging me into the math room, because Victoria asks me about it at our next SACC meeting. She reminds me that there are strict rules regarding off-camera zones, and I nearly faint with relief that there's no footage of our near-kiss.

I tell her Rick was just helping me with a science assignment, and then I launch into a detailed description of a bogus project.

I don't know if Victoria believes me because I've become so skilled at lying or if she starts waving me off just to make me stop talking all science-y stuff. But she quickly moves on to matters of great consequence. With a flourish, she sets out samples of the new Nōrealique lipstick shades on the table before me.

I need to pick a signature color that will be named *Shannon's Sugar Bliss*. After the show starts airing, it will be released for sale wherever Nŏrealique products are sold. I try to design a quilt in my head to commemorate having my very own shade of hot pink lipstick named after me, but the only pattern I can come up with is a giant pair of lips in the center of a square.

Meanwhile, I've decided that wearing a hunky football player's arm casually over one's shoulder translates to ballistic armor against things that suck. The same hallways I used to drag my black boots down with my head bowed are now a welcoming haven. Instead of a nightmare, high school is starting to feel like a dream that I don't want to wake up from.

Of course, our expensive clothing, new lipstick, and SACCs aren't actually magical. Kelly, Amy, and I are working our asses off to become popular. We have ongoing Poise Perfection Classes with Victoria giving us tips on things like how to make our peers crave our approval and maximizing lunch time as *launch time*!

We finally master the fine art of house parties too. The trick is to remain sober but act adorably tipsy and make a point of saying hello to every single person in attendance. Then we can head home once things get sloppy and people are too drunk to notice we're gone.

As the weeks pass, our extracurricular calendars get so loaded up they practically require the use of time travel in order to function. The three of us toss our hair, give sideways glances, and remain mysteriously aloof toward everyone. The aloof part is the easiest to fake since we're constantly exhausted.

By mid-October, Amy, Kelly, and I are on everyone's lips. In a good way.

"How has Amy kept the weight off?"—*Starvation. That girl should be worshipped.* "I still can't believe Kelly used to be the biggest burnout in the school."—*Not even Kelly can resist enjoying the praise.* "Have you seen Shannon's outfit this morning?"—*Everyone has. And it is fabulous.*

All I have to do now is keep moving forward with my head in the game and hope that when my old friends finally find out about the show, they'll come around. I know I'm willing to forgive them for not having all that much faith in me.

PART FOUR

The Royal Premiere

CHAPTER ELEVEN

When spring arrives and the show's teasers start airing, they're mysterious and enticing and absolutely everywhere. It's being promoted as "The boldest reality show ever conceived" and "Filmed in secret for an entire year" and "Maybe YOU are one of the stars and don't even know it." Mickey says they expect a healthy tune-in for the premiere episode.

"I'm betting the show's not even about a real high school," I hear a girl saying as I walk down the hallway, and I can't help but smile. People are going to go batshit when they find out this is all about us.

I swallow down my nervousness as I greet Amy and Kelly at our lockers and take a moment to marvel over how much things have changed for us since that devastating meeting in the guidance office. Mickey was actually right about that being the beginning of everything.

Those first weeks of school after Prom Queen Camp were like pedaling uphill with training wheels compared to the way the three of us are soaring along now. I feel invincible as I touch up my signature pink lipstick in my locker mirror. *Shannon's Sugar Bliss.* I've come to think of it as my war paint.

"You guys ready to be reality show stars?" Kelly asks Amy and me.

The first show is airing next week, and Amy is practically vibrating with anxiety. I soothe her, "Come on, girl. Just imagine you're onstage."

Amy was amazing in Westfield High's winter musical a few months ago. The drama club performed *The Sound of Music*, and her Maria von Trapp demanded everyone's attention. I was worried that she'd barf onstage, but she tapped into something deep and solid, and gave a killer performance. Grace did a decent job as Liesl, but it was absolutely Amy's show.

"There's my girl." Luke materializes in front of me and gives me a rib-crushing hug hello. His buddy Pete moves in to embrace Kelly, but she twists so that her shoulder juts into his chest when he hugs her. I try not to laugh at Kelly's look of disgust. Amy is already giggling about something with George, her own hunky football star who she met at the gym.

Just as our SACCs predicted, dating hotties has galvanized our social positions at Westfield. Although Kelly complains about playing constant *DE-FENSE* against Pete's displays of affection, Amy is genuinely smitten by her lumbering linebacker. A feeling that's clearly mutual.

Looking down the hallway, I see Deena, Grace, and Kristan huddled together, shooting us occasional glares. I thought Grace hated me as the Elf Ucker, but she downright loathes me now that I've ditched her nickname. Oh, yes. Plus stolen her boyfriend. I stand on my toes to give Luke a peck on the cheek and smile innocently in her direction.

Grace's hatred actually makes me feel strong. Like I finally stood up to the school's Alpha Bitch and now nobody needs to submit to her ever again.

The one gaping hole in my awesome life is the one that Marnie ripped out. The last time she and I even spoke was just after Buy Nothing Day, which takes place the Friday after Thanksgiving every year. Marnie is all into it as part of her anti-consumerism crusade, and the idea is to purchase absolutely nothing for twenty-four straight hours as a boycott against the frenzy of holiday shoppers. I've always supported Marns because she feels so strongly about corporate greed ruining the world and all, but by Thanksgiving, the two of us were almost completely unraveled anyway.

Plus I really, really needed a bottle of Silver Linings nail color for my New Year's Eve date with Luke.

Instead of lying to Marnie, I mentioned my Buy Nothing Day Fail, and she acted as if I'd stormed the gates of Buymart with all the middle-aged door-busting zealots.

"I can't believe how selfish you're acting, Shannon" she said, which hurt like a sewing machine needle to the heart. But it also made me realize that Marnie is not as loyal and understanding as I've always thought she was.

Apparently, for some reason, she preferred being friends with a total loser. To let a few rhinestone lip logos and a bottle of nail polish destroy our relationship showed me what kind of friend she really was. And I guess it's better I found out now, instead of waiting until we both got old like my Mom and Aunt Kate when I might *really* need her for something. I'm sad that she didn't choose to rise up the social ranks with me, but honestly she did have a choice.

And Marnie chose to watch me move on.

• • •

When *From Wannabes to Prom Queens* premieres, there are a number of dramatic clips they could choose to open the show with. There's the first day of school. Our makeover session in the Beauty Room. Or even my sprawling fall on the runway.

Instead, the episode opens with the shot of Luke Hershman leaning over my living room couch to kiss me. Right after he knocked me unconscious with a football. Except that nobody watching knows anything about the football. The onscreen image of Luke and me kissing tenderly shifts into a split-screen with my heinous before picture. Victoria brightly narrates, "See how

Shannon goes from frumpy to fabulous and snags the captain of the football team!"

Then there's a shot of Amy on our school's stage wearing a wedding dress and singing her lungs out as Maria. The split-screen cuts in with a revolting before picture, and Victoria invites, "Follow Amy's journey from withering wallflower to superstar siren."

Next, we see Kelly modeling a mini-dress as she poses at a photo shoot. She eventually caved in to pressure from her SACC and took up fashion modeling. "And watch Kelly turn from ghastly mess to model-fabulous!" Victoria says cheerfully as Kelly's shot splits with a picture of her metal minefield face from last year.

Kelly groans beside me. She and Amy are watching the premiere at my house since we can all use the support, even though Kelly acts like she doesn't need or want it. Over the past year of pretending to be a clique, the three of us have gotten sort of close. I mean, we're technically still competing against each other, and there's been plenty of casual backstabbing and confidence undermining, but we get along well enough.

Amy is always quick to cheer people up when they need it, including Victoria, and she remains sweetly introverted when she's not onstage. And Kelly's ongoing disdain for playing fashion whore manifests in biting comments that seriously crack me up.

Our classmates are just finding out that the show is about

the three of us at this very moment, so we've all turned off our phones. This two-hour premiere episode will cover our six-week stint at Prom Queen Camp, which makes sense, since they can't air any footage from the school until students or their parents sign their waivers.

Josie is in her room right now watching the show with a friend who's sleeping over, and Mom and Thomas are out on a double date with Aunt Kate and her husband. After nearly a year of secrets and anticipation, I can't believe the time is here.

Onscreen, Kelly, Amy, and I each morph from our humiliating before photos to glamorous after shots with fans blowing our hair off our heavily made-up faces. I can almost hear the director still calling "And…look!" over and over as the three of us dramatically turned toward the camera.

There were lots of blooper takes with hair blowing in our eyes and sticking to our lipstick, and one time during the group glamour shot, Amy flipped up so fast, I konked my nose on the back of her head. We had to wait for it to stop bleeding before we could go on.

As ridiculous as it all felt at the time, I must admit we look pretty hot onscreen. Amy and I are a little stiff, but Kelly is a natural at posing, and it's easy to see how her modeling career took off so fast. The name of the show melts into view and I'm a little annoyed that it reads *The Prom Queen Wannabes*, instead of the original and slightly less humiliating *From Wannabes to Prom Queens*.

"Oh God." Amy grabs my hand.

"Here we go," says Kelly from the armchair. Her alert posture betrays the fact that she's definitely invested in what's coming next. How can she not be? The three of us are being exposed in a very big way.

The room is completely silent as a commercial comes on featuring us oohing and aahing over our Nõrealique lip gloss. It is by far the cheesiest commercial ever created. They tried giving us lines, but we were all really terrible at delivering them. Hey, it's harder than it looks, okay? Anyway, they had to ditch the narrative, which makes the whole point of the commercial a little hazy, until they display the tagline, "Transform your look, transform your life, with Nõrealique Cosmetics."

As if glossy lips were our ticket off the slow bus to Loserville.

A montage of humiliating moments from boot camp plays as Victoria narrates from the *foy-yea* of our Prom Queen Camp mansion. Onscreen, we're taught to apply cosmetics as if we're three chimps who have never seen a blush brush. Then there's Amy yelling at Kelly and me for leaving hair in the bathtub drain. Again. And of course my flailing fall off the runway plays over and over about twelve hundred times. It's so humiliating I can't even watch it.

And then there are the confessional moments. "I am living with swine."—*Amy. And she is.* "I can't believe I'm trapped here with a pair of dingbats."—*Kelly. And she is not.* "I'm living in a mansion!"—*Me, said with smiling ecstasy.* I wince at the flaky image I was projecting back then.

The show ends with the three of us completely transformed, walking in slow motion down the runway/hallway of Westfield High on the first day of school. Chins held high, postures erect, we seem more confident than any of us felt that day. We are frozen midstride and tiaras are photoshopped onto our heads. The show's throbbing theme song ends abruptly as the big pink words *The Prom Queen Wannabes* are stamped across the screen.

Victoria invites viewers to tune in next week to see our peers' reactions to our amazing makeovers. Plus, she cheerfully promises a huge surprise twist to be revealed later in the season. Amy, Kelly, and I exchange looks at that, but I figure it's probably something lame, like someone at home can win a pair of spike heels by texting in a random trivia answer. Or maybe they'll be flown to meet us here in the middle of nowhere. *Great prize.*

"Well, *you* guys looked fantastic." Josie is cranky when she and her friend emerge from her bedroom. She wasn't on camera at all. "The show will definitely be a huge hit and you three will get totally famous. Congratulations. We're going to bed."

She ignores my goodnight, and I feel bad that she's so disappointed. Still, at least she no longer has a socially catastrophic older sister tarnishing her image. That is, unless everyone at school decides to turn on us now that they know about all the help we've been secretly getting.

I bite my lip and glance at my cell phone.

Kelly says, "Well, I guess it's time we face our adoring public."

We switch our phones on, and I say, "I wonder how everyone will treat us after this."

"Reminding our classmates what losers we used to be may have just broken the spell," Amy says, and I nod my agreement.

I'm relieved that my old nickname wasn't mentioned even once, but my runway fall was pretty damn humiliating. At least I resisted the urge to run away flailing.

All three of our cell phones start ringing at once. Kelly's techno overpowers Amy's ballad while mine quacks loudest of all. The bizarre mix of mismatched ringtones is unnerving.

We each take a deep breath, hold up our phones, and say, "Hello?"

• • •

The way that our peers decide to react to our huge secret is pretty damn crucial. If they choose, en masse, to not sign their permission slips, the show will probably get canceled immediately. That is, unless they decide to air it with everyone's faces blurred out, the way certain celebrities need to have their "oops" panty-less crotch shots blurred. But that does not sound like a very good show.

When Luke calls to say he loved our scene, I hear the football team whooping in the background. I was finally allowed to tell him about the show earlier today. It was only so he could sign a release for them to air our kissing scene, and he was supposed to keep it a secret, but I doubt he did. He was wildly excited by the news and invited all his buddies over to his media room to catch the premiere. Judging by the feral animal sounds coming through the phone, they either really loved the show or there is booze involved. Possibly both.

For the next solid hour after *The Prom Queen Wannabes* ends, Kelly, Amy, and I are busy fielding calls. I swear, a representative from each and every clique and sub-clique in our school checks in with at least one of us. Well, that is, except the clique of Grace and the former Alpha Queens. But we can pretty much guess their reaction.

Of course, I don't hear from Marnie, James, or Rick either, but they've probably lost my number by now. It's also possible they didn't see the show. I mean, they're not exactly television fiends. Rick's parents don't even subscribe to cable on account of it "causing brain rot." I'm tempted to send them a link online so they'll realize why I've been acting different all year long. But guaranteed they'll hear about it soon enough.

Based on the collective phoned-in responses, it seems we'll be enjoying yet another bump in status. Everyone wants to know where the cameras are hidden and if it's too late to get a bit of screen time. It's clear our classmates will happily sign away whatever rights and dignity are required in order to be on television.

I can't help but wonder how the show will portray all the incredible events that catapulted the school's biggest nobodies into the fabulous and popular alphas we are today. There's just one thing I'm sure of—there's no way it will be able to capture the reality of it all.

• • •

The Prom Queen Wannabes is the biggest thing that has ever happened to Westfield High School. By. Far.

Like, before this, Westfield's biggest claim to fame was that some alumni chick became Miss Pennsylvania back in the 1960s.

When Kelly, Amy, and I walk into school the day after our reality show's debut, the impact is immediately obvious. The first thing we can't miss is the enormous television parked in the lobby, right in front of poor old Miss Pennsylvania's framed portrait. The TV has a huge façade in the shape of the Nőrealique lips logo surrounding the screen. Nobody notices when we join the crowd of students gathered around it. Onscreen, a Nőrealique cosmetics commercial ends, and the scene changes to Kelly, Amy, and me turning dramatically in our official "show poses."

A guy from my English for Idiots Class lets out a high-pitched "Ohmygod!" when he sees us. We're greeted with hugs and squeals and open-mouthed grins as everyone looks around, probably scoping for cameras. We smile humbly, soaking up the glory.

"There's my superstar!" Luke says happily as his two best buds close in on Amy and Kelly. Everything feels perfect as Luke swings me effortlessly over his broad shoulder. I'm floating above the crowd and I'm breathless. And I don't mean Luke has me swooning. I mean he's knocked the wind out of me, and I start coughing at the sting of bile in my throat.

He puts me down. "You 'kay, babe?"

Everyone seems to be holding their breath waiting for my response, and I command myself not to projectile vomit all over my hunky boyfriend. When I nod yes and hold two thumbs up, the whole crowd gives a cheer and starts clapping. Kelly, Amy, and I share smiles of victory.

Come prom night, one of us will be wearing that tiara for sure.

• • •

A part of me hopes that Marnie will run up and say she totally understands now about this whole lips logo mix-up.

I'm telling a group of classmates-slash-fans the story of how our new cars were presented to us at Prom Queen Camp when I spot Marnie down the hall. I give her a smile and an energetic wave. She actually rolls her eyes at me and turns away. As if the fact that I'm on a reality show makes everything even worse.

"Were you totally in shock?" A girl prompts me to continue

with my story, and I realize I'm just standing here openly gaping at the person I used to be best friends with.

I snap out of it and reply, "Well, they had to give us some way to cart around our new makeup and clothes. All Nŏrealique brand of course." I pull a tube of *Shannon's Sugar Bliss* from my lips-logo purse and hold it up for them to see. Everyone laughs, but the crowd can't quite drown out the image of Marnie turning her back.

The reconciliation I'd imagined dissolves into a wispy cloud and floats away. Even though we haven't spoken in months, I feel the loss of Marnie more sharply than ever. Now I know it's permanent. The eager faces surrounding me seem like poor substitutes for having one best forever friend.

It's late enough in the school year that a number of seniors have already turned eighteen and are able to sign their releases right there in homeroom. Of course, everyone else needs parental approval, but they're all clearly dying to get their non-blurry faces on TV. Even Grace, Kristan, and Deena play along, in spite of the fact that there's sure to be ugly footage of them from this past year that can get aired now.

There are a few holdouts who refuse to sign waivers, which means they'll be shown wearing cloud faces or else be cut entirely. According to Mickey, the nonparticipants all seem to be from insignificant subsets of cliques. It's upsetting but not at all shocking to learn that Marnie, James, and Rick are opting out of my show.

"Well, at least we don't have to worry about our big revelation sending us back to social wasteland," I say to Kelly and Amy as we sit outside for lunch. We can barely eat with all the greetings interrupting us, and it's hard to tell if everyone's just excited about the spring weather or if they're acting wilder than usual because they're hoping to get on television. I watch a girl with earbuds in her ears climb onto her boyfriend's shoulders and start singing while punching the air. *Definitely grasping for screen time.*

Amy smiles hello to a girl walking by, then turns a worried look on me. "I had somebody ask me today if we've been sabotaging Grace, Deena, and Kristan just so we could win the million dollars."

"Ha!" Kelly says. "It was only a matter of time before those rumors started."

I swallow a bite of my tuna salad sandwich. "As if we could have anything to do with the crap that's happened to them."

The girls nod their agreement, but we all glance around nervously. A few times during the school year, I wondered if Kelly or even Amy could be sabotaging the queens. All three of us now have the clout to start rumors, pass judgments, and sway public opinion. But just because we can now manipulate the system doesn't mean we are above the system.

Nobody in high school is ever above the system. And if we've learned anything this year, it's that popularity can be fleeting.

I finally relax when Luke and the others sit down around us.

Amy and George feed each other fruit salad, and Luke and Pete start unpacking their large paper shopping bags filled with food. I feel happy to be associated with such charismatic people. Luke grins at me and I can practically hear a Crestmate toothpaste commercial chiming at the sparkle of his teeth before he sinks them into an enormous ham sandwich.

A few tables away, I spot Marnie sitting with Rick and James, and I wince at her homemade wrap skirt. It's nice to be passionate about something, but I just don't get how the corporate global economy is being influenced by her dressing unattractively.

She looks over at the six of us now and takes a breath that raises her shoulders. Her lips purse. James puts an arm around her waist and her shoulders settle. With a flash of excitement, I wonder if they've finally hooked up. Their shift from friends to dating wouldn't exactly make the front page of the school newspaper the way Luke and I did.

Rick's back is facing me, and by now I've almost forgotten what it felt like to have him give me that special look. *Almost.*

I picture for a moment what our senior year might have looked like as Shann-ick. He turns his head to look over his shoulder, and his blue eyes flash at me for an instant. I break eye contact and can't help but wonder, *Do these yellow pumps go with my black heart?*

• • •

The whole week is a blur of people congratulating us and inviting us to parties and even offering to let us cut in line at lunch.

Amy, Kelly, and I were respectably popular before, but now we're famous. I find myself walking around with a constant giddy feeling in my gut.

And then, I discover there's an online blog where viewers have been discussing our show. And apparently people have some conflicting opinions about the way I came across in the first episode. While some commenters think I'm kind of funny and a few even use the term "awesome," others think I seem like a flake, and one anonymous girl clams she'd love to "slap some sense" into me. For some reason, I feel tears spring to my eyes as I read on, and I want to explain to everyone that I'm doing the best that I can. Every word feels so personal.

Anilu_898: As far as I'm concerned, Shannon is beyond clueless.
Tomatlanta: She's a bit of a goof at times, and definitely spacey, but I wouldn't call her clueless.
Anilu_898: I said she's *beyond* clueless and if I want your opinion, I'll beat it out of you.

I sit at my computer late into the night, memorizing stranger's opinions of me. The most negative comments take the deepest root in my mind.

I'm exhausted, but I need to unlock the secret. I've worked too hard for too long to still be so unlikable.

CHAPTER TWELVE

Amy, Kelly, and I are invited to several viewing parties for the next installment of *The Prom Queen Wannabes*, but at the suggestion of our SACCs, we decide against endorsing any one specific group. According to Victoria, "It is best to maintain an air of exclusivity." Our most strategic move is to stay home the night of the show and perpetuate the illusion we have more important things to do than sit around watching ourselves on television.

The three of us decide we don't need to go through the whole handholding group-viewing routine again. We sailed through the ordeal of being outed just fine, and things should cruise smooth from here.

Josie is watching the show with her clique at some junior's house, and Mom is out celebrating something work-related with Thomas. I still don't trust him, but one thing's for sure—he came along at the perfect time to distract Mom from the fact that I'm on a reality show. After the first episode convinced her my life wasn't being ruined, Thomas even managed to get Mom to give me a little privacy. She'll only watch the show if I invite her to. And I haven't. I figure she'll sneak a viewing in anyway, but at least this means I won't ever have to watch it with her or discuss anything that happens.

By now nearly everyone's releases have been signed, so that might be why episode two focuses more on random high school drama than on us Wannabes. I curse myself for not listening to Josie and acting larger than life to get more screen time.

Deena McKinnley appears time after time asking for a hall pass and heading into the bathroom. I call Amy immediately, and she answers saying, "I can't believe they're going to show it."

"I'd be shocked if they didn't show it," I say. "But this is so freaky. She must be sitting at home dying."

All of us at Westfield High have already seen it, but I still exclaim, "Holy crap!" when the homemade video comes on. It hasn't been edited down a single bit, and Amy and I make gagging noises as we rewatch the entire three-minute-and-fifteen-second clip of Deena McKinnley making herself throw up.

I know that sounds pretty bad, but trust me, it's much worse. The video was taken at a crazy angle, from behind the toilet or something, so Deena's throw up is propelled toward the viewer in vivid 3D.

"Bulimia," I say. "Have your cake and be thin too."

Amy says, "I have to go," and hangs up.

I think about the anonymous website that circulated through

the school's email list back in November. The site featured only one thing. This video. The McKinnley Vomit Video.

Poor Deena. When the website first made its rounds, she was so devastated she skipped school for a week and a half. Then, when she finally came back, she had to eat her lunch in the nurse's office and be supervised in the bathroom. Deena put on about ten pounds and stayed the focus of gossip until she finally shaved half her head and got a vine tattooed on her skull. Universal high school lingo for, "Hey, everyone? Piss off."

As the show continues, I'm confused by a shot of Amy sitting in the computer lab at school. The picture cuts to the computer screen and shows one of the funky beat remixes of the Vomit Video where the clip is played backward so Deena sucks up all of her own puke. The TV screen cuts back to Amy laughing hysterically at her computer. Which makes her seem like a pretty awful person. Deena may be a mega bitch, but her having bulimia isn't exactly hilarious.

The show fails to expose the one thing we all want to know about the Vomit Video. Who the hell taped it and spread it all over the Internet?

After another commercial break featuring our awkward Nōrealique lip gloss shtick, the show comes back on with a shot of Luke hanging out at his locker with his buddies. He's talking about how much he needs a good football scholarship if he hopes to go to college. He mentions that St. James State is his top choice, and someone says, "Hey, isn't Shannon Depola's mom, like, a scout or something for St. James?"

My mouth shoots open in shock at that since before dating Luke, *I* didn't know my mom had anything to do with St. James.

Just then, onscreen, I stride past and Luke turns to watch me. I recognize the look he gives me from the video Victoria showed me at the beginning of the school year. I can't believe she didn't show me the whole clip. *He's not drooling over me! He's drooling over my connection to St. James State!* It's suddenly clear why Luke was so anxious to meet my mother.

This also explains why he threw that football so hard. He beaned me in the head *on purpose*! He was showing off, and then I actually let him kiss me, like, immediately after regaining consciousness. It's all so horribly obvious. Our beautiful, romantic fairytale relationship is a big, fat, hairy lie. I watch the onscreen shot of the two of us kissing and wonder if people can tell we have zero chemistry.

When we first started going out, I couldn't understand why I didn't get the little stomach flips that Rick gave me. Then I figured it was Luke's hotness factor that was throwing me off. Like, I'm naturally attracted to dweebs who put socks on their ears and in order to fully transform, I needed to override my innate nerdy inclinations. I remember feeling like an actress pretending to be in love as I made steady and frequent eye contact with my hunky boyfriend. I watch myself onscreen forcing my body language to convey how perfect we are together. Blinking eyes, flipping hair, touching my bare skin, parting my lips. None of it is real.

I'm already sinking into an insta-depression when my cell phone rings with the show's theme song. I'm clinging to the slim hope that maybe no one will notice Luke has been using me. I pick up the phone to Josie's anguished voice. "I can't believe he's been using you!"

"Was it really that obvious?" I wail. "What will everyone think of me?"

"Well, they'll think your relationship is fake!" Josie answers. "What was with that lame-ass shot of you two kissing?"

"I know, I know. What should I dooooo?"

"Maybe you can pretend to be a lesbian?"

I stop crying. "Can that work?"

"Probably not. You're lousy at acting. Plus, you'd have to stick with it after the show ends."

I start crying again. "I don't want to be a lesbian."

"I knew you couldn't handle this."

"You told me I was going to be great."

"That's just something sisters tell each other to be encouraging. When will Mom be home?" I answer her by gasping for air and Josie says, "Hang in there, Shannon. I'm on my way." She sounds so uncharacteristically caring it makes me cry harder.

As soon as I click off with Josie, the theme song starts up again on my phone. I make a mental note to change my ringtone back to the quacking duck. Still crying, I answer to echoed wailing on the other end.

"I'm not laughing," comes Amy's anguished voice. "At the Vomit Video. I didn't think Deena throwing up was funny at all."

"Did you not notice my *relationship* happens to be a complete *sham*?" I ask. "You were barely even onscreen this episode."

"But it's a lie." She sounds miserable. "They made me seem heartless and cruel and meanwhile my cousin has bulimia and it's an awful disease. I hung up with you because of your stupid joke about eating cake and being thin."

"Sorry," I say. "I just saw a picture of that written in icing on a cake covered in puke and thought it was kind of funny."

"Bulimia isn't funny," she moans. "I was laughing at some stupid picture of a kitten sleeping in his food dish that my *abuela* sent me. What if people think I made the video and sabotaged Deena?"

"No one will believe you would do that," I say as I silently wonder, *Would Amy do that?* She really does have it bad for that tiara. "Everything will be okay," I soothe her. "Most people know how much these shows are edited anyway."

After leaving a hate voicemail for Victoria, I consume a half gallon of fat-free ice cream while sitting on the couch comfortably loathing myself. Then of course, I have to eat two heaping hand-fuls of potato chips to cleanse the waxy taste from my mouth. By the time Josie comes home, I'm in the kitchen ready to launch into a full-on pork-out.

Josie eases me away from the Disodito nacho chips and guides me to the living room like I'm a delicate life-sized doll. "This is a very unhealthy reaction to watching a video of a bulimic," she says.

"This is a completely appropriate response to heartbreak."

"Well, the cameras are watching right now, and if you could see how you look…"

I glance down at my oversized stained T-shirt and allow Josie to lead me to the couch.

She reasons that I should give Luke a chance to explain himself, seeing as how he's so cute and all. Like his behavior should be measured on a different scale. "Lots of times, a guy that hot can act douche-y without meaning to," she says. "I know he deserves to be kicked to the curb for using you, but sister to sister? Wait and see what he has to say."

Josie also thinks Amy came across as heartless and possibly devious on this episode, which works slightly to my favor. The way she sees it, if the school were voting right now, Kelly would probably win but I'm still a close second.

"Great," I say, "the girl who least wants to be Prom Queen has the best shot at the crown."

"There are still plenty more episodes left to air," Josie reminds me, making me feel a little better. "And then there's the *live!* taping at the *Prom*," she adds, which makes me feel much, much worse. I'm not even sure I'm going to have a prom date.

• • •

As I wait for Luke by my locker the next morning, I mull over Victoria's insistence that I try to work things out. "He's been *very* good for your projected ratings," she told me over the phone last night. "And with the prize money and *tiara* hanging in the balance, you should really give him another chance."

I see him approaching and I wonder if he's planning to beg me for forgiveness.

"Hey there," he greets cheerfully. "Cool show last night."

Guess not. *Note to self: revisit earlier notes to self.*

"Why didn't you tell me you knew about my mom working for St. James before we started dating?" I cross my arms. "On the show, it looked like that was the only reason you even noticed me."

"Aw, come on, babe." He seems weary of our confrontation already. "Please don't act all sensitive about that."

"What?" I'm furious. "I'm not *acting* sensitive. I want to know if you've been using me."

He considers me a moment then leans in close. *Oh my God, he's wearing foundation.* In a low voice, he says, "I'm not using you any more than you're using me, Shannon."

I stare at him. "I'm not using you to get a football scholarship," I hiss at a volume that hopefully won't get picked up by the microphones.

"No, but you *are* in a competition to win a million bucks," he shoots back in a low voice. "And you know being my *girlfriend* can totally get you voted *Prom Queen*."

He does have a point. I squint up at him. "If you honestly think I'm using you, why didn't you confront me as soon as you found out about the show?"

"Confrontation, ugh." He shivers. "Besides, I guess I don't really mind being used." He gives me one of his easy smiles.

"I'm not using you," I insist quietly. *Just maybe your image and popularity and endorsement for getting elected Prom Queen.*

"Okay, so you're not using me. But you do have to admit, we find ourselves in a mutually beneficial situation."

I look him in the eye. *Mutually beneficial situation?* With that one phrase, he just used more multi-syllable words than he has used the whole time we've been going out. Underneath all the silly fart jokes and light underclassman bullying, Luke is brighter than I realized.

I'm suddenly glad I never let him get past second base, which in my ball field, means French kissing with hands vaguely rubbing near private bits *over* clothes. Sure, he once suggested I might enjoy getting naked under a blanket in his convertible at the drive-in, but he took my polite "no thank you" in stride and never pressured me to go all the way. In fact, to be honest, other than Grace's occasional outbursts, our overall relationship has been fairly devoid of drama. *Should've known it was all fake.*

"Okay," I whisper calmly, glancing around at our gawking

peers. "Can you fix this so I don't look incredibly stupid to everyone who watched the show last night?"

With a glint in his eye, Luke suddenly collapses to one knee and says loudly, "Please, Shannon, please don't dump me."

Suppressing the urge to laugh, I ask at full volume, "What about the way you used me?"

He smiles up at me and lowers his voice enough that the gathering crowd has to move in to hear what he's saying. "I'll admit, at first I may have been interested in getting a free ride to college, but then I got to know you. And you, Shannon, are the reason I was able to throw a grand total of over *twelve hundred* yards this season. I couldn't care less about that scholarship to St. James State." He gives his head a slight shake, indicating that he cares very much about that scholarship to St. James State. "Please don't dump me." He stands up and takes my hand in his. "You're the only girl I want to take to prom."

Nice touch, I think, but say, "I need some space to think."

He looks at me earnestly. "I'll wait for you, Shannon. As long as it takes."

Over the top. I turn away with my head held high and push through the crowd. *But not bad damage control, overall.*

I'm definitely faring better than Amy. Speculation that she was the one who spread the McKinnley Vomit Video starts buzzing almost immediately. Suddenly, people are going out of their way to console Deena over the whole ordeal. Which is an interesting turn, since when it first happened, people treated her like bulimia was the newest version of the plague.

Deena's image is helped even more by the senior assembly we have the next day. It teaches us all about how bad it is to diet, and the dangers of eating disorders, and the evil influence of skinny models. Deena bravely stands up with her tattooed head shining and shares about how hard she's worked to recover from her bulimia and how she's finally learned to love her curves. She actually cries when she talks about the awful Vomit Video. Looking directly at where Amy, Kelly, and I are sitting, she describes how degrading diets and liposuction are. Amy sinks low in her seat, and Kelly and I keep our heads down, and everyone else gives Deena a standing ovation.

Afterward, people are too distracted by the Deena vs. Amy spectacle to give too much scrutiny to my sham relationship with the captain of the football team.

It makes me sad to see Amy undone, her body language reverting back to its geeky, shy origins from before Prom Queen Camp. At least George is sticking by her side, but unless something drastic happens over the next few weeks, Amy doesn't have a chance in hell of being voted Prom Queen.

To be honest, I don't think Amy made the Vomit Video and spread it around. I don't even think she laughed meanly when she saw it. But in the dual worlds of reality television and high school, perceived truth is what really matters.

CHAPTER THIRTEEN

The producers of *The Prom Queen Wannabes* must be pretty smart, because they choose the very next week to showcase Amy's amazing singing talent. Sure, everyone at school has already heard her sing. But that isn't the same as watching her on television as she goes to an audition and gets picked to be a sexy backup singer for the variety show *All The Rave!* in New York City.

I'm relieved to see that Luke and I come across as a totally legit couple in this episode. There's footage of the homecoming game with Luke playing amazing and me looking stadium glamorous in all white as I cheer him on. Afterward, a long shot of the two of us slow-dancing together has to convince everyone that we are a couple of characters in a romantic love story. I actually squeal with happiness while watching it.

Unfortunately for Kelly, it's her turn to play the featured bitch of the week. The cameras follow her around as she presents her modeling portfolio to local businesses hiring models for catalog work. Her SACC's idea, of course. Knowing how much Kelly hates everything to do with looking attractive, I totally under-stand her pissy attitude. But people watching the show can't see how much cashing in on her looks is making her skin crawl.

And then we see the fateful day she shows up for a model interview at the same time as Grace Douglas. Grace has been the standard model for many local businesses ever since doing a garage door commercial for her stepdad back in elementary school. We're all used to seeing her in some cheesy pose or another on the cover of the *Nickel Saver,* and she's even been on few bill-boards. It's one of the reasons I felt like there was no escaping her back when I was the Elf Ucker.

The scene shows Kelly and Grace sitting across from each other in a waiting room with their modeling books balanced on their laps. Grace must have been stress eating chocolate over her breakup with Luke or something, because even through the hidden camera in the ceiling and layers of foundation, we can see her face is covered in angry red bumps.

The obvious tension in the room is emphasized by the shark attack music playing in the background. *Finally*, I think as I watch the hostile looks between them escalate onscreen. *This show could use a good bitch-fight about now.*

Suddenly, Kelly stands up and verbally attacks Grace with unbridled viciousness. She looks like a lunatic, letting Grace know what a has-been she is and adding a number of unkind references to Grace's complexion. Poor Grace seems absolutely crushed.

"Wait a minute," you may be saying. "'Poor Grace'? Isn't she that hateful bitch that you hate?" Well, yes, she is. But continuing to hate her at this point seems sort of petty.

Besides, if you could see the way Kelly rips into her, completely unprovoked, you'd feel sorry for her too. Especially when they show Grace blowing her interview afterward. She keeps covering her face with her hands, which is not the best way for a model to win over a client.

The scene is intercut with more recent confessional interviews with each girl. Kelly comes off as cold, complaining about being forced to drag her butt around on go-sees. Meanwhile, Grace is almost in tears as she talks about wanting to make her modeling dreams come true *so badly*. Kelly winning the ad ends up feeling like a huge injustice.

I've been trying to avoid the esteem-smashing message board about the show, but since I came off pretty well this week, I venture on for just a quick peek. Thankfully, I was right about me and Luke seeming swoony together and a few commentators say our dance was the highlight of the show. Grace takes a few hits for her shallow dreams, but Kelly's the one who really gets the hate on the forum this week. I seriously hope she doesn't decide to do a browser search for herself because things get pretty harsh.

Mona_184: Kelly is beautiful on the outside, but rotten to the core.

Andrewthesun: They never show her and Pete getting it on, but you can just tell she's a total slut.

JonJon_5: She'd look better if she duct-taped her damn mouth shut.

And to think, a week ago she was my biggest competition.

• • •

Kelly and Pete have a very public fight and break up the next morning, supposedly over the way she treated Grace on the show. Her defiant strut down the hallway while flipping onlookers the bird does nothing to help her win back supporters.

"What was that?" I ask when she approaches the lockers. "You forgot the cameras were on?"

"Now *you're* giving me shit?" Despite her tough-girl façade, I can see she's upset. She may have even seen the blog. "Grace is evil, okay? She attacked me and threatened to cause problems for my mom at the Snack Shack if I didn't quit modeling. She basically dumped her bitchiness all over me and I reacted."

"That's not what it—"

Kelly cuts me off. "I know, I know, through the *wonders* of editing technology, the show made me look like an unbelievable ass." She slams her books around inside her locker.

"Well, what happened between you and Pete?"

"That meathead?" She laughs. "He's a poser. Drops me the

second my status loses value. And here I thought *you* were the only one using a relationship to social climb."

"Hey, that's not—"

"Oh, come on, Shannon, don't deny it. You don't have feelings for Luke any more than Deena has a promising future as a spokesperson for Ipegag." I glance around as Kelly goes on, "I'm so sick of the show's stupid games, and I'm tired of being such a constant whore over a lousy million bucks. I'm making money modeling now. I don't need this. I'm quitting."

I stare at her. Ever since making it through Prom Queen Camp Hell, I have never once honestly considered quitting an option.

"So now that you're obviously losing, you're going to bail?" I say. "You want to be a full-time whore-model for the rest of your life? Oh, wait, I'm sorry, I mean, for the rest of your youth, which translates to about the next three years if you were paying attention during the assembly we just had."

Kelly stares at me then asks calmly, "So you really think you stand a shot at the million bucks?"

"Who's going to beat me?" I shoot back. "Amy?" I nod toward where she and George are huddled in their quiet clique of two. "She's not exactly going to win with only one vote from George. And *you* certainly aren't much competition, what with the way you *quit* the minute things get tough."

I see Kelly's jaw working in frustration. I'm baiting her. And she knows I'm baiting her. But she's also too pissed off to ignore the bait.

"That's it, Depola. It's on."

"Bring it!" I turn just in time to be caught seamlessly by Luke's bicep as he sweeps by. We move in sync down the hallway, and I see Rick out of the corner of my eye. He's talking to James, but his eyes follow as we pass and his brow furrows.

Unbidden, the scene from the math room looms in my mind. Even though there's no footage of it, it plays like a movie clip in my head. Rick cornering me. Leaning me against the desk. About to kiss me.

I kick a locker door shut with one of my red pumps, nearly taking an underclassman's head off in the process.

Luke grins down at me. "Feeling a little aggression, Depola?"

I growl back, "You have no idea."

• • •

Maybe the *Prom Queen Wannabe* forum folks are right about me being clueless, because declaring war with Kelly is not the smartest thing I've done. The whole time we're practicing our dance routine in the big Prom Queen Camp ballroom, Kelly ignores me, which totally psyches me out. I look over at her now, dancing aggressively with Raaauuul.

I wonder if she could get him to sabotage me. Amy is sharing a laugh with Victoria, and I realize what an idiot I've been this whole time. Josie told me to build alliances with people attached to the show. But I was so focused on learning how to seem popular, I forgot about building strategic relationships with people on the inside.

"Hey, what ever happened to Mickey, anyway?" I ask Victoria, wondering if I'm too late to make a power play.

Victoria waves me off. "She's in New York, taking care of show business."

"Don't worry," Raaauuul says darkly as his eyes remain on Kelly. "She has left you girls in *very* good hands."

Kelly snaps her glare toward me, and I shudder. Obviously, ignoring me isn't the worst thing she can do. I spend the rest of our practice time making eye contact with the floor.

The winter months are progressing on our show even as the trees are starting to bud in real time. I know that I had my best holiday season ever, popularity-wise, without a single rendition of "We Wish You a Tiny Pecker," but I'm not prepared to re-witness what happened to Kristan before winter break.

Despite the fact that Grace's popularity followed her modeling career into the figurative toilet, and the video of Deena unloading into a literal toilet drove her to the ugly comfort of scalp tattoos, Kristan never stopped being friends with either of them. If anything, her loyalty made her even more likable. Kristan quickly became our biggest threat for Prom Queen.

But all of that changes in the next episode.

Josie and I are watching the show together in our living room.

Partially for moral support and partially because Josie had a fallout with her bestie. "You're not the only one dealing with drama," she tells me.

The show opens with a shot of Kristan huddled with Deena and Grace in classic girl-crisis formation. Kristan confesses she's been hiding the fact that her dad got fired from his advertising job over the summer. Now her mother is threatening to leave him flat if he doesn't find a new job. She cries as she haltingly describes him being devastated over his gorgeous wife's ugly ultimatum.

"He stayed in his pajamas, eating coffee ice cream all weekend," Kristan says. "And he was still in bed when I left for school." Her friends awkwardly try to comfort her.

"It's like my mom doesn't care about what he's going through at all." Onscreen, she breaks down.

The episode gets more and more uncomfortable to watch as it follows Kristan through those first awful weeks of her parent's separation. She begins dabbling in the "natural look" which actually looks good on her. Right up until her eyebrows and mustache grow in.

"Oops, a little too natural," Josie says, and I slap her leg.

"Ouch." Josie slaps me back, and I shush her.

I get excited when I recognize the pink button-down I'm wearing onscreen and know what scene is about to play out.

Grace is alone at her locker when I approach, and I'm proud that I didn't need backup the way she did when she serenaded me. I stand, smirking at her for a moment, and she says, "Shove off, Shannon."

Clearing my throat, I start singing the carol that I made up to the tune of "Santa Claus is Coming to Town." It's titled "Padded Bras Make Grace Big and Round," and I'm surprised to hear how in-tune I sound.

"Your nipples won't twist
A bug bit you twice
A boob job might work, if not for the price.
Pa-dded bras make Grace big and ro-ound!"

I make corny gestures toward my own boobs to go with the lyrics, and Josie gives a nose laugh at my performance. Onscreen, Grace scowls at me but draws her books up in front of her chest in a way that shows my song is hitting its mark. Josie laughs harder as I continue singing, but the camera catches a look in Grace's eyes that makes something click in my brain.

I know just what she's feeling.

In that instant, watching the screen, I can sense Grace's hurt and shame because it is imprinted on me. Being the punch line to a cruel joke. The pain is still so close I can feel it.

I zone in on the glossy shade of hot pink lipstick on my singing lips. *Shannon's Sugar Bliss* is a beautiful color. But the lipstick can't make the words coming out of my mouth any less ugly. *Who the hell is that bullying fashionista onscreen?*

I've been so focused on manipulating others that I completely lost touch with who I am. I thought that hurting Grace the way she'd hurt me would make my life better. I daydreamed for years about getting even, and now as I watch it play out, I feel nothing but hollow.

I can't look at the Shannon onscreen for one more second, and I pick up the remote to click off the television.

"What are you doing?" Josie asks.

"The thing I should've done a long time ago." I look my sister in the eye. "I'm saying good-bye to the show."

"Are you crazy? You are rocking this thing." Josie lunges for the remote.

"Noooo…" The two of us start wrestling on the couch, and she rolls on top of me. I grab a throw pillow and start whapping my little sister on the side of her head until her hair's saturated with static. The two of us grapple for control—

But then.

The background music starts picking up dramatically. The two of us turn our tousled heads toward the screen as the camera closes in on Luke walking past Grace in the hallway. And it catches him giving her a wink. And a nod.

I get a really bad feeling as I sit up and watch the two of them walk swiftly in opposite directions. They meet at the door to a supply closet on the third floor.

They go inside.

It happens to be wired, and Josie lets out a gasp beside me as onscreen Luke and Grace fall into each other's arms. I put my hands over my eyes and watch through my fingers. Witness what Luke looks like when he's kissing someone he has true chemistry with. He and Grace make out so hot and heavy that even the greedy *Prom Queen Wannabes* camera pulls back and shifts to soft focus.

Josie tries to grab the remote from my hand, but I hang on tightly. "No. I want to see this."

Grace's breathy voice says to Luke, "I wish your airheaded little ticket to St. James could see us now." With that, the two of them launch into a duet of moans and kissing.

The camera zooms in on Grace's padded bra dangling from a mop handle as we hear their groans turn more primal.

The shot of the underwire cuts to a bright, loud commercial about the miraculous properties of lip stain as I stare blindly at the screen. Finally, Josie manages to seize the remote from my numb hand and she turns the television off.

PART FIVE

Project Runaway

CHAPTER FOURTEEN

I don't even cry this time. Luke and I don't care about each other anyway. Our whole relationship was just a constructed fantasy to make me look good for the cameras, and I refuse to be upset over his betrayal. I'm finished with allowing Luke and Grace to hurt me.

And I certainly don't sign on to the show's message board. Other people's opinions of me are none of my business. It's my opinion of myself that counts, and I'm ready to make some big changes so I can hopefully start to like myself.

After giving my reflection a bullhorn-worthy pep talk the next morning, I run into Mom on my way out the door. Between my crazy popularity schedule and her being busy at her office and with Thomas, it feels like we've barely seen each other in weeks.

"How's the show going, sweetie?" I notice her hair is in a tousled style instead of her usual mom-bob and she's wearing an awful lot of red. "You're certainly dressed well enough to be voted Prom Queen," she says, which means she has actually been honoring her agreement to not watch the show. "We really need to get a date in the calendar to catch up."

Or maybe she's just too busy to care. We hug and go our separate ways, and I actually hope we get that date in the calendar really soon.

Since the show started airing, I've been proudly driving my Nŏrealique Elite moving billboard of a car to school. But today when I pull up, I wish I'd driven Aunt Kate's old Coroda instead. People are pointing and talking behind cupped hands, not even trying to hide the fact that they're gossiping about me.

"Shannon's a useless bitch who deserved to get cheated on."— *Yeah, sorta.* "Grace is a slut."—*No, not really.* "What did you put for the definition of 'impute'?"—*Um, this might be a good time to open a schoolbook.*

Walking through the lobby, I'm faced with the damn giant-lipped Nŏrealique TV looping the footage of our campy poses. It's become a joke around the school to imitate Kelly, Amy, and me, posing with pursed lips and flipping hair. It started off as a funny greeting when the television first arrived, but the hair-flipping gradually took on a mocking tone.

Kelly is waiting for me at the lockers, her hands stuffed into the pockets of her fitted jean jacket. I remember my declaration of war, and a wave of panic rushes through me. She draws her right hand out of her pocket, and I flinch.

She starts laughing as she holds her hand out toward me.

"Wha…" I'm confused.

"You thought I'd pull a shiv on you or something? I just want to welcome you back, Elf Ucker."

I shoot, "Oh, like any of us ever had a real shot at becoming Prom Queen anyway."

"I know, my glorious selling out, all for nothing." Kelly laughs. "That'll teach the three of us to respect the social order." She nods toward Grace, Deena, and Kristan across the hallway. I catch Grace covering her smile with her hand as if she's feigning embarrassment for double-crossing me. But her posture clearly betrays her pride at having her affair with Luke uncovered.

I can't help but think she must really love him to let him humiliate her all that time just so he could get a football scholarship. Of course, now all of that humiliation has been transferred directly to me.

I look over at Amy and George who are completely focused on each other. She survived her backslide into the territory of the terminally unpopular just fine. Because she stayed true to George.

"Hey, are you still seeing Raaauuul?" I whisper to Kelly low enough that the hidden ceiling cam can't hear.

Kelly gives me a threatening look and glances toward the camera. Besides a conflict of interest, Raul could go to jail if things got too serious between him and Kelly on account of her being underage for another two months.

"I was just wondering." I shrug. I'm being honest. I wouldn't turn them in, and I'm not trying to psyche her out, but I do marvel at their willingness to risk a potential felony for the sake of their love.

Meanwhile, I never even gave Rick and me a shot. I wasn't willing to risk anything and claimed I wasn't sure I liked him. *Bullshit.* As if that dip I got in my stomach when he looked at me wasn't enough proof.

My mind conjures the image of Rick watching me in my car's rearview mirror at the beginning of the summer. *I should've dropped Marnie off first.*

I know what I have to do now. Tossing my books into my locker, I slam the door shut and head directly for the Nŏrealique Science Wing. I don't run, but my stride is wide and filled with purpose.

When I get there, I rush from window to window until I finally see a familiar silhouette with bad posture alone in one of the labs. *Rick.* He's hunched over, pouring a beaker of blue liquid into a graduated cylinder. He wears clear-plastic safety goggles that make his ears stick out goofily through his hair.

It's the hottest I've ever seen anyone look.

I throw open the door, and he slowly turns to face me. Our eyes lock through his goggles, and I don't want to wait one more second to get my kiss. *Just look at those tufts of hair sticking out around that elastic strap.*

I move toward him, and he pulls the goggles up to his forehead, exposing a red outline where they pressed across his nose and around his eyes.

"Hi," I say.

He leans back against the lab counter, crossing his arms. Body language closing me off.

I need to do something drastic. Something that will prove how much I like him. How much I regret my choice to do the show. I look up at the watching camera and summon all of the confidence I've been pretending to have all year long. Striding toward him, I declare, "I have some pheromones for you to experiment on."

His look of utter confusion is almost comical. With a grin, I grab him by the shoulders, close my eyes, and boldly press my lips against his.

I'm mashing my mouth around for a moment before I realize Rick isn't kissing me back. I pull back and open my eyes to see that his never closed. He's just standing there rigid, with my pink lipstick smeared all over his mouth.

Confused, I stammer, "I-I-I'm sorry. I thought this was what you wanted."

He reaches for a paper towel and closes his eyes as he wipes off my kiss. Looking around for the first time, I see James and Mr. Hoovler staring at me from the front of the room. They're frozen, holding a beaker between them as they both blink at me though their goggles.

"I'm sorry, I…" Mr. Hoovler starts to say something, but James quickly puts the beaker on a stand and hustles Mr. H out of the classroom.

Rick has effectively removed most of my lipstick from his mouth, and his cheeks have turned bright pink when he finally looks at me.

He takes a deep breath. "Um. So. What the hell?"

"I'm so sorry. I just thought…"

"What? You thought since your jock turned out to be a player in more ways than one you'd come crawling back to me? Like I've been waiting here pining away for you all year?"

"It's not like that. I just realized what a stupid mistake I made."

"Obviously. But you don't just get to call do-over, Shannon. You made a choice. Too much has changed. You've changed."

"I know. I've been acting so different and I'm sorry, but none of it is real. I promise you, underneath all of this, I'm still me." I smooth a hand over my designer dress.

"I think you need to go." Rick pulls his goggles back on, and I'm left watching him stupidly.

He shakes his head as he turns back to his beakers, and his tufts of hair wag up and down. I extend my fingers toward those tufts, and a loud sob escapes from someplace deep. Rick turns back, looking surprised through the clear lenses. I spin around and charge down the hallway, my pumps clomping as I force my legs to carry me away from the pain of his rejection.

I have to accept it—I'll never see that special look from him again. And it's entirely my fault that it will stay trapped forever in the rearview mirror of my mind.

I pass Luke on my way back to my locker, and he grabs my arm. "Hey, listen, Depola, I'm really sorry you had to find out that way. Grace and I—"

"You and Grace deserve each other, fuckhead," I say, which isn't exactly a carefully articulated response but it will have to do. I shove past him and display my signature flailing run that I've worked so hard to keep off camera.

Kelly and Amy rush over as I fall against my locker and start weeping. "I-I-III'm getting what I d-deseeeeeerve."

"Easy there. Nobody deserves to be ugly crying on national television." Kelly puts an arm around my shoulders.

"Come on, it'll be okay." Amy comes around my other side.

I swipe my snot with my sleeve and allow the two of them to guide me down the hallway. "How did I get so caught up in this?" I ask between sobs. "And now Rick doesn't want me anymore."

"Rick Shuebert?" Amy makes a face. "He doesn't really seem like your type."

"He's *exactly* my type," I practically screech.

"You're young, Shannon. You'll get over it," Kelly says. When I start crying even harder, she adds, "Hey, listen, we're all in this up to our necks. Everyone's just doing their best to get through it."

"You're right." I nod and take a shaky breath. Looking back and forth between the two of them, I say, "This reality show is hell."

"Who said anything about the show?" Kelly steers us into the girl's bathroom. "I'm talking about high school."

CHAPTER FIFTEEN

I refuse to come to the door for Victoria when she shows up with my clothing allowance. Josie finally convinces her that it will be best for everyone if she just gives me a little space. *But we'll take that sizable check, thankyouverymuch.*

I tell Josie to keep the money, and I drag armloads of fancy outfits into the bathroom where the cameras can't see me. Settling myself in the tub, I begin tearing seams and shredding fabric. I haven't held a needle in my hand since Victoria caught me sneaking a few stitches into a patch of material back at Prom Queen Camp. She'd acted so horrified you would've thought she caught me setting fire to the curtains.

The quilt I'm designing in my head will be covered with appliqués of hearts, smoke, and broken science beakers. I'm calling it *Chemical Properties of Heartbreak,* and it perfectly expresses my pain over blowing things with Rick.

Now the image that replays in my mind is of him wiping my lipstick off his mouth with disgust.

In spite of my exquisite emotional agony, it feels amazing to be sewing again, as I violently cut and tear expensive designer clothes for material.

Josie is worried about me, so I tell her I'm just depressed over the horrible episode of *Wannabes* with Luke cheating on me. But when she catches me throwing away the remains of my shredded wardrobe items, she decides it's time to get Mom involved.

Josie sets her up so she can watch *The Prom Queen Wannabes* on BubeTube in her study. When Mom emerges hours later, she hurries over to hug me tearfully. Josie has cleared out to a friend's house for a sleepover, and I lay my head on Mom's shoulder a moment before pulling back.

"Oh, sweetheart. I had no idea you were going through so much."

"Well, now you get to say I told you so."

She shakes her head. "No. I get to feel horrendous guilt for not protecting you. I thought the show might get you over your self-esteem issues. Then I saw how self-confident you seemed this year, and I figured everything was working out."

I laugh. "Sure, everything worked out just great."

Mom hugs me again, and I soak it up. She says, "Well, I'm not helping Luke negotiate any scholarships now. I can't believe he cheated on you that way."

"It's fine, Mom. I'm over him. You should get that bonus. Especially since we're clearly not about to become millionaires."

Mom laughs. "Did you ever really think this was a good way to become a millionaire?"

"Yes," I say, "I guess I did. But I can see now it still wouldn't have been worth the price. Marnie isn't speaking to me, and she's worth a cool mil at least." I don't add in the cost of losing Rick.

Mom pats my shoulder. "I guess there are some lessons you just have to figure out the hard way."

"And some lessons I've needed to learn in front of thousands of viewers." I pull my over-processed hair into a rough ponytail and flop onto the couch. "I can't believe how caught up I got."

"Go easy on yourself, sweetie," Mom says. "We all have our blind spots."

When Thomas comes over, he assumes my presence in the living room means I want to watch one of the stupid old black-and-white movies that he loves so much. Mom sits beside me rubbing my arm while he works on his super-fattening cheesy dip in the kitchen.

The phone rings, and I look up at one of the cameras faithfully recording my abject misery. I resist the urge to rip the damn thing off of its mount and instead ask Mom, "So, any chance that TV contract you negotiated has an exit clause?"

She turns toward me, but before she can answer, Thomas hurries in, holding the phone to her. "It's Kate," he says. "She sounds upset." He stands, nervously squeezing the spatula, and I'm touched by the way he watches my mother take the call.

Mom's voice rises in alarm as she clutches the phone to her ear. She squeaks ominous one-word questions like "When?" and "How?" *Please, not Aunt Kate's dormant cancer.* I start to pray silently, feeling stupid for thinking I'm the only one in the world who has problems.

"I'll be right there." Mom clicks the phone off and turns to us. Her eyes seem wild. "Kate's husband, John, just died." She says it so simply. I'm almost relieved for a moment that it's not Kate's cancer before I feel the full weight of what she's just said. I've known him my whole life. *He can't be dead.*

"I'm an awful friend," Mom says as she staggers about gathering her purse and keys. "I didn't even know he was back in the hospital. Things progressed so fast…organs started shutting down…"

"Stop," Thomas says firmly, facing Mom and forcing a hug on her. She collapses into his embrace. "You are an excellent friend, and you need to be the strongest version of yourself, because Kate needs you *now*."

Mom stands up straighter in his arms and nods. "You're right. Kate needs me." With that, she draws away from him and strides toward the door.

"Whoa, hold on. I'll drive you," he says.

"Oh, right." Mom seems caught in a cloud of shock. "Let me get some things. I'll probably be staying the night." Her eyes focus on me, and I wave her off, indicating that of course I'll be fine.

She heads to her bedroom to pack a bag, and Thomas and I stand awkwardly in the living room, the only thing we have in common gone. "Kate's lucky to have her."

I nod. "They've been friends for forever."

"It's a rare friendship that lasts a lifetime."

Even though I know he's just making polite conversation, I can't help but crumple onto the couch. My life has turned to crap, and I need Marnie. Just like Kate needs Mom.

After a few moments of hyperventilating with my face in my hands, I take a hitching breath and rub the blur from my eyes. I expect to find myself alone in the living room, but Thomas is there, watching me with concern. *Wow, a guy who doesn't bolt at the sight of emotions? He's a keeper, Mom.*

Thomas doesn't offer to hug me or anything—I suppose that would be weird—but he does walk over to the hutch to grab a tissue. Handing it to me, his eyes flick toward the hidden camera. My mind goes straight to *Is he having inappropriate thoughts? *ick** But when I feel the weight of the tissue in my palm, I stop freaking out. Something wallet-sized, flat, and weighty is wrapped inside it. I'm careful to not react.

"No need to return that," he says.

My heart is throbbing, but I keep my voice even. "You sure you don't want my snotty tissue back?"

Thomas gives the slightest smile as Mom reappears from the bedroom with an overnight bag over her shoulder. She pulls a tired smile from someplace deep and looks back and forth between us. "Thanks for understanding. And for the ride."

Thomas and I assure her that the ancient movie we were going to watch can wait. As soon as they leave, I head to the bathroom. My camera-free zone.

Sitting on the edge of the tub, I look at the tissue cupped in my hands a few moments. *How did Thomas know?*

Finally, I unwrap the object he's privately passed to me. It's exactly what it felt like. A cell phone. A disposable cell phone that isn't set to record every conversation I have. A beautiful untraceable private cell phone that I can use to call Marnie.

• • •

I know I have no right to ask my ex-bestie for anything. Or to even expect her to take my call, but I need to try. I make a silent plea to the wart gods of friendship and dial Marnie's number. She answers after the second ring, which I think is a good sign, until I realize my name didn't come up on her caller ID. Her picking up just means Marnie answers calls from Unknown instead of letting them go to voicemail like I do.

"Uh, hi?" My voice cracks. "It's me. What's up?"

"Shannon?" She says my name with a whoosh of air. Like

I surprised the breath out of her. When I don't reply, she says, "What's up? Well, let me see, *other* than the fact that we haven't spoken in about five months?"

I immediately start sobbing. What the hell was I thinking? I don't deserve to *speak* to her.

"So what?" she snaps. "Luke cheats on you and I'm supposed to clean up the mess?"

"It's not that. We never even really liked each other."

"Then why the hell were you two going out?"

"I don't knoooow," I wail. "I've spent the whole year manipulating people so they'll vote for me to be Prom Queen. I don't even know who I am anymore! And now, here you are, being nice to me, and I don't deseeeerve it."

"This is *not* me being nice."

"You didn't hang up." My voice hitches. "That's nice."

I continue crying, and she asks, "Would you feel better if I did hang up?"

"Infinitely! I've been so selfish…" The line goes dead. "Hello?" *I can't believe she just hung up on me!* As I sit, staring at the phone in my hand, it starts vibrating. I hit Answer, and before I can say anything, Marnie shoots, "There. Feel better?"

"I…I'm not sure…"

"I can't believe you thought running for Prom Queen was a good idea."

"I know! I'm a complete imbecile."

"What the hell made you agree to even be a part of that show?"

"I don't know. I just really wanted to escape my life for a while. You know, see what it would feel like to not be the Elf Ucker."

"I knew it! Shannon!" Marnie sounds so annoyed with me I want to hide under my bathroom sink. "I warned you that focusing on that horseshit made it worse. Now look at where it's brought you."

"I know. I know!" I'm more frustrated with myself than she is. "I thought that getting even with Grace would make me feel better. But making her feel bad just made me feel even worse."

"Yeah, I heard that song you made up. Much more creative than 'Tiny Pecker' but equally wrong."

"Watching myself sing it to her on TV made me see how ugly I was acting."

"Nice if you could've seen that a little sooner. Like maybe *before* blowing senior year."

"I'm sorry. This was supposed to be our best year ever."

"Yes, it was."

"I will still be saying I'm sorry to you when we are both one hundred."

"That's a start."

"I hate myself."

"You should always love yourself, but it is good to acknowledge when you've been acting like a jerk or a conformist."

"I've been mean and selfish and small-minded," I list my offenses, eager for Marnie to forgive me.

But she just adds, "And *shallow*, not to mention becoming part of a branding spectacle that is sucking off the teat of a brainwashed consumerist system."

"Um, okay. There's that. *Plus*, I blew things with a great guy who actually liked me for me."

After a pause, Marnie asks, "Have you spoken to Rick?"

"I went by the lab the other day and er…saw him. Actually I kind of tried to kiss him." I cringe at the image of him wiping his mouth.

"You're lying!"

"I wish I was lying. He totally rejected me. Thought I was just rebounding from Luke. It's hopeless."

"Wow. I thought he still liked you," Marnie says.

"Well, he's over me now."

"I was shocked when I came back from the Bahamas and found out you two didn't hook up."

"Um, I was surprised when I saw that you and James *had*. Marnie! I'm so happy for you guys. Is he a great boyfriend or what?"

I can hear the smile in her voice as she tells me about James realizing they were perfect for each other during a late-night study cram. Of course, Marnie already knew this, but sometimes boys need a little help catching up. She shares about the ups and downs of their relationship, and the time we've spent apart dissolves in our whispers and giggles.

It feels so good to be talking to her that I start crying again.

Softly at first, but when Marnie asks, "Are you okay?" I curl myself into a ball on the bathroom rug and just go with sobbing. I don't hold back. Big wails mingle with anguished moans as I let myself feel every real emotion coursing through me. I cry long and loud over blowing things with Rick. I cry for Aunt Kate losing her husband. And I cry because of how horribly I've treated my best friend. And yet here she is—listening.

"Shannon?" Marnie's voice sounds concerned. "Are you okay?"

"Fine. *hic* I'm fine."

"You sure?"

"No, actually, *hic* I'm so *not* fine. But I'm not going to spend the whole night crying on my *hic* bathroom floor if that's what you're worried about."

"Um, why are you on your bathroom floor?"

"Cameras." I let out a shaky sigh. "Actually, Marns, do you think there's any *hic* chance I can—"

"—come over to my house for a sleepover?" she finishes my sentence for me. Just like old times.

CHAPTER SIXTEEN

Marnie and I hug for a full minute when I arrive, and then she tosses my bag on the couch and drags me directly to the kitchen. There, she teaches me how to mix a green clay mask out of regular household ingredients that aren't part of the "big beauty brainwash machine," as she puts it. "We need to purify your pores from all that Nőrealique shit."

"I need to purify my soul after the way I've acted all year." I laugh as we slap green goop on each other's faces.

"Well, it *was* for a shot at *One! Million! Dollars!*" Marnie says, and I love that she totally nails the cheesy way they announce it on the show.

While our masks dry, the two of us move to her bedroom where she has sewing supplies already laid out on her bed. I almost start crying again at the sight. I'm pretty sure just puffs of air would come out of my tear ducts at this point. As we sew, I talk about Rick and the fact that even the sound of his name fills me with deep regret.

"So, the two of you haven't even spoken since you tried to kiss him?" Marnie asks.

"Honestly, I don't know what I'd even tell him," I say. "'Sorry for getting my stupid lipstick on you'?" I flop myself across her bed, bury my face deep in her pillow, and give a cleansing scream.

Then I remember the clay mask still drying on my face. *I'm the worst friend in the universe.* I raise my head to find smears of green all over Marnie's pillow. "Oh no, I'm so sorry." I grab a tissue from the nightstand and start scraping the green gunk off her pillowcase.

"Would you please stop that? We do have a washing machine." She grabs my hand holding the tissue. "And I know Rick really did like you. Maybe he just hates Nŏrealique lipstick."

"Yeah, right," I say.

"Honestly, Shannon. Since finding out about the show, he blames Nŏrealique for turning you into a…um…" She covers her mouth with her hand.

"Turning me into a bitch, right? Rick thinks I'm a total bitch."

Marnie looks me in the eye, swiping at the clay on my face with a tissue. "Listen, he was really hurt when you started dating Luke."

I cover my head with my hands. "Why didn't anyone stop me?" I look at Marns. "I mean, besides those times when you tried to stop me."

Marnie's mom knocks softly on the door. "Girls?" she calls. "There are two women here who'd like to talk to Shannon?"

When Marnie opens the door, her mother's eyes are wide. "They're awfully fancy," she says.

Mickey and Victoria look like a couple of well-dressed mannequins that someone set up in the middle of the homey living room as a prank of some sort. Victoria's body language says she's afraid one of the cross-stitched pillows might jump up and bite her. Mickey's body language says she's flat out pissed.

"Hi, Mickey," I greet casually. "What brings you to the middle of nowhere?"

Victoria squints at me. "Is that mask one of ours? You know you're only to use Nŏrealique products. That includes skin and hair care."

Marnie gives a loud laugh.

"May I please see Shannon alone for a moment?" Mickey smiles tightly and unclenches her arms as Marnie and her mom obligingly head for the kitchen. Without breaking eye contact with me, Mickey tells Victoria to go outside and keep the car running. Victoria looks happy to escape all of the domestic handmade crafts.

Once we're alone, Mickey looks me up and down in a way that's designed to make me squirm. "You and I need to discuss a certain contractual matter or two."

I squint at her. "How did you know where to find me?"

She ignores my question with a wave of her hand. "Am I right in assuming you planned to spend the night in this unapproved location?"

"Unapproved?" I look around and wonder if she really finds overstuffed furniture that repulsive.

"Yes, *unapproved*." Her jaw is tight. "This *Marnie* person didn't even sign her release. Staying here overnight will disqualify you from winning the *One! Million! Dollars!*"

"Disqualify me?" I snort. "How about, *I quit*?"

"Shannon," she snaps. "Prom Queens are not quitters."

"I lost all interest in being a damn Prom Queen."

I glare at her until she relaxes her shoulders and tries a new approach. "I shouldn't be telling you this." Her voice lowers conspiringly. "There's going to be a huge twist that will put you, Kelly, and even Amy back into the running for that prize money."

I laugh. "It's enough of a miracle that the three of us were ever popular at all. Just give it up already."

"Okay, Shannon. I can understand you're feeling things are hopeless, but let me explain the show's direction."

"Not interested," I say as I turn toward the kitchen. *I should've walked away in the first place.*

"There's going to be a viewer vote!" Mickey calls out.

"Don't give a shit!" I shoot back then turn. "Wait, you mean Westfield's seniors aren't even voting for their own Prom Queen?"

"Not unless they call in." Mickey smiles.

"How much did you pay our school to let you do all of this?"

"That's none of your concern." Mickey gives a slick grin. "What you should be focused on is the fact that this voting system ups your odds of winning. For three-in-one odds at a million bucks, you'd at least buy a lottery ticket wouldn't you?"

"Keep your lottery ticket. I'm done. I've got my old Advisement Coach back, and she's worth ten million."

I take another step toward the kitchen, and Mickey calls out ominously, "What about Rick?"

I turn. "What about Rick?"

Mickey places her hands on her hips, opening her body language aggressively and displaying both thumbs. "I didn't want to resort to this, but we have footage of your *Rick* person discussing his science project with his advisor on the first day of school."

I narrow my eyes. "That's what he was supposed to do."

"Yes, he was to *start* the discussion of the project on that day, but it is clear from the footage we have on file that Rick and his partner, James, actually began their experiment earlier. If this video were to come to light, they would not only be disqualified from the Pennsylvania State Science Fair, but there would forever be a black mark on their names within the larger science community."

She's bluffing. Rick and James banned from science? Impossible. But then, as distracted as I was that first day of school, I do remember they'd already picked pheromones for their project. I wonder if using the wrong wording with Mr. Hoovler could really ruin their whole science geek careers.

I can't believe Mickey is actually trying to blackmail me into staying on her show.

"You're to say nothing to anybody, including this Marnie character," Mickey warns in a low voice as Marnie comes out of the kitchen.

"Everything okay, Shannon?" she asks me while eyeing Mickey suspiciously.

Mickey's eyes are two drills boring holes in me. *I can't risk Rick's whole future.* I close my eyes and turn to Marnie. "Sorry. I have to head home. No cameras. No clearance."

Marnie looks at me in disbelief. "So just quit the damn show already."

"I'd love to, believe me." I am mentally pleading with her to figure out that I'm being blackmailed right now. "But I signed all these contracts. I really need to talk to my mother first and find out what my rights are."

"I can't believe your mom would let you sign a contract that you can't get out of." Marnie's eyes are narrowed. I know that she can smell the lies on me and wish she would just trust me. But that's way too much to ask of her at this point.

Picking up my overnight bag, I give her a huge hug. "I'll text you," I whisper, but she still looks angry.

"Thank you for your, er, hospitality." Mickey gives a nod to Marnie and her mother and turns to go.

"Nŏrealique is a tool of the man!" Marnie calls and holds her fist up in the air.

I turn and grin at her as Mickey ushers me briskly out the door.

Once outside, she leads me to my Nŏrealique Freus while Marnie watches from the front door. A homemade wreath covered in berries hangs from the center of it. I try to use best friend telepathy to convey the fact that I have to do this for Rick and James and even for sweet, innocent Mr. Hoovler, but Marnie just stands there with her arms crossed.

Before climbing into the slick black SUV where Victoria waits in the passenger seat, Mickey hisses at me, "You *will* act surprised when they announce the big twist in the voting." She turns away, but then lunges even closer. "And I better not catch you with that girl again. I'm *always* watching."

With a growl, I fling myself into my Freus, glance in the rearview mirror, and nearly scream at the dried green glops on my face. Then I picture Rick sitting behind me, looking at me *that way* at the beginning of the summer.

I have to win him back.

Something that *real* is worth fighting for.

CHAPTER SEVENTEEN

We only have a few weeks before prom and there's a big assembly in the auditorium for all the Westfield High seniors. Kelly, Amy, and I stand onstage with huge fake smiles as our classmates are commanded to "Settle down now."

With a flourish, Victoria strides onstage and makes the announcement, "For the first time in Westfield High history, students will not be voting for their own Prom Queen." With an enormous grin, she flings her arms wide and proclaims, "America will!"

I act as surprised as I'm able, and Amy actually gives a small jump as if the news just goosed her in the butt. The room erupts with squeals and clapping which isn't really what I was expecting. I figured our classmates would be pissed to hear the election is being outsourced to a bunch of strangers. Then again, I suppose having our prom televised *live!* will mean more opportunities to win the new holy grail of adolescence. Airtime.

My fake surprise turns into actual surprise when Grace,

Deena, and Kristan stride out from behind a curtain and move beside us onstage. The three of them look colorful and showy and have obviously been treated to Nŏrealique extreme makeovers.

Victoria announces, "And in our other surprise twist…Grace Douglas, Deena McKinnley, and Kristan Bowman will be joining in the race for the crown! Each will have her own call-in number at the *live!* finale at the prom!" Victoria practically levitates with enthusiasm. "That's right, these former Alpha Queens will have a shot at winning that *One! Million! Dollars!*"

I notice Grace, Deena, and Kristan are all wearing lips logo pins now too. The three of them face off as if to confront Kelly, Amy, and me onstage. It's a little cheesy, like, what does Victoria expect? That we'll start grabbing hair weaves and clawing each other's eyes out?

I scan the crowd, trying to find Marnie. I tried to call her from my bathroom last night and left a message about Mickey blackmailing me, but she didn't respond. Now I'm afraid she'll think I'm staying on the show because I have better odds of winning the money with America making the decision.

"Nŏrealique is a tool of the man!!" I spot her right away, standing in the back of the auditorium with her fist in the air. Getting her protest on, she chants, "Nŏrealique is a tool of the man! Nŏreal—"

Nobody joins in, and Marnie is tackled by a guy dressed in all black who comes out of nowhere. "Hey!" I yell and head to the edge of the stage, but more men dressed in black appear and hustle the six of us behind the curtains.

"I'll see you all at prom," Victoria announces gaily to the crowd as if a student hadn't just been silenced by force. "Be sure to look your best, because the cameras will be rolling!"

The show must have been planning the voting twist for a while, because within a day of the assembly, the giant Nőrealique big-lipped TV in the lobby includes dramatic, windblown shots of Grace, Deena, and Kristan turning and posing for the camera. They look fresh and natural, especially compared to the tired shots of me, Kelly, and Amy that everyone sees in their sleep by now.

The Queens start campaigning right away. Deena proves that sometimes a few curves can be a good thing as she adopts a sexy '50s pin-up style of dressing. Plus, she's grown her hair into a smooth, short style so you can't even see her scalp tattoo anymore. Kristan pulls herself together and adopts a waxing and bleaching routine that's better suited to her body's needs. And with Luke back on her arm, Grace has that tiara directly in her crosshairs.

I send a text to Marnie telling her how proud I am for her demonstration of rebellion during the assembly.

Marnie: They've taken over our mindspace!

Me: Westfield High had its price and I guess Nőrealique paid it.

Marnie: Sold out by our own school.

Me: I need to find a way to fix this.

Marnie: There are some things that are beyond fixable.

I need to find a way to try.

• • •

Things on *Wannabes* start building up for the *live!* finale at the prom. They even air a recap show of previously unseen footage. None of it is as earth-shatteringly original as the teasers made it out to be. But the recap does give them an excuse to air my mortifying runway fall twenty-six more times.

As my flailing descent is being shown for the fourteenth time onscreen, I look over and catch Josie laughing silently. When she sees I'm watching her, she sucks in her lips and shrugs apologetically. The clip plays again. Onscreen, my arms pinwheel madly as my body flies off the runway ass first. I look ridiculous.

But for the first time, instead of feeling blinded by humiliation, my face cracks into a smile.

When they repeat the clip yet again in slow motion, I watch my wrists flap and my face twist in surprise, and I actually give a small snort through my nose. Josie stares at me a moment before giving a squeal of glee and adding her laughter to mine.

I guess it's a sibling's job to help us learn to laugh at ourselves. Josie smiles. "Well, at least you won't be known as the Elf Ucker ever again."

"Yup, from now on, I'm just that chick who ate it on the runway at Prom Queen Camp." We start laughing again, and I decide to quit trying to flee from embarrassment now, before an even *more* humiliating version of reality finds me.

I've been waiting for them to air my pass at Rick in the science lab, but I guess they decide that's more humiliation than one girl should have to endure. Or maybe they just don't want to show someone wiping off their lipstick in disgust.

Now that Deena, Kristan, and Grace are included in the audience vote for Prom Queen, they join us at our next practice for our *live!* prom performance. Amy, Kelly, and I have been practicing all year long, and now the three of them are jumping in less than two weeks before Prom.

The routine we've been perfecting ad nauseam consists of Amy singing like a superstar, with Kelly and I as her backup singers-slash-dancers. Or, more accurately, lip-syncers-slash-sway-and-snappers with a few twists and kicks thrown in for good measure. I've worked hard trying to keep up with Kelly, whose sways, snaps, twists, and kicks are quite excellent I assure you.

"Girls?" Victoria faces us, holding her arm around a thin,

well-groomed man with an impish face and completely bald head. "This…is Anthony!" Except she says his name like "Aaaaaan-tho-neeee." I glance at Kelly in time to see her face fall. *Where's Raaauuul?* I wonder.

"We've run into a bit of a problem with Raul." Victoria says his name flat. "He's being investigated for having a relationship with a minor that shows a conflict of interest." She looks pointedly at Kelly.

"*Alleged* relationship," Kelly corrects.

"Regardless, our legal team uncovered a felony charge from his youth that he tried to cover up."

"His juvenile records were supposed to be sealed," Kelly says.

"Still…" Victoria shakes her head in condemnation.

Kelly shouts, "When he turns twenty-three, they're getting expunged, okay? Raul is *not* some sort of criminal!"

"*Any*way," Victoria goes on with her game-show host voice, "we are *very* lucky to have Anthony here from the popular show…" She pauses and raises her arms for dramatic effect. "*Make Me A Star!*" At our non-reactions, she throws her hands down. "Come on, am I the only person who watches that one?"

Anthony looks crushed, but once we reshoot the scene with the six of us displaying a proper level of joy and awe at his presence, he recovers quickly. Anthony has Raul's enthusiasm times twelve, but none of his Latin hotness. With flamboyant gestures, he explains he has some *fabulous* ideas for our song and dance number.

Each of us has a fresh talent tryout, since apparently they neglected to show Anthony the recorded evidence that I cannot sing or dance. Kelly blows the dancing almost as bad as I do. I'm not sure if it's on purpose to protest Raul's absence or if she's genuinely too upset to dance without him. But aside from Amy nailing her song, Grace, Kristan, and Deena basically come off as fresher, more talented versions of us.

Anthony claps. "Okay, okay, people." Gesturing to Kelly and me, he announces, "You and you are out." Giving a hug to Deena and Kristan in turn, he squeals, "You and *you* are in." And with that, Kelly and I are released from performing backup for the stupid song we've been forced to practice for months. Deena gives us a smug look of victory, but Kristan actually apologizes.

"So now we don't have to do anything for the show?" Kelly seems relieved.

"Oh, yes, you must do something," Anthony insists. "America will be voting during the fabulous *live!* prom recording, so you each need to get equal camera time—even if we *did* have to watch you three bitch it out all season. Oops, did I say that out loud?" Anthony covers his mouth mockingly as Grace and Deena laugh like a couple of drunks.

"This sucks," Kelly grouses.

"At least you have skills," I say. "You can do some sort of painting or dance or *something*. What the hell am I supposed to do? Plunge off a runway? It's the only thing I seem to be good at."

Kelly snorts a quick laugh, but Amy puts her arm around me. "Don't say that about yourself. You're very talented."

Kelly says, "Yeah, we just don't know at what yet."

I have sudden inspiration and call to Anthony, "Hey, can I maybe sew a craft as my talent?"

"I've worked with Liza Minnelli and now I'm running the freakin' 4-H?" Anthony says. "Perhaps you'd like to display your prize hog?" He waves me off. "Do whatever you please. I must get back to my *real* talent now. Ready, girls?" He claps quickly and goes back to shouting "fabulous" at Kristan and Deena who are stretching and doing high leg lifts. Clearly, as Amy's backups, their job will be trying to upstage her.

Grace gives me an unattractive snarl and turns to Kelly. "You want to have a walk-off on the runway on Prom Night?" She sounds like she's challenging Kelly to a duel to the death.

"You're kidding, right?" Kelly looks at her as if she's just asked for a sleepover.

"Well, we've got to do something," Grace says. "Are you afraid my fierce walk will shame you?"

Victoria must be eavesdropping, because she comes prancing over, grinning like a deranged beauty queen. Which, of course, she is. She hugs Grace, which is really strange to watch since it's the first time Victoria has shown any sign of human affection. "What a fabulously *fabulous* idea!" she says. "Our sponsor will provide all of the designer outfits, of course. A runway

competition promoting Nõrealique Fashion! You're *fabulous*!"
Anthony's *fabulouses* seem to be rubbing off on her.

"No way am I doing modeling as my talent." Kelly shakes her
head. "I'll paint a picture or something and show it like Shannon."

Victoria frowns. "That's not a tiara-worthy attitude, Kelly."

Anthony calls out, "Start counting down the days, girls! Prom's
less than two weeks away!"

I sigh. *Fabulous.*

• • •

"I need to find a way to convince Rick I've changed." I'm talking
to Marnie on my cell phone, and my butt is sore from sitting in
the bathtub. Marnie and I decided that if Rick found out about
the blackmail, he'd try to convince me to quit the show. But
he cannot appreciate the level of ugly Nõrealique is capable of.
Marnie casually asked James a few questions about the science fair,
and she's pretty sure they didn't break any rules. Unfortunately,
we've witnessed the ways a little crafty editing can alter reality,
and neither one of us wants to risk the boys' future.

"Well, I don't know that you've *totally* changed," Marnie
teases me.

"Um, I'm supposed to be out campaigning for call-in votes
right now," I tell her as I shift to grab my scissors. "Instead I'm
hiding in my bathtub. I've definitely changed."

"I hear you moving around," Marnie says. "What the heck are you working on anyway?"

I can't tell Marnie what I'm really doing and bite my lip as I eye the stack of prom magazines piled high on the sink. Fashion porn.

Victoria has been on my ass about how much time I'm spending in the bathroom and threatened me with breach of contract for hiding from the cameras. A part of me would love to see that court case, with the prosecutor trying to prove what I was and wasn't doing on the toilet. But to keep the peace, I started bringing piles of magazines in with me as a cover.

"Oh, I'm just looking through magazines, finding the perfect prom dress," I tell Marnie my patented lie.

"Oh, sure, you've changed," she laughs. "I'm working on sewing my dress myself."

I wince involuntarily at that image and immediately want to slap myself. *I wonder how long it takes to undo an entire year of thinking like a Prom Queen.*

I lean over and grab a magazine off the top of the stack so I'm not lying about looking through them. "Some of these pictures of people standing around pretending to laugh make the prom seem like agony."

Marnie chuckles as I flip the pages loudly into the phone. And then I stop. And I gasp.

"What is it?"

I fold the magazine open to the page. It's a Nőrealique ad. And I'm in it. "I'm an advertisement!" I burst.

"What the—"

I've posed for about four kajillion glamour photos, so I knew this was always a possibility, but it's still a shock. I can't help feeling thrilled at seeing the full-page spread of my smiling face. I look impossibly fresh and smooth and awake. I'm wearing a bright pink wrap dress and my blonde hair is dramatically blowing back and…"Wait-a-second."

I pull the page closer to my face and screech, "My ears! Marnie, they totally photoshopped my ears off!"

"Those bastards!" she hisses.

I cup my left ear. "I feel like I've been violated."

"You *have* been violated," Marnie says. "Extreme airbrushing violates and disrespects *all* women. They make us insecure and keep us chasing impossible ideals. I'm sure you're impossibly skinny in the photo too."

"Yes! I look like I'm weak and starving, but Marnie—they *took* my *ears!*"

"Don't worry," she says. "We'll get even somehow."

I eye the real project I've been working on and a new idea starts to take form in my mind. *And I know just how I'll force them to listen.*

• • •

Aunt Kate has been leaning on Mom more than ever since her husband died, but Thomas has been a real superstar, acting supportive and helping with the cooking. Since the cell phone incident, I've even started thinking of him as a potential fatherly-type figure that might not be so horrible to have around.

He's finally wrangled Josie, Mom, and me into watching his favorite movie with him. The black and white film was directed by a fat bald guy with big jowls. Still, it beats the agony of watching rerun episodes of *Prom Queen Wannabes* that are playing every hour in anticipation of the *live!* Prom finale.

The movie's so old the credits run before the film, and as they're still rolling, Thomas slips me a pad of paper. "Let's play hangman. Go ahead and guess a letter." I catch Mom shoving a handful of popcorn in her mouth to hide her hint of a smile.

"Oh, I love hangman," Josie says. "I think I have an app for it."

"This one's for Shannon." Thomas glances at the spot where the camera is watching us. "And I like low tech."

"Because you're old." Josie pokes him and turns her attention back to the movie.

On the pad, I see Thomas has drawn a hangman's noose with six spaces to one side of it. As I reach to take it from him, Thomas uses his thumb to flick the top page quickly. I catch just a peek of something scrawled underneath. I take the pad and lift the corner of the top sheet, careful to block the camera's view. In teeny tiny print, Thomas has written, There's something I need to tell you. Just guess a letter and pass the pad back.

I narrow my eyes at him and glance at Mom, but she's absorbed in the movie. I obediently write an E on the top sheet and pass him the pad.

Taking it, he starts writing again, and when it's back in my hands, there are E's in the second and the last spaces. On the teeny-tiny writing page, he's written, You need to know, I'm in love with your mother.

I smile and write back, Okay, I think she likes you too.

Then I guess the letter Z, since I don't want to solve the word before he finishes this bizarre game of asking me for my mother's hand in marriage.

Before handing the pad back, he draws a head in the noose and writes, Don't hate me, but I'm an actor. My real name is Charlie. The show hired me to date your mother.

A cloud of black birds onscreen descends on a screaming woman while I stare blindly at the pad. I feel like my insides are being pecked apart. *The man sitting on my couch is an actor pretending to be my mother's boyfriend?* Looking over at Mom, I see she's clutching a cushion to her chest as a screaming woman flails for her colorless life. I squeeze the pen in my hand and envision stabbing Thomas with it. *Oh, I'm sorry, I mean Charlie.*

I take shallow breaths and mentally command my mother and

sister to *Run!* Thomas is begging me with his eyes and glancing at the camera. I take a deep, cleansing yoga breath that would make Victoria very proud.

"Are you okay, Shannon?" Mom is looking at me.

I can feel Thomas/Charlie pleading with me to keep quiet. *Let's give the guy a chance to explain.* There'll be plenty of time to murder him later. I say, "I'm just not a fan of horror."

Mom leans over from her chair to pat my leg. "Just remind yourself it's not real." I have to swallow to keep myself from shouting *Nothing is real!*

I draw a knife sticking out of the head in the noose with blood dripping down. Then I draw hair and a goatee so it looks like Thomas/Charlie and write back, Why are you telling me this? You need to stay the hell away from my mother! Then I think a moment and add, So that cell phone you slipped me had a trace on it? Is that how they found me at Marnie's so fast? Has the show been listening to my conversations with her this whole time?

I'm so sorry, he writes back. I had no idea what I was getting into when they hired me. And no, the cell phone is clean, but they have a tracer on your car. I've been trying to figure out a way to tell your mom the truth. He holds a hand to his forehead, shading his anguished expression from Mom's view. I can kind of relate to the conundrum of trying to prove to someone that your love is real after screwing up very, very badly.

Through our back-and-forth cryptic hangman exchange,

Thomas/Charlie explains he recently sold his business for a comfortable profit and had always wanted to try acting. Being on a reality show seemed like a good start, and the show hired him to distract my mother from what I was doing. She's a tough nut to crack, he writes, which I know is true. But once she allowed me in, I came to realize she's the most amazing woman I've ever met. Which is probably also true.

From her chair, she gives Thomas/Charlie an adoring look, and my chest throbs.

I cautiously continue our exchange, trying not to look too obvious for the cameras as Thomas apologizes over and over. I will do absolutely anything to make this up to you, I swear, he writes and goes on to say that he's hated watching my downslide over the past year as I listened to my SACC's bad advice.

I try to absorb the fact that Nōrealique would actually hire a person to seduce my mother as we sit on the couch watching innocent people get their eyes pecked out. I have no doubt the show would use that science lab video to ruin Rick and James. Especially if it guarantees a bit of drama.

The hangman game ends with the drawing of my mother's fake boyfriend hanging, stabbed and dismembered, on the page. Sketched black birds fly away with his fingers in their beaks. I figure he'll be lucky to look that good once Mom learns the truth. Studying the letters he's filled in, I finally guess the word.

<u>B</u> <u>E</u> <u>W</u> <u>A</u> <u>R</u> <u>E</u>

• • •

I'm sitting on my bathroom floor with the contraband cell phone from my mom's artificial boyfriend pressed to my ear.

"This is getting freaky," Marnie says. After I texted her about Thomas/Charlie, she did some investigating and discovered a connection between Nőrealique and the places that replaced Grace with Kelly as a model. "I'm almost positive they were bought off by your *illustrious sponsor*."

"They're not *my* sponsor," I say. "I tried to quit, remember?"

"Sorry. I think as a student at Westfield High, they actually qualify as *our* official sponsor."

I shudder. "Moving on, I think I may finally have an idea how to convince Rick I deserve a second chance. I'm going to need your help."

"Of course you've got it," Marnie says, and I can hear her grin through the phone.

"Please stop acting like this is some sort of fun adventure."

"Come on, Shannon. Things are always fun when we do them together."

There's an insistent knock on the bathroom door that makes me jump. "What the hell are you doing in there?" Victoria's voice is sharp.

"Oh, nothing," I say loudly. I hiss into the phone, "Just make sure Rick comes to the prom." I scramble to hang up and hide the cellphone.

When I open the door with a fake smile for Victoria on my face, I'm horrified to see Mickey is standing right beside her.

"How the hell did you guys get in here?"

"Josie let us in," Victoria says brightly.

"Sorry, Sis," Josie calls from the living room. "They wouldn't leave." I curse myself for not finding a way to warn her.

Mickey tells me darkly, "I'm afraid we're going to have to search you now."

"Like hell you will." I make a break for my bedroom, but the skinny ladies are fast and surprisingly strong. "You can't do this!" I insist as Mickey holds me down and Victoria checks my pockets.

"Check her socks!" Mickey commands.

"What the hell are you doing?" Josie runs into the hallway just as Victoria pulls the contraband cellphone out of my sock and holds it up in victory.

"I knew it," Victoria shouts, her hair wild and her grin deranged.

"That's mine," I insist. "You can't take that!"

"We most certainly can," Mickey says and starts quoting a section of the contract that I signed. I slump to the floor defeated and hope that Marnie heard my plea to get Rick to the prom. I don't know how I'll communicate with her now.

Josie bends down to help me and accuses Mickey and Victoria, "Haven't you taken enough away from her?"

I thank Josie as I stand up, and Mickey gives us a sneer. "One more week and you can have your sister back."

"Let's all just focus on what matters here." Victoria smooths her hair and announces, "It's almost time for Prom!" I slump back down to the floor. "First order of business is finding you a date."

Slouching at the kitchen table a few minutes later, I'm trying to sell Mickey and Victoria on the appeal of the lonely girl, dateless at the prom, getting her chance to shine and maybe even win the crown. "That would make *great* television," I say, "and probably sell a ton of lipstick." The two of them aren't buying it.

"Your SACC is quite adamant that a dateless girl can never be voted Prom Queen," Victoria says while Mickey pokes at her smartphone.

They make me look through a huge photo album filled with model headshots of potential escorts. "Going stag is for unpopular girls," Victoria says. "You are beautiful and on television and you're *blonde*. Just pick a date, for pity's sake."

I refuse. The prom is my last chance to win Rick back. Showing up with big-biceped man-candy on my arm will not help my cause.

"Fine," Mickey says finally. "We'll just pick a guy and have him shadow you around so he *appears* to be your date."

"It's all about appearances," Victoria says brightly, and I resist the urge to smack her. But just barely.

•••

With the cameras constantly watching and Mickey's threats still looming, Marnie and I are having a hard time communicating. From what she's been able to convey through miming, it seems she's having a tough time convincing Rick to go to the prom. Either that, or she's trying to tell me that she's dealing with some nasty constipation.

I shouldn't be surprised Rick doesn't want to go. Besides the fact that everyone attending must have signed releases, he's never shown anything but detest for the tradition of prom. Or as he calls it "spending tons of money and dressing up for all the people who've seen us in sweatpants and T-shirts for the past seven years." *Unless the prom is made mandatory for graduation, I'm seriously boned.*

I resort to wrapping up the *Chemical Properties of Heartbreak* quilt I made. I pin a note to it that says "Please, please, please meet me at the prom" and blackmail Charlie/Thomas into making sure the giant package makes its way safely into Rick's possession. Thomas tells me he's glad for a chance to prove how committed he is to my family, but really all it proves is how committed he is to keeping his giant secret from my mother. I tell him he needs to come clean to her right after the prom.

Prom night is shaping up to be doomsday in all sorts of ways.

PART SIX

Prom Queens Gone Wild

CHAPTER EIGHTEEN

I realize that it is a tradition to go a little over-the-top cuckoo for prom. Girls get their nails done, go tanning, sit in hair salons for hours, and boys, well, *shower* I suppose. But I'm not exaggerating when I tell you that this year, Westfield High goes completely apeshit over prom. I mean: Ape. Shit.

The prom is being thrown at the same mansion where we had Prom Queen Boot Camp. "How fitting," Kelly said when the announcement was made. "The actual location of my personal hell."

Like me, Kelly has been assigned a handsome escort from a binder, so despite the yearlong efforts of teams of experts, Amy is the only one of us who managed to score an *actual* date to the prom.

By the time I arrive at the mansion, a row of limos are lined up across the front like black and white piano keys set end to end. As I coast by in my old maroon Coroda, I see Luke Hershman gallantly helping Grace out of a huge white SUV limo with the Nŏrealique lips logo emblazoned on the side.

She's wearing a pale pink dress that's classy yet sexy, and I have to admit it looks great.

But the ethereal white dress I have on is better.

I park in the employee lot and start to unload a huge black garbage bag from my back seat. I'm not at all graceful despite my bride-worthy gown. My personal stylist picked it out as representative of my Per-style-ality™. *In my dreams.* But if I'm about to go down in the annals of reality show history, at least I'm beautifully dressed for it.

My makeup is simple, and instead of Nőrealique, I used all "no brand" wholesale products that I ordered online. After being "airbrushed to deaf," my eyes were opened to how unrealistic beauty standards are in the media. My goal is to stop buying things that use advertising that offends me.

Through a series of private notes at home, I filled Josie in on my plan, and using more notes, she begged me to change my mind. Finally, I broke our silent exchange and said simply, "I need to be true to myself," which finally got her to smile and nod. The show actually *aired* me saying that line in one of their finale teasers. Except it's edited to seem like I'm being true to myself in an I'm-choosing-to-wear-this-shade-of-Nőrealique-lipstick-because-I'm-still-trying-to-get-crowned-Prom-Queen way that's pretty ironic.

I walk across the lot toward the mansion, and a studio assistant wearing a headset runs up to help me with my giant black Heffybag. I shake her off. "I can handle it, thanks."

Her eyes widen. "It is recommended that one carry nothing larger than a small clutch to a formal affair," she recites robotically. "You cannot go on *television* carrying a huge garbage bag…thing… like that." She looks at my black plastic lump with revulsion.

"Fine, you carry it." I heft my bulky burden into her skinny arms. "But I need it to go right to the prep room. It's very important."

"Sure, it'll be there." She grunts under the strain as she hustles ahead of me, her knees wide and headset askew. Into it, she calls, "Cue Bodacious Date number two, Eagle S has landed, repeat, Date two on deck."

Ugh. I glance around and see a smiling male model in a tailored tuxedo striding toward me.

I grab the wispy edge of my skirt and haul ass up the front steps. When I reach the columned porch, two men dressed in old-fashioned formal attire primly open the doors for me. The male model catches up to me and gallantly tries to take me by the arm.

"Hello, I'm Todd," he says as I bat at his hands.

"Hi, Todd. Go away."

Everyone standing in the formal *foy-yea* freezes to stare at me slapping away my "date." With a final shove that sends Todd reeling backward, I scan the enormous ballroom.

All the apeshit nutso planning has resulted in a huge gang of dolled-up teenagers trying to look either sophisticated or subversive with varying degrees of success. A giant stage has been set up in front of the gold big lip curtain at one end of the ballroom. Cameras and light stands are planted all around it like trees, and the Nŏrealique posters are still hanging on the walls.

I don't see Rick, but I spot Marnie right away. She's wrapped in fluorescent green material and is holding hands with a bored-looking James. She waves happily when she sees me.

I move closer and I take in the Day-Glo prom dress that she's designed and sewn. I picture the reaction my stylist would have to the wide, wild skirt of glowing green tulle. Shining satin peeks out unevenly, and I see loose threads hanging at crazy angles, and it is beautiful. Marnie is beautiful. She lives by her convictions and is not ashamed of flaws. *Just when I thought I couldn't love the girl any more.*

I smile and say, "You two look so great together."

"That dress is amazing!" Marnie reaches out to touch the white fabric of my gown.

"Thanks." There's a pause before I need to ask, "Is he here?" Marnie shakes her head. "*Aaargh!*" I'm in agony. "Rick *has* to show up!"

James makes a *pbltt* noise with his lips.

"You'll see," I tell him. "I've really changed."

He gestures to my amazing dress. "Oh, yes. We can all see you've changed, Shannon."

"I *have.*" I want to point out that I could have quit this stupid show weeks ago if it wasn't for the two of them and their science project, but I just turn to Marnie. "Did he say he's coming?"

"He wouldn't say for sure."

"But you guys told him I *need* him to come, right?"

James says, "I don't think he's up for another big ol' bucket o'hurt from your highness." Marnie jabs her elbow in his side, and he adds, "I'm just saying."

"All I want is a chance to make things up to him." I start to panic as I scan the crowd. *Where is he?*

Just then, my heart does this happy little flippy thing as I see him walk in from the foyer. He's wearing a cool pale-blue retro tuxedo that I recognize as the exact shade of his eyes. Those eyes are scanning the crowd, and before I know it, they find me.

Everything around us fades as we look at each other from across the room for what seems like forever. I feel a smile pushing at my lips. Rick squints in a way that I can't read from here and…

"Oh shit!" I spot a smiling Todd pushing his way toward me. I close my eyes and shoot down into a full squat behind Marnie and James. "Stall Rick," I command. "But make sure he doesn't leave, no matter what."

"I thought you wanted to talk to him!" James says. "What head games are you playing now, Shannon?" Through the sea of colorful dresses and black tuxes, I see Rick's pale-blue pant legs with his matching blue sneakers moving toward me. But Todd's black pant legs and polished shoes are closer.

"Marnie, meet me back by the prep room," I say as I squat-run away. I hope Rick doesn't see me, because I'm pretty sure my squat-run is not flattering from any angle.

I glance back and see Todd's handsome face creased with confusion as he scans the crowd. I don't see Rick. The girl wearing the headset who carried my garbage bag in is suddenly leading me by my elbow. "I thought I *lost* you. And where is your date?" I shrug innocently, and she drags me to the giant library that's been partitioned off as a backstage preparation area. The scene is wilder than when people on a stranded island show finally get a tableful of real food.

Deena and Kristan are huddled on one side, primping and fawning in front of a full-length mirror. Deena's short hair is so glossy it looks plastic, and they have on similar black and silver beaded dresses. Deena fills hers out better, but Kristan's seems to draw all the light from the room and reflect it off her perfect features. Meanwhile, Grace looks like she belongs in a prom catalogue with her classic pale pink. She's even practicing cheesy poses.

I move quickly to the other side of the room with my fellow Wannabes. Amy looks frightened but amazing in her red sequined dress that shows off her curves. Her lips are the same shade of red as her dress, and they're so shiny I'm afraid they'll shatter like glass if she moves them. She gives me a tense grimace, proving my fear wrong, and says, "I can't believe this is it!"

"Sure, you're excited," says Kelly. "This is your big public debut as an amazing singer. The rest of us are just appearing *live!* as a bunch of sellouts." She wears a dark eggplant dress with an uneven hem that hints at her artsy side. Her hair has thick eggplant streaks that match her dress, and I can't help but think it would look awesome with a tiara stuck on top. Not that she has any more or less of a shot at winning than the rest of us. Looking around I realize, based on the final few episodes, the race for the crown is fairly even. I wonder if, unlike the Miss Pennsylvania title, this thing may actually come down to talent.

"Where's your painting?" I ask Kelly.

She shrugs. "I haven't felt inspired to paint lately."

"But I thought this was your chance to show some of your work," says Amy.

Kelly's small diamond nose ring glints as she flares her nostrils. "Our illustrious *sponsor*, Nõrealique, has paid a large fee to have my modeling 'talent' featured instead of my artwork. I'm having that walk-off against Grace after all."

"What?" I'm angry. "They can't *make* you do that!"

"They're not *making* me," she sighs. "We really need the money."

"Wait? You mean—" Amy starts.

"Yeah, that's right," Kelly says. "They just kept sweetening the deal until my inner-whore finally surfaced."

"How much did they—?"

"Enough, okay?" Kelly's head dips to the right, which in body language means she's on the verge of getting emotional. "It's enough for me to move my sister and Mom out of the trailer and into a house and for Mom to stop depending on the kindness of strangers who just want to get into her pants. It's enough to make a *difference* and so I'm doing it. I took the money and now I'm going in front of America to sell a bunch of stupid clothes like the whore that I am."

"Oh, honey." I pat her shoulder, and she looks at me with tears in her eyes. "Our dates are whores. You are not."

She groans and leans into me. "I miss Raul. And I can't believe I'm banned from all contact with him until I turn eighteen."

Amy wraps her arms around both of us and squeezes tight.

"Um, Amy, a little personal space?" says Kelly, and we all laugh as we detangle.

"Okay, people! Let's save the emotion for when the cameras start rolling!" Mickey strides in and stops to examine me. "Dress looks great, Shannon, but you need serious help with hair and makeup."

I just smile and say, "No thanks, I'm fine."

Mickey snaps her fingers and points at me, and I'm immediately ambushed from three directions by makeup brushes. "Keep it natural looking," I command as I try to block a mascara wand.

"And finally." I feel lipstick being applied to my lips. "*Shannon's Sugar Bliss*. Your signature shade for your big moment." But now my hot pink war paint feels too heavy on my mouth.

"Okay, ladies, this is it," Mickey commands. "Ready to *fight* for that crown?"

Kelly claws the air with her eggplant manicure and gives a nasty "Grrr!" It makes the Queens look a little nervous. I laugh and then say, "Ouch!" as my hair gets pulled by a hot iron. Mickey looks pleased. She explains that the show will begin with us performing our talents and then the voting lines will open for the second hour of the *live!* show. Shots of us enjoying our prom as well as highlights from the past school year will be aired as voters call in.

The huge-lipped Nőrealique television that's been on display in the school lobby has been moved onstage in the ballroom. It will display a running tally of our scores, and at the end of the show, Victoria will crown one of us the winner. Or, more accurately, Victoria would be de-crowning all the losers, since it's much more dramatic and humiliating to give us all tiaras and line us up onstage, then, one by one, rip the crowns off our heads.

Mickey says. "Remember, this is your final reality-show moment, girls. Be sure to make it a good one."

I intend to.

CHAPTER NINETEEN

I spot Marnie at the door to the library-turned-dressing-room, arguing with a man in a headset wearing all black. She points to me as she pleads with him, but he shakes his head and keeps his hand up, blocking her way. I rush over to the door and say, "It's okay, she's with me."

"Nobody but Prom Queens and Wannabes in this room," he says gruffly.

"Fine." I take Marnie's hand and head out.

Mickey calls after me, "We're about to begin, Shannon. You need to stay here."

"Gotta pee! Real bad! Right now!" I pull Marnie down the hallway to the extravagant marble ladies room.

"Is Rick still here?" I ask as soon as we're inside.

"For now." Marnie admires the fabric of my dress again. "We're doing our best, but I don't think he'll hang around all night."

"Argh!" My frustration echoes off the marble walls, and I take a deep breath of perfumed toilet air. A few female prom-goers are milling about the bathroom, each admiring my dress. Then one of them points to Marnie's one-of-a-kind green Day-Glo creation and covers her mouth, snickering.

I grab Marnie's hand off the skirt of my dress and tell her, "We're trading."

"Wha…?"

"I mean it, Marnie, please trade me prom dresses."

"Come on." She shakes her head. "There are about a thousand dropped stitches on this thing and you're going up onstage."

"Yes, I see the dropped stitches, but Marnie I would be so honored if you'd please allow me to wear the dress that you sewed."

She eyes my dress. "Who's the designer?"

"Okay, so it's some *fabulous* new guy working exclusively for Nōrealique Fashions. But not that awful one who says he won't design clothes for fatties. And anyway, this is a chance for you to rescue me from my sentence as an unwilling on-air promoter of their fashion products."

"So this is a case where *not* boycotting will make more of a statement," she says.

"Shannon! Are you in here?" A desperate-sounding voice echoes off the tiles as the clicking of heels grows closer.

Marnie and I dive into separate stalls.

"Shannon?" It's the frazzled girl with the headset.

I balance my crystal slippers on either side of the toilet seat and hold my breath.

"I saw the bottom of your white dress, Shannon."

I sigh and step down off the toilet. With a flash of inspiration, I lift my dress and move my shoes into position. "I must be nervous or something because my stomach is a mess," I call out.

I make a farting noise with my mouth on my forearm and Marnie joins in from the stall beside me. "That's awful!" she says. "What crawled up your butt and died?"

Trying not to laugh, I continue mimicking flatulence and let out a couple of convincing groans. "Oh, yeah. That's better," I say between fart sounds.

Finally the assistant calls, "I'll just wait outside. Please hurry."

"You betcha," I say and pull the white dress over my head. Standing on the toilet, I look over the divider into Marnie's stall. She's laughing hysterically as she claws her way out of her asymmetrical creation.

"Too bad the cameras weren't rolling for that." I toss my white dress, and it floats down to her. Then she heaves her wadded-up Day-Glo green ball over the divider in my direction. "And don't worry, I'll make sure breaking your boycott is totally worthwhile."

With a smile, she finds the label in the back of my dress and tears it out. "Some sacrifices are easier than others."

"Careful," I tease. "That was the reasoning that led to me dating Luke Hershman."

I hear her laugh as I pull her green dress over my head.

Marnie looks so heavenly when she emerges in my white

dress that I can't help but think I'd make a pretty decent fairy godmother myself.

I give her a hug just as the freaked-out assistant reappears in the doorway. "*Ugh!*" The girl wrinkles her whole face. I sniff the perfumed air and then realize she's referring to my dress. "What are you wearing? We are about to go *live!*"

"I'm ready," I tell her and give Marnie a wink as I lead the disgusted girl out of the bathroom.

When we reach the library, my wardrobe switch is met with gasps of horror. Fortunately, we're out of time and there isn't a spare gorgeous designer gown lying around.

Gathering my garbage bag from the dusty corner where the assistant-wench stuffed it, I squeeze between Kelly and Amy on the custom Nŏrealique-lip-shaped couch with my project on my lap. Marnie's dress is big on me, and her rough seams scratch a bit, but I smile, thinking about how beautiful and happy she looked in my white one. Patting down my huge plastic-covered heap as best I can, I feel the anxiety in the room swell as the television monitor counts down from ten to "Action!"

Victoria stands onstage and launches into a recap of how this whole spectacle is the "most unusual reality show ever conceived." The camera pans to the crowd, showing our classmates grinning and nodding energetically. Suddenly, the monitor shifts to the same view I'm facing in the library. I look over my shoulder to see a longhaired cameraman zooming in on the Queens posing and primping. He smoothly swings the shot over to us Wannabes sitting on the lip-shaped couch. Kelly and I are mostly obscured by my black garbage bag, and Amy is making unflattering warm-up shapes with her mouth.

"You girls ready back there?" Victoria calls from the front stage.

We nod dumbly at the camera, and Kristan gives a loud "Woo!"

"Well, okay then!" Victoria practically squeals. "Performances will begin right after *this* commercial break!"

The monitor flips from Amy, Kelly, and I sitting like lumps on the lips couch to the commercial the three of us shot earlier in the season. "Okay, runway girls, let's go." An assistant herds Kelly and Grace toward the door.

"Hey, Kelly," Grace shoots. "Don't pull a *Shannon* and fall on your ass." The shot of me sprawled on the ground is one of the most-played clips of all time, so Grace's comment is pretty funny. But it's also a really stupid thing for her to say. Kelly straightens up like she's just resolved to win the whole stupid walk-off.

Which she does. Grace looks like amateur-modeling-day-at-the-mall compared to Kelly's fierce runway strut. Watching their "fashion show" on the monitors, it's obvious. *Grace should head straight for the after-prom.*

When they're done, Victoria goes in for a congratulatory hug, but at Kelly's glare, she reroutes and gives a feeble handshake to Kelly's forearm. "Remember," Victoria says to the camera, "when the polls open, you can vote for Kelly by dialing or texting

888-555-5401, that's oh-one to vote for Kelly." She glances over, and I think she actually expects Kelly to hold up a giant foam finger or something. But Kelly just stands with her hands on her hips, looking ultra model-esque. Victoria puts an arm around Grace's shoulder and recites her voting number next. Grace holds out two wiggly number fingers and smiles pleadingly at the camera.

Victoria announces, "After the break, we'll see Wannabe Amy Waller performing with our other two Original Queens!"

My arms are sticking to the plastic garbage bag, and I realize the other girls must be headed to the stage already because I'm alone in the giant library. I look at the ornate light fixture on the ceiling and take a deep breath. The show is going much faster than I'd imagined, and I'm not sure I'm ready for this. I look around at the old books lining the walls and have a sudden urge to snuggle up with one of them and be left alone.

"Depola!" a headset-wearing assistant barks. "You're on standby in five. Better move stage-left with your, er…parcel."

I stand, staggering awkwardly under the bulk of my black plastic bag, and make my way to the side of the stage where I'm hidden from view.

The music starts pulsing, and Amy and the girls charge through a cloud of smoke. I can feel the energy of the crowd rising from where I stand watching. Kristan and Deena are really great dancers, and it turns out those dresses they're wearing are very stretchy. They perform mirrored leaps that slide into splits and high kicks that show they're both wearing sparkly shorts underneath their gowns.

Amy's singing is totally rocking the whole room, but the other girls don't give up trying to grab the spotlight. The two of them go off-routine with growing enthusiasm, and before long they're both gyrating back and forth trying to out sex-face each other. Finally, Deena "accidentally" whacks Kristan in the head with a high kick and sends her sprawling. The crowd absolutely loves it.

I want to abandon my big black yard bag and run flailing from the prom. *There's no way I can follow this high-octane performance.*

Wild applause explodes as the song ends. Victoria announces the call-in numbers and all three girls do their cheesy number-fingers. For the eternity of another commercial break, I carry my bag toward the middle of the stage, shuffling my feet and wishing I were wearing my old boots rather than these clear crystal pumps.

The monitor in front of the stage shifts to a ridiculous shot of an enormous wad of levitating black plastic. Marnie's asymmetric florescent green hem peeks out from the bottom, and Victoria's voice comes from offstage. "And lastly, we have Wannabe Shannon Depola with um…her act."

Crowd energy? Gone.

The silence stretches out until someone coughs uncomfortably. I drop my plastic bundle in front of my feet with a *splat*. Looking at the camera, I laugh nervously. Off to one side, I notice a small team of uniformed paramedics standing by, probably hoping I pass out right now. They may get their wish.

Victoria is twirling her finger around in a circle, indicating I need to start doing something before she forces the cameras back on herself.

The crowd of my peers stretches out before me, watching with open pity. I'm doomed. Then I spot Marnie. She looks downright angelic in my white dress, and I'm filled with hope as she grins at me encouragingly. My swirling thoughts stop. No more tangents.

With a deep breath, I point my finger in the air, displaying an item that shocks the prom-goers into a collective gasp.

"This," I announce, "is a finger cot!"

The murmuring starts as I'd expected. "I dropped one of these in tenth grade gym class and was given the nickname…" I shout, "The Elf Ucker!"

Victoria gasps, laughter breaks out, and *this* time, I laugh right along. "Yes, that's right. It's me, the Elf Ucker." I give a small curtsy, and the room quiets down to see where I'm going with this…*where am I going with this? Oh yeah.* "The reason I never explained about the finger cot is because I use it for a hobby that I thought was super-embarrassing." The murmurs start up again, this time sprinkled with a few *Ooooo*'s. "Okay, okay. It's not actually *that* embarrassing."

I lunge for the bag at my feet. Crawling over it, I rip off the black plastic in giant strips, wishing I'd used a much less durable trash bag—or at least thought to wear stretchy shorts underneath my gown. I feel a side-seam give a little and steal a glance at the monitors where I see myself sprawled awkwardly with my enormous Day-Glo green butt in the air.

Snickers start erupting from the crowd as I step on a corner of the trash bag. My crystal pump slips on the plastic and I fall forward onto the bag. *Nice way to bookend my reality show experience*. At least the cameras won't cut away as long as I continue humiliating myself.

Out of the corner of my eye, I see a flash of white floating toward me. It's Marnie. James is giving her a boost onstage and she moves to help me.

I'm intensely grateful, not just for her support, but also because now I'm not the only girl in a prom gown pawing about onstage. The two of us laugh together at the ridiculousness of our situation as we rip into the bag. Finally, we each latch on to an end and hold up my project together.

I hear someone in the crowd gasp, probably some 4-H fanatic. Looking at the television monitor displaying my handiwork, I have to admit it is a truly beautiful quilt. The colors and patterns swirl together in a mesmerizing dance. The crowd actually seems somewhat impressed. At least the snickers stop.

"The hobby that I love," I say, "the one that I thought was more embarrassing than living with the nickname Elf Ucker… is *quilting*." I pause, waiting for gasps of horror that never come.

So I go on. "High school isn't easy for any of us. We all have parts of ourselves we're ashamed of and want to hide. Some of us are desperate to fit in. Maybe even dream of being voted Prom Queen. *What a great concept for a reality show!*" I mock, winning a few laughs.

Glancing to the spot where Marnie emerged from the crowd, I spot James grinning at her. And beside him I see Rick, eyeing me skeptically. *He's still here!* My heart starts beating harder, and I feel a renewed focus.

I pull up the edge of my gown and wipe off my signature pink lipstick into a perfect lip shape. Holding it up I say, "I didn't need Nŏrealique lipstick to rescue me from being a wannabe. I was a little odd, maybe, but at least I was genuine. This show is what turned me *into* a Wannabe."

The camera's little red light continues blinking as Victoria strides angrily across the stage toward Marnie and me. I hold the quilt up higher. "This quilt represents what I gave up to become popular," I say. "It's a friendship quilt for my best friend. Those of you at home may not recognize Marnie without a blur across her face." To her, I say, "Thanks for signing that release."

Victoria pauses just outside the camera's frame and gives me a warning glare. Gesturing to a patch on the quilt, I say to Marnie, "This is a chunk of the flannel nightshirt I wore for the sleepover when we made up hand motions to go with every song on your '18 hits from the '80s CD.'" Marnie laughs and I point to another square. "This dragon appliqué represents our brief and embarrassing gaming phase." Tears are forming in Marnie's eyes. "And this tree is the big gnarly one behind my house where we'd sit and talk about our dreams for hours." I look at the crowd. "I mean *literally.* We discussed what we dreamt about at night, for *hours.*"

I look back at her and say, "Marns, I am so, so sorry for choosing some stupid popularity contest over our friendship. This quilt is my gift to you, I've titled it *Warts and All,* and it's a promise that I'll never let anything come between us again."

Our classmates applaud, and I'm glad to see Rick is standing in front still paying attention. Marnie glides over to me in her swirling, angelic, "sellout" prom dress and gives me a tackle hug. My eye catches Victoria's look of relief at our heartwarming exchange.

And that pisses me off.

Victoria is the person who labeled Marnie a "popularity liability" and suggested I dump her.

Turning back to the quilt, I flip it around to display the back side. It has an enormous Nőrealique lips logo with a giant buster sign slashed through it.

"But this is no peace quilt," I announce to the crowd. "This company is a *bully* who photoshopped the hell out of me for their advertisement." Victoria immediately starts slashing at her neck for the camera to cut. "Transform your look? Transform your life? How about transform the *WORLD*?"

Victoria moves in front of me, and Marnie shouts, "Makeup companies bully us into feeling insecure so we think we need to buy all their crap to be beautiful! We are *all* uniquely beautiful!"

"Okay, thank you for that Shannon and Marnie," Victoria laughs as if we aren't at all serious.

"Schools should be an ad-free zone!" Marnie shouts. "Nőrealique has hijacked our mindspace!"

I love watching Marnie get her public protest on. Victoria shifts to stand in front of her, trying to deliver a singsong wrap-up over Marnie's rant.

So it's up to me to start up the chant, "Nőrealique is a tool of the man!" Marnie immediately joins in and we lead the crowd punching the air.

"Nőrealique is a tool of the man!"

"Nőrealique is a tool of the man!"

Victoria lunges for me angrily, and with a grunt, I toss the quilt over her head. Running to the edge of the stage where Rick is standing, I call, "I'm sorry for acting like such an idiot all year." His face is unreadable, but he uncrosses his arms.

A disheveled Victoria finally frees herself from the quilt, and her heels clack on the hard wood of the stage as she barrels toward me.

"This is the real me, Rick!" I yell dramatically as I dodge the charging ex–beauty queen. Taking a deep breath, I do a perfect swan dive toward Rick as everyone watches, including the cameras. It's a magical moment. The crowd lets out a whoop. *This is really good TV.*

Except for here's the thing—I got sort of used to being held by Luke, a football player…who lifts weights. Luke made me feel as light as a feather. *Rick*, on the other hand, is a science geek who lifts glass beakers. I am *not* as light as a feather. I'm a teenage girl who is suddenly barreling through the air at full speed.

Bless him, he does seem to try to catch me with his scrawny little science-y arms.

Instead—he breaks my fall. There's a loud cracking noise that sounds suspiciously like bones snapping. *Oh my God, I broke him!* We are nose to nose and I have a closeup view of his expression of pain. The entire room is silenced by my eager display of affection gone awry.

"I'm so sorry!"

Rick is in obvious agony as he says, "Well, *that* was a different way of campaigning for Prom Queen."

I'm sprawled on top of him, glowing green material wadded around us. "That wasn't about votes," I say, leaning in toward him. "That was about *this*." My heart beats strong and fast. *This is it…*

"Um." He winces. "Can you maybe just shift a little off of my right leg?"

The crack I heard must've been his thigh bone.

"I am so sorry!" I leap off of him and am horrified to see a red stain moving quickly over the light blue pants of his tuxedo. "Are you bleeding?!" I scream, "Holy crap! *We need a doctor!*"

"Paramedics!" Victoria calls gleefully from the stage.

"It's not blood," Rick says. "But…"

Before he can say anything else, I'm shoved roughly aside and the paramedics move in. One of them places an oxygen mask over Rick's face, successfully killing any chance of me getting a kiss.

He struggles to push the mask away, and I feel myself being pulled back. Rick's arms flail as his body is strapped down and wheeled away on a stretcher.

"I'll wait for you," I call out with all the melodrama I can muster. Which looks perfect on the monitors as Victoria announces the number for people to call if they want to vote for me for Prom Queen. *Because nothing says "Prom Queen" like a crazypants chick stage-diving her crush and breaking him in half.*

"The call-in lines are now open!" Victoria announces as she smooths her hair. Suddenly, Kelly rushes onstage, calling out to the cameras, "Raaauuul! Meet me on the rooftop at midnight on my birthday!" She waves her arms as Victoria uses her skinny body to try and block her. "I love you!" Kelly yells into the camera as she continues wrestling Victoria until the monitors finally cut to a commercial.

"That didn't exactly go as planned," I mumble to Marnie as we fold up her quilt.

"That was *awesome!*" Marnie says, and I can see she's still high from our spontaneous protest.

"Yes, it was." I can't help but grin at her. "But I'm afraid Rick is going to be on crutches for a while."

"He'll be fine," she says. "That was probably just a beaker of formula that broke in his pocket. He was all excited about some breakthrough he had in the lab this afternoon, and he brought a sample to show James."

"So the two of them were working on a science project here at the prom?" I laugh.

"Science geeks," Marnie shrugs. "Got to love them."

"Yes, I guess we do." But now I wonder if the only reason Rick even came to prom was to share his breakthrough with James.

Marnie hugs our friendship quilt as she looks over to where *her* science geek is grinning at her from the edge of the stage. She pulls her eyes back to me. "Thank you for all of this, Shannon. The quilt is beautiful. And the flash rally really made my—"

"Go on, and get over there," I scold. "James is waiting. And our friendship will always be here."

Giving a happy squeal, she hugs me with the quilt between us and heads over toward her boyfriend. She stops, and James gives me a thumbs-up before easing her and the quilt gently off the stage. *So that's maybe a better way to get down for a kiss.*

"Don't think you're off the hook, miss," Victoria yells after me as I head backstage. "You are going to pay for what you've done."

I reach down and grab the hem of my asymmetrical skirt. I hold up the perfect impression of my wiped-off lips burning pink on the fluorescent green fabric. "Hey, Victoria?" I pull it up and use it to make kissy stamp marks on my butt. "You and Nŏrealique can both kiss my ass."

CHAPTER TWENTY

By the time we come back from the commercial break, all the Wannabes and Queens are sequestered in the library, and the huge Nőrealique television onstage displays all six of our faces, each with a red bar above it that tracks the number of call-in votes we get.

The Nőrealique commercials are all plugging their tagline: *Transform your look, transform your life, with Nőrealique Cosmetics.* I smile when the monitors blast with the sound of the crowd in the ballroom calling out, "Transform the *WORLD!*" over that last part.

The camera pans the ballroom when the commercials end, and I can't help but search for Rick even though he must be at the hospital by now. I seriously hope the only thing I broke was his beaker.

To distract myself, I check out the scores on the monitor and am surprised to find I'm not totally behind. In fact, all six of our quivering little red bars are fairly even.

From the stage, Victoria happily narrates a collection of commemorative clips documenting our journey. Watching, I can't help but notice they show us Wannabes joking around together and seeming relatable intercut with shots of the Queens snipping behind each other's backs. Nŏrealique must be angling for a Wannabe to win so this whole reality show becomes one huge drama-mercial for their brand.

On the other side of the library, Kristan squirms as she gradually drops into last place. Amy grabs my hand as the three Wannabe scores inch into the lead. I don't know about the power of lipstick, but the power of editing to sway opinion cannot be denied.

Kristan Bowman yells, "*That's it!*" in a voice so evil there's no way it could've come from that beautiful face. "*That crown's been mine since the sixth grade, and you bitches wrecked everything!*" With that, she launches herself across the room and tackles Kelly.

What the...? I see Deena closing in on Amy, who ducks just in time to avoid getting punched in the face. Deena screams, "Liposuction is violence against women! Love your body! Embrace your curves, bitch!"

The next thing I know, all the girls are wrestling with each other on the floor, and I start laughing at how ridiculous they all look. Hair and makeup and sequins blend into a swirling mess of screams and swearing.

Then *Whammo!* I land right on top of the pile.

I look up in time to see Grace Douglas, straddling me in her pink gown, as she swings her fist at my face. "You stupid Wannabe slut!"

I duck her punch and laugh. "*Wannabe slut* makes it sound like I'm just a slut-hopeful. Like I'm not really a slut…"

Grace doesn't get the joke. "*This* is for stealing my Luke!" she yells, and everything goes white as my nose explodes in pain. Using the back of my hand, I swipe it and see there's blood. A *lot* of blood.

"Oh, come *on*!" All of my past fantasies of attacking Grace Douglas come together in my mind, and I throw a punch that lands directly on her high cheekbone. *So that's what that feels like.* I use the hem of my dress to wipe the flow of blood from my nose as my knuckles scream in pain.

The cameraman's red light flashes, and his face shines greedily. The monitor shows the *live!* onscreen version of our battle with shots of ripping tulle, clawing French manicured nails, and angry, makeup-smeared faces. I hear Victoria's voice narrating, "The Prom Queens and Wannabes are backstage, *literally* battling it out as they fight for that crown. We did *not* expect this level of hostility, folks." She sounds more excited than genuinely surprised.

I roll out of the way as Grace launches toward me again, and I hear her *thud* belly-first onto the floor. The cameraman can't help but laugh out loud at that. Wobbling, Grace stands up and grasps the neckline of her pink gown with both hands. "My bras are contoured, not padded!" she shouts and gives a violent tug on her neckline, exposing the top portion of her breasts. "I'm proud of my ta-tas!"

I stand up and grab her hands before she can display any more. "Put your girls away," I tell her, blocking the camera with my body. "Don't give these bastards the satisfaction."

Looking around, I can just picture how the six of us look. Going at it on TV sets and computers all over America, clumps of processed hair flying, mascara running, and spittle soaring in slow motion. Our dignity stripped for the sake of entertainment.

You know how sometimes you'll tune in to a reality show and find people in the middle of throwing drinks or pulling weaves or acting all in a way that can only be described as cray cray? You watch these battles and you wonder, *Where do they find these people?*

Trust me, with enough pressure, under the right circumstances, you could be one of us. You could catch yourself screaming, throwing books, and scratching at eyes.

And if you're like me, you might stop and look around and ask yourself, *How the hell did I end up here?*

"This is insane!" I jump up on the Nŏrealique-lips couch, whistling loudly. "Listen up! Is this going to be our fifteen minutes of fame? Or our fifteen minutes of *shame*?" I point into the camera. "We shouldn't be fighting each other. This stupid show has been manipulating all of us this whole time!"

The bitch-fight slows down as I tell them about my mother's fake boyfriend, Charlie, and the modeling gigs they paid for Kelly to get.

"I know someone sent a phony text to break Luke and me up." Grace is nodding her head at me. "I always figured it was you."

I laugh. "The Elf Ucker didn't exactly have the Alpha Queen's cell phone number, did she?" The girls begin to disengage from the fight, looking like a bunch of drunk celebrities ready for their mug shots.

Deena says quietly, "I'm willing to bet they're the ones who made that…video of me." Amy limps over to put her arm around Deena consolingly.

Glancing at Kristan's face, I see one beautiful eye is swollen shut. Deena's dress is ripped, displaying a left shoulder that's probably going to need stitches, and Kelly is groaning about a cracked rib. Amy rubs her head and accuses, "Hey! I'm missing a chunk of my weave." Sure enough, there's a wad of orange frizz lying on the floor.

I jump off the couch and stride toward the cameraman who is happily capturing our group meltdown. I see myself on the monitor, blood smeared underneath my nose and Marnie's glowing green creation in shreds. It actually looks a little better.

"Viewers at home, please stop calling and texting in votes," I say into the camera. "Obviously none of us deserves any type of crown. Nőrealique has suckered you into watching us behave badly so they can sell you lipstick. This show is an ad wrapped inside another ad."

Grace moves in behind me and I flinch. But she just turns to the camera and says, "Nőrealique sucks! That garbage made my face breakout."

Kelly joins us, looking all tousled, and adds, "Yeah, Nőrealique is shit!"

"This is more like it," I say. "Declaring war on our manipulating sponsor instead of each other."

Amy and Deena move into position beside us, looking like a couple of Prom Queen zombies. Amy's orange weave sticks out in every direction, and the side of Deena's head shows a swirl of scalp-tattoo where she's lost a tuft of hair.

Lastly, a one-eyed Kristan steps into the camera's frame. She holds out four fingers and wags them solicitously, imploring viewers at home to vote for her. The rest of us turn toward her, and she raises her hands in surrender. "Just kidding?"

The monitor shows they've cut away to Victoria onstage looking very uncomfortable. The giant television displays our votes, which have taken a huge jump, particularly mine. In fact, I've pulled ahead of the pack. Apparently, insane pleas asking viewers to stop voting has had the rebound effect of making me the crowd favorite.

I can't believe I allowed myself to get so sucked into this

stupid contest that I nearly lost Marnie and may have lost Rick for good. And here I am possibly *winning* the damned thing? *Hell. No.*

Onscreen, Victoria announces, "It looks like Shannon Depola is in the lead. Unless something drastic happens in the next fifteen minutes, I think we can predict who will be crowned Prom Queen *and* winner of the *One! Million! Dollars!*"

I look around at the girls. "Come on! Let's go make something drastic happen!"

With that, we shove past the surprised cameraman and are nearly out of the room before I remember. "Wait! Girls! *Grab your tiaras!*" We all rush to the mantle where our color-coded crowns are waiting. Slamming the diamond tiara on my head, I see Kelly considering her amethyst-encrusted one with a look of contempt. Finally she plunks it on top of her disheveled hair. "I suppose I've earned this son of a bitch, huh?"

"I think we all have," I say.

Smiling, Kelly and I follow our army of angry, ragged Prom Queens down the hall to the ballroom's double doors. The cameraman follows us, his red light flashing in anticipation.

"On my count of three." I call, "One! Two! Three!" Together we run full-tilt into the big wooden doors.

Which is a mistake. Because they are locked. The six of us bounce off of them and land on the ground in a comical heap of gowns and crowns and drying blood.

"Okay!" I shout as we drag ourselves apart. "Let's try another set of doors."

"Or we can knock?" suggests Grace.

I laugh. "Very funny, this is a *crusade*! We're storming the gates of Nőrealique's castle! We're bringing this bitch down!"

As I rant, Amy knocks.

There's a click as someone on the other side pushes the release bar and the door opens a crack. A guy from my Spanish class peers out at us. "Who ordered a half-dozen crazy Prom Queens?" he quips as the six of us press past him into the ballroom. Once inside, our classmates stand, staring at us with gaping expressions. Breathing heavily, the girls wait for me to execute some elaborate plan of attack that I haven't had a chance to come up with just yet.

I scan the crowd, looking for Rick or Marnie or…and I see it. Up on the stage. The Television. That damned Nőrealique lip-shaped television that has enslaved us all year. It displays my high approval rating, but I'm finished being judged. This Ucker is ending *my* way.

"*To the LIPS!*" I announce. The girls whoop and holler in a way that's quite terrifying, and our classmates clear a wide path as we rush the stage.

We close in on Victoria standing protectively in front of the Nőrealique TV, her skinny arms outstretched. Which is definitely a mistake. I don't know how she could've just witnessed the violent scene in the library without realizing that putting her ninety-eight pounds up against the six of us is pretty unhealthy.

Kelly is the one who grabs her, but I can't say for sure who flings her. I just see Victoria reeling through the air with her arms windmilling as she soars off the stage. And she doesn't even have the benefit of a science geek to break her fall. At the sound of her blood-curdling screech, I glance over, expecting to see her limbs bent at impossible angles. Instead her eyes are huge as she reaches into her mouth.

"My tooth veneers!" she shouts, displaying the nubs that are left of her front incisors. "And my nails!" In horror, she holds up a hand featuring jagged claws and starts screaming again and again until two paramedics rush over and kneel beside her.

I join the other girls clawing at the television. It's so massive we're not making much progress in taking it down. We tear chunks of the lip façade off, which only makes the lips look chapped. Kelly climbs on top and rocks it back and forth, but the screen just continues rating us.

"Changing your look does not change your life."—*True*. "Friends matter, not popularity."—*True, true*. "Oh, wait." Kristan takes a step back. "Did my score just go up?"

We all stop and watch her red bar wiggle a smidgen. "Give it up, Kristan," says Grace, snatching the crown off her friend's head and smashing it into the screen. The glass behind the flat-screen breaks, and a rainbow of colors bloom out of the cracks and smear across our photos and scores.

I pull off one of my crystal pumps and use the heel to hammer punctures across the screen. "You have no right to judge us!" I shout.

Finally, with a loud groan, the giant Nŏrealique television falls backward, knocking Kelly to the floor as it sparks and finally goes dark. *Unplugging it may have been another way to go.* I watch as flames peek out from the pile of rubbish.

The curtain behind the stage is pushed open by the falling television, and the same command central that I saw at camp is visible through the opening. As the flames begin to lick higher, dozens of people dressed all in black can be seen scrambling from view like cockroaches.

The room is silent for a beat. Then a cheer goes up from our classmates. The six of us stand unsteadily for a moment before we all start laughing and jumping up and down and punching the air in victory.

And then with a *whoosh,* the sprinklers blast on. The crowd's cheers morph into screams as we are all immediately soaked. Clusters of charging teenagers in wet formalwear rush about, many of them holding teeny beaded bags over their heads. *Bet they wish they'd accessorized with trash bags now.*

The paramedics lift a hysterical Victoria onto a stretcher as the room begins to empty out. I imagine Rick is probably at the hospital watching our prom burn down on television. *We didn't even get to dance together.*

The other Prom Queens clear out with the rest of our classmates while I'm absorbed watching the chaos unfurl. I shove my dripping hair back off my face and sit on the edge of the stage, my feet dangling. The sprinklers continue spraying the empty room as men in reflective jumpsuits shoot white foam over the dying flames.

I pull my crown off my head and throw it down on the floor. *What were they thinking, anyway?* Turning high school popularity into a game show? I look down at my scuffed tiara sparkling on a pile of rubble and decide I should probably keep it as a souvenir. Or sell it on eBid. *Hell, there's probably blood on it, which will get an even better price.* Leaping down, I reach for the tiara at the same moment it's grasped by a guy's hand.

That is, a guy's hand that happens to be attached to a pale blue sleeve. My heart dips. *Rick.*

We each keep our hands on the tiara as we stand up to face one another, and I look him over. The right leg of his tux is stained a deep purple down to his knee, and the pant leg is split all the way up to his hip, revealing a bandage around his thigh. He turns to scan the charred remains of the ballroom. "So this is what they get for trying to turn you into the Prom Queen, huh?"

I laugh. "That'll teach 'em."

Taking the tiara from my hand, he looks at it carefully. "This thing has caused quite a bit of trouble, hasn't it?"

"I'll just throw it away," I say. "I'm so sorry…"

Rick holds a finger to my lips. He looks me in the eye in that way of his that makes me feel like I'm really being seen. He says, "You thought you had to change everything about yourself in order to earn this thing."

I bow my head and look down at the drenched wreck of my shredded dress. I feel a gentle pressing as Rick places the tiara on my head. His eyes are smiling when I look up at him. "Don't you know? Shannon, you've always deserved to wear a crown."

With that, I reach up and wrap my fingers into the back of his hair. He mirrors my moves and, if you know anything at all about body language, mirroring is a sign that a person is totally into you.

We slowly draw close. He's finally out of my rearview mirror and right in front of me. My mind reels with the knowledge that he's about to kiss me. The whole scene of debris and dying flames fades as Rick and I become the only two people at the prom. I close my eyes. Sense his lips moving toward mine until…"*Ow!*" I wail in pain as his nose bumps my broken one.

"Wow, am I sorry." He looks so upset I can't help but laugh.

"I guess we'll call that even," I tell him and we stand, just looking at each other. His gaze grows intense, and he takes my face in his hands. Gently *turning* my head so our noses won't bump, he kisses my lips, softly at first then with growing firmness.

It's the most awesome, wonderful, fulfilling kiss of all time. And more than that. It's entirely *real*.

We sway a bit as we continue kissing, and I imagine we're dancing at a beautiful ball, instead of standing alone in the wasteland that is our prom. Happily, I place my head on his chest, close my eyes, and sigh.

Bleep bleep!

My eyes shoot open, and I see a cameraman, circling around, filming our intimate moment. I raise my head as he pulls the camera away from his eye and holds it out to examine its side. "Damn, battery," he grumbles.

"Hey, buddy," I say. "Would you mind pissing off?"

Rick pulls back to look at me. "Now, that's not language very becoming of a Prom Queen, is it?"

"Yeah." I grin. "It's a good thing I'm not the fucking Prom Queen."

We laugh and he bends down to kiss me, and everything goes all happy ending.

THE WRAP-UP:
BACK TO REALITY

Except that I was wrong.

About being the fucking Prom Queen.

After the show's final closing scene of me and Rick embracing in the rubble, I was a lock for the crown.

And since Mom negotiated my contract to death, I couldn't even be disqualified for leading the rebellion coup that wrecked the prom.

I actually won the *One! Million! Dollars!*

At first I considered splitting it with the other girls, especially since the whole point of charging in and ripping down the Nŏrealique television was to reject the competition. But, come on, we're only talking about a lousy million bucks. Split six ways, it wouldn't be all that much. Besides, that's the sort of thing someone might do if they were overly concerned with making everybody like them. I'm *so* over that.

Anyway, the girls are all doing just fine.

Six months after graduation, Kelly is still making money

modeling, plus she's studying pre-law in college. Raul met her on the roof of the clock tower at midnight on her birthday, and they've been going strong ever since. Kelly's not thrilled about him having a juvie record and figures if she's destined to become a groupie to outlaws like her mom, she may as well get her law degree and get paid for it. My mother has been sort of mentoring her, and we've stayed close.

Amy and George are as happy together as ever, and Amy has relaxed on the extreme dieting, although she and George still love working out together. Amy looks amazing and recently became a regular singing backup on *All the Rave!* It seems clear our wall-flower has a bright future in performing.

The original Prom Queens have mostly recovered from the road trip to madness that was our senior year. Deena decided to go to college to become a social worker, specializing in eating disorders. She's even managed to stretch her fifteen minutes of fame, appearing on talk shows, encouraging tearful guests to love their natural curves. Her first piece of advice? Go on a media fast to get away from the impossible skinny ideal. She says, "Those unrealistic photoshopped images are poison." Then she shows examples of airbrushing and labels them with pink Ms. Yuk stickers that she designed as warnings. I have to admit she's pretty badass.

And I discovered a little something interesting about Grace. It was right after the prom burned down to the ground. The cameras were done with us, but we still had to be checked over by paramedics for any injuries.

She and I were sitting there in the parking lot in our ruined gowns, waiting for them to finish with the other girls. Grace turned to me and said, "So you quilt, huh?"

Whatever. I waved where Rick was waiting for me, and he gave me his shy, loopy grin. "Yes, you were paying attention. I quilt," I told Grace distractedly. "What's it to you?"

"Yeah, well, that's pretty cool."

I looked at her skeptically. And that's when she leaned in and confessed, "I've been crocheting for years." Her wide grin showed she'd chipped a tooth at some point during our prom.

"So you mean that brown wool beret you wore last fall…?" I asked.

"Guilty!" She raised her hand and rolled her eyes. "Totally made by hand. By the way, I'm sorry for that whole Elf Ucker thing."

"Yeah," I said with a short laugh. "I guess I kind of let that one get to me."

It's not like the two of us started our own Stitch-n-Bitch after that or anything, but she and Luke are going to St. James State together, and I'm genuinely happy for them.

And Kristan? Well, that's a pretty remarkable story.

Our show was crazy popular with our extreme bitch-fight finale getting about a gazillion hits on BubeTube. We were such a sensation, an investigative journalist decided to do a behind the scenes story about *The Prom Queen Wannabes* and ended up uncovering some pretty wild stuff.

It turns out, the show's producers were responsible for Kristan's father getting fired. Nörealique switched their ad accounts for the new clothing line to his agency and got him canned to create drama for the show. After the story broke, Kristan's dad sued the studio, the ad agency, and Nörealique and settled out of court for enough money that her mom took him back.

Kristan found a job at a place where she gets drooled over and worshipped every single day. She's an assistant groomer at the Snuggly Doggie Boarding Kennel, and I hear she's the crowd favorite.

Mickey and Victoria got fired since Nörealique's stock dumped into the crapper after our uprising on *live!* television. You can find huge bins of their lipgloss and mascara for twenty-five cents a tube at clearance warehouses like Sob Lots. Girls actually started wearing baseball caps and T-shirts that have lips with a buster sign slashed through them as a symbol of anti-beauty-ad anarchy. In fact, I helped Marnie start the nonprofit website that sells them.

My mom's boyfriend, Charlie, quit acting and now he's working on a book about reality television. He came clean to Mom, and after she broke every dish in our kitchen, she forgave him. It's too bad the cameras were all ripped out by then, because the whole scene would've made for really good television. But the Depolas are officially done satisfying the voyeuristic urges of America. That is, at least until Josie finds a reality show that will have her.

Forgiving Charlie was the most stellar leap of faith Mom has ever taken. She says if I could swan dive off a stage into Rick's skinny arms on national television, she can certainly give Charlie a chance. I don't point out that my swan dive lacked a graceful landing, but I do think she and Charlie will be just fine.

And me? Well, now that my hair's back to its natural brown color, people have stopped assaulting me with, "Hey, you're that girl! From that show…?" My favorite was when people used to recognize me and start flailing about, pretending to fall down.

After my completely unreal year of living on a reality show, it has been *really* nice to spend time just hanging out with my best friend. Thankfully, Marnie decided to stay local, majoring in women's studies at the community college instead of paying big money for a "designer diploma" as she puts it. I'm taking business classes there as well, and things are finally back to me and Marnie, sewing buddies, best friends, just the two of us.

Well, except for when it's the four of us, since we do a lot of hanging out with James and Rick too. We are no longer friends of least resistance; we're totally inter-dating friends by choice. I'm working on a fairly amazing and massive wall-quilt to commemorate our circle that I'm simply calling *Real*. Both of our prom dresses are incorporated into the design.

Rick and I finally got around to that very small gathering, just the two of us, and I can tell you, he's an amazing boyfriend. We miss each other a lot while he's away at school, which is tough at times, but we're making it work. To be honest, after getting through our senior year, this long distance thing is cake.

I'm pursuing a career in the textile arts and have been silk-screening my own fabrics and piecing them into wall hangings that I sell online. Who knew the embarrassing habit of quilting could lead to such a cool gig? Rick has been super-supportive and marvels over the creative designs I come up with. He tells me, "Don't ever stop daydreaming." Which isn't something that you will ever find written on a poster hanging in a guidance office. But it should be.

Sometimes when he's visiting home, the two of us will hang out together on the couch watching a movie or sitcom or anything that's *not* a reality show. Rick will start this goofy game where we see who can hang the most stuff from their ears. I refuse to use socks, but one time I watched a whole movie with a ruler, a pair of scissors, and a pack of PostThis Notes tucked behind one ear. Rick thinks it's adorable that I always win the game.

I figure the two of us have earned the right to embrace our unique Per-style-ality™ which happens to fall someplace between "eccentric" and "full-on geek." And when Rick leans in toward me with that perfect tilt of his head that means he's about to kiss me? Well, let's just say it feels great to know that nobody's watching.

click

ACKNOWLEDGMENTS

Tiaras and sashes go to the fabulous Ammi-Joan Paquette, Aubrey Poole, and the entire cast and crew at EMLA and Sourcebooks Fire. Without your wisdom and support, this book could never have made it to the runway. Miss Congeniality award goes to Derry Wilkens for your boundless enthusiasm, and royal scepters shaped like giant pens go to my favorite writing folks: Alison, Amanda, Shana, Steph, and Michelle. Thank you for all the valuable manuscript makeover tips. Plus, a special gold crown for Mr. Mortimer, the best English teacher anyone could wish for.

To the Real Clergy-Wives of Intercessor: Cathy, Katie, Melanie, Maria, Dorene, Jamie, Joan, Bari, Maggie, and Vicki. Thanks y'all for never pulling my weave. To happy-Sue, my quirky quilter girl, and to the amazing, beautiful, and multitalented Courtney CADET. Special mention goes to Christine, Nancy and Chrisi, Sue, Lisa, Laura, Rhonda, The Other Laurie, Shawna, and all the Freaks and Geeks who helped make HS such an adventure.

To Mom, Dad, and Gerry. I'm beyond blessed to have such

incredibly deep (and wonderfully twisted) roots of support, and to Jenna for encouraging me to try my wings. To Zach, Christina, Jackson, and Alessia, thank you for keeping me grounded in love, and to Katie, Alan, and the girls for always keeping things real.

And especially and always to Brett, Aidan, and Trinity. I mostly write books just so I can publicly say how awesome you guys are. Thank you for making it all worthwhile and for keeping the laugh track rolling.

ABOUT THE AUTHOR

Laurie Boyle Crompton is the author of YA novels *Blaze* and the upcoming *Adrenaline Crush*. She grew up in Butler, PA, where she was never in danger of becoming Prom Queen despite looking fairly cute in a tiara. She now splits her time between Queens and New Paltz, NY. Visit Laurie online at www.lboylecrompton.com or check out her activist artwork at www.dreamer-girl.com.

Blaze

Laurie Boyle Crompton

Blaze is tired of spending life on the sidelines. All she wants is for Mark the Soccer Stud to notice her. When her BFF texts Mark a photo of Blaze in sexy lingerie, it definitely gets his attention. After a few hot dates, Blaze is contemplating her imminent girlfriend status when Mark dumps her.

Blaze gets her revenge by posting a comic strip featuring uber-villain Mark the Shark. Mark then retaliates by posting her "sext" photo, and suddenly Blaze is in an epic online battle to the (social) death.

Praise for *Blaze*:

"High-schooler Blaze is self-deprecating, hilarious, and geeky in the coolest way possible…One of the most relatable anti-love stories we've come across in a while." —*Seventeen*

"Funny, cringe-worthy and heartbreaking. Don't miss out." —*RT Book Reviews*, 4 ½ stars

Things I Can't Forget

Miranda Kenneally

Kate has always been the good girl. Too good, according to some people at school—although they have no idea the guilty secret she carries. But this summer, everything is different...

This summer she's a counselor at Cumberland Creek summer camp, and she wants to put the past behind her. This summer Matt is back as a counselor too. He's the first guy she ever kissed, and he's gone from a geeky songwriter who loved the Hardy Boys to a buff lifeguard who loves to flirt...with her.

Kate used to think the world was black and white, right and wrong. Turns out, life isn't that easy...

Praise for Miranda Kenneally:

"A must read! I couldn't put it down!" —Simone Elkeles,
bestselling author of the Perfect Chemistry series

"An incredibly well-written, beautiful story that balances romance,
drama, and comedy perfectly." —*Bookish*, on *Stealing Parker*

If He Had Been with Me

Laura Nowlin

"If he had been with me, everything would have been different."

Finn and Autumn used to be inseparable, but middle school puts them on separate paths going into high school. Yet no matter how distant they become or who they're dating, Autumn continues to be haunted by the past and what might have been. While their paths continue to cross and opportunities continue to be missed, little do they know that the future might separate them forever.

Praise for *If He Had Been with Me*:

"Friendship, love, secrets, hope and regret…this book
has it all! *If He Had Been With Me* is a page-turner that
you won't be able to put down." —*Girls' Life*

"This sweet, authentic love story masks complex characters
dealing with complex issues…First-time author Nowlin
keeps the story real and fast paced." —*Booklist*